LOVE REFUSES TO DIE

LOVE REFUSES TO DIE

ELLEN FRAZER-JAMESON

FOURTH DIMENSION
of South Beach

Published by
Fourth Dimension of South Beach

Cover quote from William Shakespeare's *Romeo and Juliet*

ISBN: 978-0-69285-873-8

Cover design and typesetting: Gary A. Rosenberg
www.thebookcouple.com

For Christian,
who caused my heart
to dance to a different beat.

prologue

"Love denied blights the soul we owe to God."

—Shakespeare in Love

Julianne struggled to tie a silken wrap over her naked body as she stumbled down the narrow cottage stairway to answer the hammering on the fist-sized metal knocker. Dawn had not yet broken over the shrouded mountain range on the coastline of Spain's Costa Blanca. She wrenched open the heavy wooden door, determined to give whoever had so rudely awakened her a piece of her mind.

A young lad confronted her. His sullen expression telegraphed the fact that he cared little for social niceties and was there only to carry out his obligation and be on his way. Without a word, he thrust a thorny delivery of red roses into her arms. She recoiled. Here was the warning she dreaded. A dozen blood-red roses twisted into a wreath. A small white card edged in black with the words written in red ink. ROMERO RIP.

Revenge was always inevitable; she knew that though she had tried for years to deny the stark reality. The needle sharp thorns of the wreath ripped holes in her heart, and she flinched as the cruel jagged prongs threatened to draw blood from her trembling hands. Romero had presented her with a rose the first time they met, and she now reflected, how could the symbol of love also inflict such excruciating pain?

From the day she had issued a murder contract on her international drug-smuggling criminal lover, Julianne had known her own life and that of her family was destined to be in danger. She never doubted that one day she risked being betrayed by the lowlife she had persuaded to carry out the death sentence. There's no honor among thieves, she reminded herself. It would be only a matter of time before he agreed to yet another contract with whoever was prepared to pay the highest price.

Julianne carried the wreath through the overgrown garden. She headed for a shed by the wall that marked the boundary of her property, almost hidden under a leafy, low-limbed olive tree. She placed the wreath on a dust-covered workbench and on her way out turned the rusty key in the lock and put the key in her pocket. She was not yet ready to tell anyone about the dangerous and unwelcome delivery.

★ ★ ★

Caught up in a tangled web of deceptions, lies and betrayals, Julianne's daughter Kira Mae had been framed by the master criminal Romero and named an accessory in the death of his fiancé, a local celebrity, the celebrated Festival Queen, La Reina, Senorita Michella de Jesus Santa Castellana.

Kira Mae admitted that she was guilty of loving a man who was already betrothed to another but she was innocent of all implications in the murder of Michella. Kira Mae, then a naive twenty-year-old, served a prison sentence for her alleged part as an accomplice in the crime as did Romero, who was guilty of the murder.

Desperate to avenge her daughter, Julianne arranged to have Romero killed the day after he escaped from prison and long before he had served his sentence. A tiger defending her cub, she vowed that no man would betray her beloved daughter and escape retribution. Especially the one who had ruthlessly entangled both her and Kira Mae in a twisted love triangle. Julianne was not proud of the fact that she too had been a victim and been seduced by Romero. Her only defense was that she had not known the extent of his wanton womanizing, nor thank God had Kira Mae. As long as there was breath in her body, Julianne would fight to keep the truth from Kira Mae.

Julianne tracked down and enlisted the services of a petty crook, a gang leader that Romero had also framed and abandoned. He too had served a prison sentence thanks to the dubious testimony of Romero, who did everything he could to reduce his own years of incarceration. Prison was not to be his only punishment. Romero would be forced to pay the ultimate price for his contemptuous disregard for his fellow human beings. Without mercy, he destroyed lives and walked away.

Julianne made it her mission to bring his evil reign to an end and ensure that he paid with his life.

Now she faced the realization that, despite the passing years, her own life was under threat. Whoever had delivered the wreath was not playing games. They knew what she had done. Her life was on the line.

Fear had ruled her for far too long. Fear had fermented into a poisonous cocktail of pain, grief and outrage. She knew her ordeal was not over—she just did not know how it would end.

Romero was the only man she had ever loved. The only man to whom she had ever given herself freely. His callous betrayal of her and her daughter had shattered her heart but not her spirit. Her mind and emotions were warped by the terrible revenge she had taken upon him, but her heart also cried out for a love that had never been hers to lose.

At his graveside as she threw a rose onto his coffin, she danced and whispered the words, "Adios gypsy boy. Not a tear will we shed."

Julianne's triumph was short-lived. The night terrors had begun hours after she attended his funeral. In the sanctuary of her own bedroom, she awoke from a nightmare covered in sweat. The very life was being choked out of her. Romero's coal-black eyes stared into hers. His strong hands, once so gentle and seductive, gripped her throat and applied murderous pressure. His body overpowered her. His rage filled the room.

Julianne was powerless. She imagined that her open mouth resembled the Munch painting *The Scream*—

soundless, terrified, inescapable. Seemingly locked in that moment before death, Julianne accepted the inevitable. She was destined to die.

A sudden awakening to consciousness returned her to the comfort and safety of her own bed, but the experience had felt so real that Julianne questioned whether the waking state was the dream. Too frightened to move, she lay rigid under the covers and waited for the dawn light to enter her room and chase away the shadows of the night. *Romero was a killer, why would he not kill her?*

★ ★ ★

Julianne's mind tortured her in the weeks, months and years following Romero's escape from prison and his subsequent assassination. Her heart was pierced. She prayed, without expectation, for just one moment of peace. Her prayer remained unanswered. Guilt and shame and regret were constant companions. Every night she was forced to push the boulder of her fears up the mountainside only to find the following morning that it always rolled back to the bottom of the pit of despair.

She wore a golden cross, obsessively locked her doors and windows, questioned the motives of every new person who crossed her path and viewed the world through eyes haunted with suspicion.

The day Romero died, she felt as if she died too.

Now the sum of all her fears was delivered direct to her door, revenge and retribution.

She did not doubt that the blood-red roses were destined for her grave. But she refused to give up without a fight. Julianne sought strength from her personal mantra, "Hell hath no fury like a woman scorned."

chapter one

"Expectation is the root of all heartache."
—William Shakespeare

Julianne arrived back after having been away from home for too long. Each time she traveled, it became harder to face the inevitability of her return to the scene of her crime, the Costa Blanca in Southern Spain. Despite misgivings, her heart was filled with expectation and anticipation as she approached Villajoyosa—the village of joy—on the train from the airport. The familiar landmarks along the coast from Alicante airport delighted her. The train was reliable, clean, filled with tourists and students and provided a sense of normalcy and security.

Villajoyosa provided a safe haven. The place where she had built her business empire and overcome the challenges of the past to find success. The place she had entrusted to nurture, shelter and protect her family. The family flourished here, but for Julianne there was no such sanctuary.

The decision to remove herself from her family home and take up a solitary odyssey around the world had been almost as unbearable to Julianne as the pain she had experienced on the day Romero died. In a time warp where she felt like a ghost and was never fully able to trust her own emotions, Julianne was frozen. How could she have been so blind? She berated herself as the most gullible fool on earth. Even after so many betrayals, she had still refused to admit the inevitable. Without mercy, Romero had cruelly and willfully manipulated her.

From the safety of her window seat she stared out at the familiar dry, barren landscape, wiping a tear from her eye. The woman who had been so full of life and enthusiasm had hardened her own heart and become a dried-up vessel, fearful that never again would her being fill with joy or feel love. She prayed that she could still appear to be a fully functioning human being. She rehearsed the moment when she would arrive home and be forced to put on an act for the loved ones who now felt like strangers.

Julianne gazed at the railway line alongside the highway, where graffiti-scarred blue bridges spanned dried up riverbeds and entryways. She recognized the large metal statue of a black bull on display in an empty field. Ghostly silver trees stood guard around the edges of the orange groves and grapevines, fruits that continued to flourish in spite of the rugged conditions.

Brilliant white villas with sandstone and terracotta barrel roofs dotted the countryside, proudly displaying their fanciful turrets and towers.

Typically windows were shuttered against the fierce rays of the noonday sun. Julianne knew how it felt to shut out the sunshine, to live inside with only gloom for company. Even views of the sparkling blue ocean as the train made its unhurried journey along the tracks failed to raise a smile.

A sense of dread slowed her footsteps as she set out to walk the short distance from the train station to the Galleria de Artistas, The place was her pride and joy when she had arrived on the Costa Blanca in what seemed like a lifetime ago but was actually only seven years previously. Then she was already a fugitive, on the run from her British homeland and a high profile and glamorous life in London. Her idyllic existence in the capital city had been shattered by the exposure of the dark childhood secret she had tried the better part of her life to conceal. When the powder keg of shame and guilt was ignited and with fury exploded into violence, Julianne took flight along with daughter Kira Mae.

In the tight-lipped residents and the traditions of centuries old Spanish village life, they found acceptance and an unwritten code for people to mind their own business. Villagers asked few questions. If their businesses depended on it, they were polite, if not they took the view that even the mountains have secrets. Tourists, they observed, failed to show much curiosity about their fellow countrymen. The lure of sunshine was enough to convince them of the sense of an expat's desire to leave behind the cold and rain of the British weather.

Along the cliffside, the so-called "hanging houses," the most emblematic image of Villajoyosa, broke through her reluctance and elicited a degree of interest from Julianne. City walls built to ward off attacks from the nation of Berbers had lost their function in the eighteenth century. Instead houses, now brightly painted in vibrant shades, were built along the walls.

To descend from the mountainside level of the town's pretty main street to the sea front below, a series of railings and ornamental marble plazas were carved into the stone, each level landscaped with fountains and statues overlooking the ocean. Julianne admitted inwardly that even in her terminal sadness, the optimism in the air in Villajoyosa put a spring in her step. Joyful memories of the past, inspired by the town, allowed her to pretend that life was still full of potential and hope.

She had long since ceased to believe that things could ever be the same, but she was at least reconciled with her eldest daughter. However, it seemed inconceivable she would ever find it in her heart to forgive the man who had betrayed them both and forced her to make the decision to order his murder. She could not deny her part in his death and her guilt ensured that Romero was never far from her mind.

Julianne halted as the Galleria de Artistas came into view. As she composed herself, she applauded her choice of the setting, a one-story detached whitewashed building, highly visible on the junction of several roads and next to a crosswalk. Floor to ceiling windows showcased the art and fashion displayed inside. Julianne stepped closer to admire the opulent display of the Galleria's signature clothing brand, Wear 4 Art Thou? There was no time to re-acquaint herself with the brand she and her daughter, Kira Mae, had created.

A heartbreakingly beautiful child at the top of the marble steps that led up to the gallery stared down at Julianne. She had chocolate-brown eyes, waist-length shiny black hair and painted rosebud lips. Her lipstick matched her nail polish and coordinated with the jewels in her ears. She was a mini fashion plate in her rose pink T-shirt with the motif of the Eiffel Tower, leggings and fur-lined boots; Julianne stared in wonder at her.

"Isabella? What about a hug for your mother?" she called.

With a shy smile, the girl nodded. Julianne could stand it no longer. Desperate to embrace her daughter, Julianne ran up the steps and swept her into her arms and kissed her, again and again. The child did not resist. She reached out and stroked Julianne's long blonde hair and Julianne felt her heart beginning to thaw. How could she have thought she could walk away from her beloved child for so long and feel nothing? She had promised herself it would be better for everyone if she stayed away. Now she was not so sure.

"She's been counting every minute since you phoned this morning," called a young woman from the doorway.

As the ice inside her heart turned to tears of joy, Julianne looked over the head of the small girl to where her grown-up daughter, Kira Mae, stood coolly observing her mother in silence.

"Kira Mae, so you do still know who I am?" asked Julianne. What was meant as a joke came out as an accusation.

"Oh, yes, you resemble someone I used to know," said Kira. For a moment she hesitated, then made her way down the staircase and put her arms around her mother and sister. Their relationship went through periods of great strain when each blamed the other for bad decisions and their joint history often erupted into explosive recriminations. Clearly today neither was ready to reopen old wounds. Not yet anyway.

"What about me?" called out a small voice.

All three turned to acknowledge the other child, almost identical in appearance and dress to Isabella, who held her arms up and waited to be included in the group hug.

"Angel," said Kira Mae, "we would never leave you out."

Julianne choked back a sob. "Now all my girls are together again," she said. "May God preserve us!"

The prayer was one that Julianne uttered a dozen times a day. She prayed even more fervently the next day when she received a menacing delivery of a wreath of red roses.

chapter two

"If you have tears, prepare to shed them now"'

—Shakespeare's *Julius Caesar*

Julianne and Kira Mae each held a child by the hand as they made their way into the Galleria. Julianne had willed the fashion emporium into creation, but she was fascinated to see how Kira Mae had taken her original vision and brought it to life.

Featuring "Art to Wear" from all over the world, the selection of merchandise was a feast for the senses: bejeweled gowns, painted dresses and creations of every description. Center stage were the exclusive designs created by Kira Mae who, thanks to international publicity and celebrity endorsement, enjoyed her status as one of the foremost new young designers of her generation.

Kira's extraordinary talent made it possible for Julianne to promote her daughter by capitalizing on her global connections within the fashion industry and her previous life as a jet- setting brand ambassador for one of the icons of the luxury market, Maria de Angelis, a legend second only to her mentor Mary Quant.

Kira Mae stayed home and designed, Julianne traveled

the world sourcing materials, ideas and designs. Now Julianne felt a familiar stab of sadness as she recalled the day she arrived home unexpectedly after a particularly successful research trip.

She remembered as if it were yesterday. The plan was to surprise her daughter Kira Mae and the girls, so she had taken a taxi from the airport and instructed the driver to take her directly to the Galleria where she could drop off her large suitcases full of merchandise. She trotted up the steps to the Galleria full of energy carrying a custom-made outfit she specially commissioned for Kira Mae during her stay in Bali. It was the middle of the day; the entrance was locked.

Julianne peered into the deep recesses of the showroom, convinced she could see figures moving in the background. She rang the doorbell again, her nerves now beginning to fray—she had endured an almost twenty-four-hour journey from the Far East. Standing on the doorstep, a heavy suitcase at her feet, she felt hot and bothered. And angry. What if she were a client, left to stand outside the Galleria in the hot sun?

A car engine started up in the small private car park alongside the showroom and startled her. She looked out to see the vehicle reverse at high speed and drive off into the back streets of the town.

She could have sworn that the driver was Paolo, her lawyer and lover.

Julianne had seen Kira approaching, key in hand. Not at all her usual immaculate self, she looked flustered and confused.

"Mum, what are you doing here?" she said. "Why didn't you tell us you were coming?"

Avoiding her mother's eyes, she reached down to pick up the oversized Louis Vuitton travel bag. She had still not kissed her mother or welcomed her home.

Julianne wished it were possible to ignore the uncomfortable sensation in her knotted stomach.

"Was that Paolo I saw drive away?" she asked Kira Mae as she followed her into the showroom.

"I don't think so," said Kira.

A strange answer, thought Julianne. It either was or it wasn't.

Paolo, an Italian lawyer, had been a fixture in both their lives since the dramatic events of six years before when Kira Mae had been charged with being an accessory to murder. He represented Kira Mae in court, plea bargained and obtained for her a much reduced sentence based on her young age and the malicious influence and lies of Romero. Paolo was their friend, confidant, surrogate father and husband and business partner. There was no reason why he should not be at the Galleria. Julianne was determined to find the explanation for Kira Mae's secrecy.

Finally after she heaved the large suitcase down the corridor and into the stockroom, Kira Mae remembered her manners.

"Good to see you," she said. "How was your journey?"

Julianne walked toward the office at the back of the building that led outside. She couldn't resist opening the door just to check. But check for what?

Julianne felt that all the joy had been taken out of her return home. She sat down behind the desk and started to look over the pile of papers in her in-tray while Kira Mae unpacked the suitcase.

"Want me to hang up the new merchandise?" she called from the next room. "You can show me it all properly later. I can't wait to hear about your trip."

Julianne had thrown the dress she was carrying on to a spare chair. She did not any longer feel like making a grand gesture of presenting a gift to her beloved daughter.

Kira Mae came into the office. "Let me move my things from your desk," she said. "I would have cleared up if I had known you were due back. Coffee?" she added.

Julianne shook her head. A familiar sense of unease had overtaken her. "I'm not staying long," she said. "I only came by to bring the new stock—and a gift for you."

She didn't move to give it to Kira, just nodded her head in the direction of the chair where the dress now threatened to slide to the floor.

"My plan was to stop by here and then head over to the villa. I want to see the girls."

Kira shook her head. "They're at nursery school. You can come with me to collect them and then I'll take you home. They'll be thrilled to see you. They ask all the time when you are due home."

Julianne slumped back in the chair. "I'm exhausted,

Kira," she said. "Don't play games with me. What's going on?"

Kira looked innocent. "What do you mean? We've been pretty busy here. I can't wait to show you everything we've done."

"And who do we mean by *we*?" said Julianne.

"Paolo and me and a few other people," said Kira, looking away. "It's good to have you back," she said over her shoulder as she headed out the door. "I'll tell you all about it. Promise."

Julianne knew her daughter well enough to be sure that something was amiss.

Much as she tried, Julianne had never been able to totally trust Kira. Not since the two women had shared the love of Romero. Still they had to make their relationship work, especially since there were two children to be considered, Kira's daughter and Julianne's daughter. Both were fathered by the same man, except that Kira Mae did not know that Romero was the father of her mother's child. She had been in prison already pregnant with Romero's child when Julianne had been forced to admit her own pregnancy. Julianne had allowed Kira Mae to believe that Paolo was the father, and he had not denied it.

Fact was, at that time Paolo and Julianne were not intimate though she clung to him for the support she needed during Kira Mae's term in prison. Later, Julianne and the lawyer would become friends with benefits.

The girls, Angel and Isabella, were born just a month

apart and were as alike as two peas in a pod. Most people assumed they were twins and as they were being brought up together as sisters, not nieces, the family lines were conveniently blurred.

Romero had been forced to face the consequences of his betrayal. When he chose to love both mother and daughter, and then later to frame Kira Mae for a murder she didn't commit, a Greek myth was enacted and Julianne felt cursed to make him pay for his sins.

Sometimes she felt murderous enough to believe that Kira should also have been forced to pay.

At the small village school the five-year-olds attended while Kira worked at the Galleria, Julianne stood by the car and waited for the girls to run down the pathway to greet her.

"Mama JoJo," they chorused and attempted to climb up into her arms.

Both girls called her Mama even though Angel knew that Kira was her mother. Julianne was grateful that their few Spanish neighbors and friends did not feel it was their business to pry. The locals were reserved people and family was sacred. Some of the older women might remember snatches of gossip from the time of the births but no one really knew the details. Besides, all foreigners who choose to live in a small out of the way village where English is not universally spoken were likely to have some kind of secret history.

People here kept themselves to themselves and that was the way Julianne liked it. When they entered the school system the fact that all four had the same surname meant that no questions were asked, and to all intents and purposes, Angel and Isabella were sisters.

★ ★ ★

Filled as she was with love for her daughters, Julianne felt a mixture of pride and unease. Where was Paolo?

Paolo Grazia was Julianne's business partner, lover, best friend and lawyer. When she was away she knew Paolo would be there to protect her family.

"Paolo's on business in Rome," Kira said. "He'll be back for the weekend. We have something we need to tell you."

Julianne kept her head down and pretended to listen to an account of what happened that day in school being told by Isabella. Nausea washed over her. Without being told, she knew what Kira and Paolo had to tell her. Fact was she had suspected for a while. She just hadn't wanted to heed the warning signs.

chapter three

"This above all: to thine own self be true."
—Shakespeare's *Hamlet*

Home for Julianne was a whitewashed cottage in the village of San Juan, a beach resort just north of Alicante. As the girls and the business grew, she vigorously resisted all attempts to move her from the original home she had set up on arriving from England. The place still held memories of an earlier time of optimism when she was working hard to set up her business and win the love of Romero. It was a fantasy, but Julianne clung to the few times when her life had felt perfect.

Kira Mae lived with the girls about an hour away in a pretty four-bedroomed villa with a pool close to the Galleria in Villajoyosa. Julianne traveled so much that it did not make sense to keep moving Isabella from house to house.

As Kira always said, "It's as easy to look after two of them as one. Easier in fact as they keep each other company."

The collaboration worked well. Mother and daughter worked in partnership and shared the vision for their business but they also lived independent lives.

Kira, still only in her midtwenties, relished the role of mother and she loved Isabella as if she were her own.

They had an unspoken agreement that the events of the past would not be allowed to intrude on their success, but the old hurts often manifested themselves in heated arguments about how to run the business, how to bring up the girls and a hundred other totally non-related issues. Both agreed that they must never reopen old wounds. Julianne knew if they opened Pandora's box, all hell would break lose.

Julianne's main ally was Paolo, the wonderful Italian lawyer whom she had met when Kira Mae went to jail for a crime she didn't commit. Paolo was also Kira Mae's confidant. He was the only person other than Julianne who knew the whole story of their tangled relationships and he adored both women. He maintained client confidentiality and kept the peace.

Now Julianne wanted to delay the time when she would hear what Kira Mae wanted to tell her—what she and Paolo wanted to tell her.

"Drop me at the cottage," she told Kira, "I need some sleep. I'll come over to see you and the girls this evening."

"Fine," said Kira, visibly relieved to have been given a reprieve. The girls were playing happily in the back of the car on their tablets, sharing a game as usual.

"Say good-bye to Mama JoJo," said Kira.

"Bye," said the girls, hardly looking up.

Julianne resisted the temptation to make an issue of the fact that after just half an hour of having her back, she could be dismissed so easily. *Better than being clingy,* she thought.

"Give me a kiss, Isabella," she said leaning over the front seat. "Angel, a kiss for me, please."

Both girls obliged and to ensure that she would be missed, Julianne added, "See you at your house later. I have presents for you."

That got their attention. "Yay," they shouted in unison. "Can we have our presents now?"

"Later," said Kira. "Say good-bye to Mama JoJo."

She leaned over to kiss her mother's cheek. "I'll cook." Julianne took a moment as she always did on arriving at her cottage to stand outside and pay homage to the premises where she had set up her first boutique. *La Dama Escalata.* Perched high on a hillside, the white-washed stone building was covered in purple and white wisteria.

She loved to recall the image of her first attention-grabbing window display: a shimmering, scarlet Roberto Cavalli evening gown in his signature shiny satin with net inserts on the fishtail skirt where it fanned out in ruby ostrich feathers. A glittering rhinestone belt encircled the size zero waist and was replicated by the spaghetti straps on the sweetheart neckline. The dress had the power to transform every woman into a goddess and every man into a slave.

But all that felt like more than a lifetime ago.

The large window of the downstairs room where she had first boldly displayed her *Dama Escalata* sign was now closed up with wood-grained shutters. The small black railing around the upstairs balcony needed a coat of paint. She never saw or indeed heard from the owners of the property. All communication was directed through the lawyer's office with whom she had signed the first lease seven years before. The lease arrived annually, ready for her renewal signature. She sent it off with a check for the year's rent, and continued to live in the cottage she called home.

Always her memories returned to Romero. The first time she had visited the office of the lawyer who executed the lease, Romero began his seduction. He took her completely by surprise on the narrow stairway as he pulled her into his arms and kissed her passionately.

Julianne had spent some of her best and some of her worst days in the cottage. The window area that had been her showcase was now a closet for her own clothes. There was a small kitchen, big enough for someone who didn't cook, and upstairs three small bedrooms and a bathroom. The downstairs had a small comfortable living room and one of her favorite features, a fireplace.

It was in this cottage that her dreams had first been shattered by Romero.

She wandered around the cottage. Everything was just as she had left it. Neat as a pin.

She lay down on her colorful double bed, exhausted from her long flight from the Far East and looked around. Julianne retained her signature white furniture but added glorious splashes of color upstairs with traditional accessories; the room came alive with throws and cushions and bright Spanish paintings on the wall.

There was a flamboyant series of oils of a female flamenco dancer as she twisted and stomped her way through a dance in a flounced red and black dress.

She had initially resisted the lone male flamenco dancer as it reminded her too strongly of Romero. He was a flamenco musician. But she relented and agreed that it completed the collection.

And she liked being reminded of him.

How strange that she could not stray too far from that which had hurt her so much. Who would have dreamt that the need to avenge her daughter would have turned her into a murderer?

She might not have been the one to stab him in the heart and spill his blood on the wooden floor, that was the job of the hired hitman, but no court in the world would have declared her innocent of the crime she had ordered.

Above the small fireplace that Julianne had uncovered and restored, hung a landscape of the hauntingly beautiful Spanish countryside. Her emotions responded to the starkness of the mountain range and the unforgiving rocky wasteland.

She loved the sanctuary of her bedroom, the romantic Mediterranean-blue painted walls, plump jewel-colored pillows and the sensual smells of her candles and incense. Surrounded by her favorite things, she felt safe. Wherever she traveled in the world, to the best hotels and in the grandest suites, no place delighted her like her own home.

Disturbing emotions still arose in her and she tried

to maintain her serenity by taking slow breaths. The inner and the outer Julianne were two distinct entities. Outwardly she was confident, glamorous and in control. Inside she was constantly on the verge of falling apart.

Here in the tranquil atmosphere of this little house she could nurture herself. Reconcile the inner and outer. Feel whole. Love herself and hold on to her sanity. Julianne kicked off her shoes, gave a sigh of relief and fell asleep.

* * *

It was evening by the time she woke up. She checked her phone. Kira Mae had left several messages. Perhaps she thought Julianne would avoid the impending visit. Julianne sent a text.

"What time shall I come over?"

Paolo had also left text messages to welcome her home. Julianne refused to respond. She did not want to preempt anything he might have to say.

Julianne drove herself to Kira Mae's house. The villa was not fancy, a simple one story brick structure, but well-furnished in the rustic Spanish style that allowed for kids to jump on couches and for newspapers and magazines to be piled sky-high on coffee tables. Goodness knows what the maid did all day. It certainly wasn't housework. A trail of clothes led out to the outdoor pool.

Julianne resisted the urge to tidy up as she was in the habit of doing. She and Kira Mae had long since exhausted all arguments on that front.

Instead she said, "Let me know if there is anything I can do."

"No help needed," Kira Mae replied. "You go out to the girls. They're at the pool."

Julianne walked outside to where the girls played next to the pool. They squealed and ran over when they saw her.

"Presents, presents," they chanted.

Julianne smiled. She held out dolls in national costumes from her Asian travels and a couple of handmade wooden instruments.

It had become harder for Julianne to find unique gifts for the girls. Even in the most exotic locations it seemed that all the stores sold the same selection of children's toys and games.

"They can go in the pool now if you can stay out there to supervise," called Kira Mae.

"Awesome," called the five-year-olds. Like twins they seemed to speak each other's words and thoughts together.

"Of course, I'll watch them," said Julianne. They were already dressed in their bathing suits and Julianne settled down in a lounge chair alongside the pool.

Hours every day in the water ensured that the girls swam like fish, ducking and diving and racing each other.

Julianne watched mesmerized, and unbidden came the enduring combination of pride and pain. The rhythmic splashing and the dancing shadows on the sparkling blue waters of the pool lulled Julianne into a familiar reverie.

Was fate really to blame for her choices? What would she change given the chance?

Isabella was her daughter, the daughter of Romero. Their affair had flared briefly and for Julianne magnificently. He was the first man she had ever given herself to in every respect, the first man who convinced her that she could love and be loved.

Sadly, the passion of their brief affair was a lie. Romero was a master manipulator who used women to his own ends. He had a fiancée and also a wife, as well as a criminal record as long as his arm. Romero was a Don Juan, a serial seducer. An accomplished manipulator of women and a man who always got all of his needs met. His fiancé Senorita Michella de Jesus Santa Castellana, his childhood sweetheart, who outlived her usefulness and was killed by Romero in a fake car crash, was high born and well connected. She brought status and respectability to the rogue, Romero.

Annabelle, his wife, was the best kept secret of all. Julianne was completely in the dark until the receptionist at the lawyer's office in Alicante, where she signed her lease, let the cat out of the bag.

She asked innocently, "How is the other English lady? The one who is married to Mr. Romero Rosario? We haven't see her lately."

Julianne was shocked rigid. The "other English lady" was Annabelle Anstruther. Julianne was a guest in Annabelle's villa. She had no idea that her childhood friend, now visiting her sick father back in Britain, was married to the local heartbreaker. When Julianne confronted

Romero, he claimed to have married Annabelle as a business expediency to give her Spanish residency.

Julianne knew she was a fool but still she trembled with passion when she remembered the first time she became aware of Romero. The image of him was burned into her soul.

At a local Spanish restaurant, she fell hopelessly in love with Romero. He certainly knew how to attract attention. A flamenco guitarist, he perched high on his stool and cradled his instrument in his arms and stroked it as if it were a woman. He was the most handsome man she had ever seen. Exotic, mysterious, challenging. Perfect features, black flashing eyes, black hair that curled and flicked as it crept on to his collar, long tapered fingers. Matador jacket, tight black trousers and boots of black leather with studded heels.

Striking without mercy into the very depths of her being, he sang songs of love and betrayal and Julianne felt all the pain of her past released and honored. Never before had she experienced this depth of delicious, dangerous passion. Romero seduced with his music, with his presence and his complete disregard for the physical longing he provoked. He knew only too well that he could reduce any woman to a state of helplessness with his ungodly siren call. The ancient spell he weaved was as powerful as any drug.

Julianne could not know that she was merely a pawn in his wicked game. Her heart broke when she was confronted with the fact that as he captured her in his web, he also seduced her daughter.

She wished she could turn back the clock and heed the warning look given by the restaurant owner, Pepe, as he watched Romero's classic manipulation on that first momentous evening.

As he left the stage, Romero strode toward the table where mother and daughter sat at a ringside seat. Without looking directly at either of them, he placed on the table—between Julianne and Kira Mae—one perfect rose.

The consequences of that action would be tragic. Kira Mae went to prison, framed for a murder. Romero went to prison, and when Julianne heard of his escape, she made the most dangerous decision of her life.

She betrayed Romero to the underworld criminals who had also served prison sentences because of him. When he thought he was coming for a welcome home to Julianne, he was instead confronted by a contract killer. Julianne led the killer to Romero and his death was later confirmed in a phone call by the coded message—*"The roses have been delivered."* Julianne never saw Romero dying on the floor. The hitman Gio Lopez stared into his eyes, and at the moment of death, Romero knew that he paid the ultimate sacrifice for his betrayal of Julianne and her daughter, Kira Mae.

Julianne and Kira Mae were left devastated—both had borne him chidren.

Kira Mae knew only one version of the story. She believed Romero was killed by an ex-colleague because of his many betrayals. That much was true.

As to her mother's unexpected pregnancy, she wanted

to believe Julianne's made-up story of an old flame who had visited and comforted her while Kira herself was in prison and carrying Romero's baby. Though she had her own ideas, she suspected Paolo.

It was never up for discussion that the same man, Romero, had made both mother and daughter pregnant. Julianne dreaded the day when that devastating secret might be revealed.

Lost in memories of the past, Julianne didn't hear Kira Mae come out to the pool deck.

"It's past the girls' bedtime," she said. "I'll dry them off and take them in."

Julianne followed Kira Mae into the villa and helped tuck the girls into their little matching Princess beds. She kissed them good night. To make herself useful she set the dining-room table and checked the food. Chicken and a cold salad was all that appeared to be on the menu.

Julianne wished she could find a good excuse to leave before Paolo arrived. Kira had informed her that Paolo was traveling back from Rome earlier than he had planned. Julianne wanted to run away and bury her head in the sand. Instead she popped a pill, her favorite brand of painkiller, and washed it down with a glass of white wine.

Sure, her doctor had told her not to take the pills with alcohol but, when her heart pounded and her nerves were frayed, the double combination was the only one that calmed her down.

"Just the one glass," she promised herself.

Paolo's plane was delayed, and Kira Mae suggested they go ahead and eat.

"No need," said Julianne. "I'm not hungry. Come sit down and tell me all the news."

Kira Mae appeared reluctant to talk; she could barely look at her mother but did pass on some titbits about the shop. Julianne found it hard to focus. Businesswise she was pretty much up to speed and checked emails every day when she traveled.

"Could you refill my glass, please?" Julianne asked, as Kira turned on the television.

"Thought I heard one of the girls," said Kira, getting up again for the hundredth time. She rushed out at the first sound of a car in the driveway. Julianne turned off the television and strained to pick up a hushed conversation as Paolo entered the villa by the gate to the pool.

Julianne was feeling more relaxed than before she started drinking but still felt anxious.

Paolo entered the room and threw some papers down on the coffee table. He walked toward Julianne and showed no signs of awkwardness as he extended his arms to embrace her.

"So good to have you back," he said. "We all missed you."

"Let's eat and you can tell us all about your travels and the exciting new stock for the Galleria. Did you get the contract I sent for the new manufacturer? We need to sign him up before someone else discovers him."

Paolo was his usual charming, urbane self, Julianne

reflected. A gentleman. He was always in control of the situation. A smooth operator.

Throughout dinner, Kira Mae kept getting up from the table and fussing over the food. Backward and forward to the kitchen she went. One more dish, one more piece of cutlery, a spare plate, an extra salt shaker.

Julianne stayed put and tried to ignore the look of disapproval from her daughter when she held her glass out for yet another refill.

Even she knew that her voice had a slightly sharper edge than she had intended when she asked, "So, what did you want to tell me?"

Julianne caught Paolo shooting Kira Mae a warning look and an imperceptible shake of his head that said, "Not now."

"Kira Mae gave me the impression that it was urgent," said Julianne. "So am I to be let in on the secret?"

Kira Mae looked to Paolo. "Shall I tell her or will you?"

Paolo, handsome as ever, a real silver fox, looked uncomfortable. "Now is not the time," he said. "Your mother has just come back from a long trip. Let her settle in first."

Kira Mae was not to be placated. With both feet, she jumped in.

"I know about Isabella and Romero," she said. "I know he is her father."

Julianne froze. Glass halfway to her lips, she stared at Kira Mae, then turned her attention to Paolo.

"You told her?" she challenged him.

"I had no choice," he answered. "She had already guessed. I merely confirmed."

"Thank you, Mr. Lawyer," said Julianne, her voice loaded with sarcasm.

Kira Mae raised her voice. "How could you think I would not know? I spend almost every minute of every day with Isabella. She's the spitting image of Angel. The spitting image of Romero. How long did you think I could go on being made a fool?"

Julianne took a large gulp of her wine, almost finishing the glass in one go. She could not dispute what Kira Mae had said. Both girls were as dark as their mothers were blonde. To cover up her discomfort, Julianne held out her empty glass in Paolo's direction.

He ignored her so she reached for the bottle.

"She's already had enough," said Kira.

Julianne narrowed her eyes and threw an angry look at her daughter. "I'll say when I've had enough," she said. "My only intention was to protect you. You did not need that extra burden on top of everything else. Yes, I thought I could keep it from you."

Julianne shook her head sadly. "So now that you all have the information, what do you suggest we do about it?"

Kira Mae spat out the words she had clearly been nurturing. "I hate you."

Julianne flinched. "I guess I deserved that," she said, "but it doesn't diminish my love for you. I knew nothing about you and Romero when he and I"—she hesitated—"did what we did."

Paolo came to Julianne's defense just as he had for Kira Mae in court.

"Romero is the villain of the peace, Kira Mae," said Paolo. "He betrayed both of you. Trust me: he was a ruthless, murderous criminal; he got what he deserved."

Kira Mae looked daggers at her mother. "I know you killed him. It was you, wasn't it?"

Julianne sprang to her feet, "We both danced on his grave. You were happy enough to know that he was dead. I told you, no one knows what really happened, the police said it was one of his accomplices."

"Paolo told me," Kira Mae shouted.

Julianne stood up and stared at Paolo. "I don't believe what I'm hearing. What did you tell her? You know he was killed by one of his own. Those who live by the sword die by the sword."

Paolo sensed that Julianne was on the verge of tears, and he held out a hand to comfort her. Kira Mae moved between them.

"He told me," she repeated. "Everything. How you made Paolo tell you where Romero was so you could lure him into a trap. I know it all. You're a murderer and you killed the man I loved."

Kira Mae collapsed into one of the few chairs that was not heaped high with children's clothes and toys and began to sob.

Her cries brought Paolo to her side. Sensing victory she looked up at her mother.

"Darling, please. Tell her everything. Tell her. Tell her everything."

"For God's sake, Kira," he said.

Kira smiled in triumph. "Paolo and I are in love," she gloated. "We are lovers."

Julianne turned away. If her daughter had stuck a knife in her heart, the pain could not have been worse. Julianne grasped her stomach in anguish as if she had been physically attacked.

Paolo also looked as if he had been struck. He left Kira's side and walked across the marble tiled floor toward Julianne. "This wasn't meant to happen, any of it," he said.

Julianne looked him in the eye. "Judas," she spat out.

As if in slow motion, she approached Kira Mae who had uncurled herself from her chair and now attempted to maneuver closer to the safety of Paolo's arms.

She was not quick enough. Julianne aimed one perfect stinging slap to her daughter's cheek. The blow left its mark. Kira Mae's tears began again.

Paolo recalled the last time he had been witness to such a scene. Kira Mae was in prison charged with murder when Julianne discovered her daughter was pregnant by the man she loved.

Julianne reacted then as now and slapped her daughter. But this time was different. She did not immediately retract the punishment and ask for forgiveness. Instead she picked up her purse from the table and checked for her car keys.

A slight slur could be detected as she addressed Paolo and Kira Mae. "I wish you a happy life," she hurled at them as she headed for the front door.

Having delivered her parting line, Julianne found her exit blocked. Isabella and Angel stood hand in hand in the doorway, in their matching pink Little Mermaid pajamas, in tears.

"It's OK," she told the girls. "Everything is alright. Go back to bed."

Kira Mae pushed her way past her mother, took both of the girls by the hand and steered them back to the bedroom.

"There, there," she cooed. "Come on now. Nothing is wrong. Do you want another story?"

Drama over, the girls were led back to bed and as Kira Mae settled them, Paolo pleaded with Julianne. "Come outside. Please let me talk to you. You're upset," he said.

"Damn right I'm upset. Is there some other way I should be?"

Paolo had the grace to look sheepish. "I'm sorry," he said. "Please let me try to explain."

"I can't think how you are going to talk yourself out of this one, Mr. Lawyer," Julianne told him as they stood a distance apart by the pool. "You sleep with my daughter and in your pillow talk tell her secrets that should have gone to the grave with you. I trusted you more than any man alive."

Paolo reached out a hand to her.

"Get away from me," she raised her voice, "there is no way you can ever make this better."

Julianne moved as fast as her high heels would allow around the pool. Paolo was right by her side.

She wanted to pull away but had become so used to him being there. The reassurance of his touch turned her anger to tears.

"I'll drive you home," he said, "and bring your car back tomorrow."

Julianne held on to his arm. If she lost her right-hand man, she might as well lose a limb. She had no greater ally.

"How could you do this to me?" she asked.

Paolo shushed her as Kira Mae had shushed the children.

"Watch where you're going," he said, as they walked toward his car. "Hold on to me. I'll look after you."

Julianne allowed him to lead her, but in a moment of clarity she realized that she had lost him forever. There was nothing he could say to make it right. Paolo, the man who had refused to allow her to fall apart, had delivered a death blow to her heart. Julianne would have preferred to refuse Paolo's offer to drive her home, but she knew she was in no condition to navigate the mountain road in the dark.

Huddled in the passenger seat of his car she closed her ears to the explanation he tried to offer.

"Kira Mae went through a hard time," he told her. "She was overwhelmed with all the responsibilities of the Galleria, the girls, running the house, the need to fulfill orders to build up her own designer brand. I told her constantly that she needed to take the pressure off. You were traveling all over the world and she refused to worry you by admitting that she couldn't cope. So I did what I could to help."

"Yes, I bet you did," said Julianne, her voice loaded with sarcasm.

"You know I've always been here for all of you. I love you and your family. This is my second home. When you went away I started to stay over at Kira's to help with the school run in the morning."

Guilt was playing its usual undermining tricks on Julianne. She should have been at home, she should have done the school run and she should have helped her daughter more in the business. Would have, should have, could have. Instead she had run away. Always in flight mode. When she couldn't cope, Julianne ran away.

"Kira Mae promised to talk to you when you came home. She was to tell you honestly that she needed more resources. She needed help. She needed you."

Guilt on top of more guilt.

Julianne's mind flew back to the early years when she had made the choice to leave Kira Mae with her grandmother in Scotland while she pursued her dreams at night school of a career in fashion.

Kira Mae would plead with her, "Please, Mummy, come home. Why do you have to go to work?"

Julianne would try patiently to explain and then promise a treat to make up for all the time they spent apart. "Mummy loves you. We'll be together soon. I'll buy you something nice."

The anger and sadness she felt toward Kira Mae and Paolo turned inward. Tears of recrimination stung her eyes. This was all her fault. She was the one whose loyalty was in question. Bad mother.

Paolo drove slowly and took the hazardous mountain turns at a snail's pace, always aware that another vehicle could approach on the opposite lane where there was barely room to pass. "Kira Mae came to rely on me more and more," Paolo admitted. "I like being relied upon. You know that, I've been there for you long enough. But you weren't there for me. You never seem to need any of us."

Julianne protested, "But you know more than anyone that I can only be that independent woman when I have you there as my foundation. My rock."

Paolo took the chance that he would be rejected and patted her hand.

"I bitterly regret what happened between me and Kira Mae," he said. "I blame myself totally. I'm the adult. I shouldn't have allowed it. My only defense is the one I have spent years deriding when people do things they shouldn't do. I was drunk. We were both drunk. It only happened the once. I was ashamed. It was my responsibility to ensure it never happened again."

Paolo turned to face her and for a moment she feared for their safety up there on the rocky mountain road. "I hated myself. It was like a curse that I should be the one who repeated what happened years ago. Even if by some miracle you forgive me, I can't forgive myself."

Julianne dried her tears. Now she wanted to scream and rail against the unfairness of the Fates who had condemned her to feel again the pain that she had endured when Romero slept with her daughter.

"Maybe I was wrong but I thought it would be better if we didn't tell you. Kira Mae refused. She has a crazy idea that she and I will build a life together. She says she's in love with me, that we are in love. It's not true. She's like a daughter to me. You are the love of my life Julianne. Always have been, please believe that much at least."

They drove on in silence until Paolo pulled up in front of Julianne's house. The place that a few hours before had been her haven of safety and sanctuary.

Now Julianne felt there was nowhere she would find peace.

"Do you want me to come in?" asked Paolo.

Julianne shook her head. "What for? So you can comfort me and we can pretend everything is alright? That you haven't just ripped my heart out? Would I feel secure and know that no one and nothing will ever harm me because my protector is by my side?" She gave a deep sigh and before it turned into a sob said, "I don't think so."

Paolo, as always, left the driver's seat to go round and open her door. As she made to walk away, he grabbed her arm. "Promise me you won't do anything silly."

She shook him off. "Silly, me? I'm the adult around here. I have to be responsible. After all, I'm truly on my own now. My knight on a white charger has moved on to the next damsel in distress."

Paolo flinched.

chapter four

"Most dangerous is the temptation that doth goad us on to sin in loving virtue."
—Shakespeare's *Measure for Measure*

"You're hurting me," said the showgirl as Kira Mae stuck a pin in her skinny behind.

"Stay still," said Kira. "These outfits are so flimsy that there is nothing for me to get a grip on, and it doesn't help that there is no flesh on your boy body. We've got to be ready for the producer by this afternoon."

Kira had more than a dozen of these fittings to complete before lunchtime and her brusque manner did not endear her to the young models. Her commission was to design a whole new set of costumes for a major show in Benidorm on the Costa Blanca, a show that attracted some 500 visitors every night. The most popular was the James Bond theme and it was now Kira's job as a visiting designer to come up with outfits for six sequences for a dozen female dancers and half a dozen men.

Kira had been beyond excited to get the commission. This was the first time she had been asked to design theatrical costumes. Unlike clothes intended for real life, the show costumes were meant to be over the top, outrageous, showstopping. She needed to come up with the ideas and make sure that the costumes would be serviceable as the girls high-kicked and danced through three hours of high-octane routines.

She turned back to the girl in front of her. "Sorry," she said. "Put it down to jealousy. I wish I had a body like yours and was as fit as you. It would give me the energy to spend all day running around after two five-year-old girls. Doesn't help that I am always running late to collect them."

Kira Mae, as usual, had taken responsibility for picking the girls up from school. Julianne objected. "I'll take my turn on the school run," she said pointedly.

"After all, Isabella is my daughter, not yours."

Their conversation about the school run had been mercifully brief, and Kira was determined that she would not be anywhere in the vicinity when Julianne returned the girls.

The maid would be there and give the girls a snack to keep them going till dinner time.

Paolo had not returned to her house after dropping off her mother the night before. On the phone he had cut her off short.

"You handled that really badly," he told her. "I just hope your mother is alright. Have you forgotten how fragile she is?"

Kira Mae refused to feel sorry for what she saw as the necessity of getting everything out into the open.

Where her mother liked to bottle up her emotions, Kira Mae thrived on drama.

"I'm going back to Rome," he said. "I'll try to work out the best course of action. I'll call you."

"Love you," said Kira Mae.

Paolo hung up the phone without responding.

Kira was under no illusion that Paolo and she were a couple, though she was trying to pretend differently. She had made all the running in the intimate relationship that had developed between them. Paolo had refused her approaches on so many occasions, especially when she had drunk a couple of glasses of wine.

"You're all family to me," he told her. "We must not be disloyal to your mother. She doesn't deserve this, please don't try to force the issue. There's a good girl. You know what happened last time she came home; she felt so unwelcome she left again almost immediately.

"Your mother is an important member of this family. I won't have you being cruel to her. Now please, be a good girl."

Kira Mae had pouted and he wanted to laugh as she displayed all the signs of the child he was accusing her of being. On the one night when things had gone too far and he slept in her bed at the villa, Paolo remonstrated with Kira. "I'm a man. I'm only human. I don't want to blame you for this, but it must not happen again. And your mother must never know. Please promise me."

Kira Mae had turned from him and with a triumphant smile on her lips she said, "She stole Romero from me. Now it's pay-back time."

Paolo thought back to the scared young woman he had first encountered in a cell in a jail in Rome six years before. Lost and frightened. Way out of her depth, having been duped into carrying contraband across the border from Spain into Italy. He had been assigned by the British embassy, where he was a staff lawyer, to take charge of her case. Relying on his powers of intuition, he could honestly claim that he never doubted she was innocent of all charges. Her crime: a fatal obsession with fantasy and romance.

The revelations of intrigue and double-dealing he heard from Kira and her mother, Julianne, were hair-raising even for a trial hardened lawyer. Both women had been having affairs with the same man. At least one of them, the prisoner daughter, was pregnant with his baby.

Kira Mae had accepted a plea bargain, and, while she served her two-year sentence and subsequently gave birth to her baby in a brand-new state-of-the-art prison in Rome, Paolo became Julianne's champion.

The admission that she too was pregnant by Romero brought from Paolo the assurance that he would be there for Julianne and Kira Mae no matter what. In the years since the babies were born, Paolo was the Numero Uno man in all their lives.

Paolo had pleaded with Kira, "I am not proud of myself. Please promise me that we will keep this between ourselves. No good will be served by telling your mother. And, I give you my word, there will be no repeat performance."

Kira nodded as if she agreed but then had dropped the bombshell. "If I don't tell her about us, is it OK if I tell her I know about her and Romero? And of course that I know Isabella is his daughter."

"You will destroy us all if you do," he warned her. Kira refused to listen. It was already too late—he had known what was coming.

chapter five

"The fault is not in our stars, but in ourselves."

—Shakespeare's *Julius Caesar*

Julianne needed an escape. She always needed an escape, she admitted to herself. A history of self-harm meant that when she felt stressed, the danger was that she would revert to old behavior. The treatment and therapy she had undergone over the years offered relief, and indeed there were times when she truly felt that she was cured, but once that propensity was in the genes, a permanent cure was not considered an option.

Like an alcoholic who for the rest of her life must abstain from alcohol, Julianne needed to be ever-vigilant of her mental health. Unfortunately, like millions of other people, it was not in her control. Once tipped over the edge by some emotional upset, chemical imbalance or sheer inability to cope, she was always in danger of finding that self-harm was her chosen form of medication.

Refraining from alcohol was also a discipline she tried to impose because she knew that the alcohol often gave her the Dutch courage and loss of perception to go ahead and inflict harm upon herself.

Kira Mae and Paolo tried to act as gate keepers, ensuring that she did not have too much to drink, but it was useless to try to impose their restrictions on her.

Her emotions in a complete turmoil after the revelations about Kira Mae and Paolo, Julianne knew she needed to be extra vigilant. In a strange effort to remove herself from the pain she was feeling here and now, she made a decision to return and face demons from the past.

Her childhood had been the start and the source of all her early pain and it was there that she began to develop the coping strategies that would enable her to maintain a functioning life. The abuse she had suffered in her childhood following the death of her mother from cancer left her with wounds that would never heal.

She had sworn that she would never return to the scene of her misery. But she made a decision that she would gather up her courage and try to obliterate the memories from the past.

A solicitor's letter from England, delivered to her solicitor in Spain, contained the highly unexpected news that the cottage where she grew up had been left to her in her father's will.

Her first thought was to completely reject the information. She wanted nothing to do with the scene of the crimes. Her father had spent some years in jail, not for the abuse he had inflicted upon her, but for his part in a wide-ranging pedophile ring that had operated at the boy's school where he was a master. Julianne was proud of the fact that she had broken her silence to pass on information to the police that along with other evidence had led to the decades old investigation achieving the imprisonment of many of the men who had been responsible for crimes against minors in their care.

Paolo had been instrumental in helping her provide the information to the authorities in England but he ensured that she was kept well away from the squalid realities of the case. In England the case had attracted much attention and after her father had gone to jail the house where he lived had fallen into rack and ruin.

Local kids had gone up there to use the house as target practice. A local solicitor contacted Julianne. Though she intended to cover her tracks and leave no forwarding addresses for anyone in England, the solicitor managed to find her.

Her father died in prison. A fitting end for him, Julianne concluded.

"What are your intentions for the property?" asked the solicitor. "Do you wish me to rent it out or sell it?"

"I want nothing to do with it," said Julianne.

The house fell further into disrepair until the solicitor again contacted her. He informed her that a well-known British actress, Amber Grace, who ran a charity offering safe homes for children who had been abused, was living in the Devon village and had made enquiries about acquiring the cottage. Amber had an idea to enlarge and convert the house into a safe home and suggested that the new house should be named after Julianne. Little did she know that the very thought of being connected with the house of shame where she grew up filled Julianne with horror. Instead she agreed to consider the possibility of attending the annual village fete and seeing firsthand the work that had been done on the newly extended building.

Amber sent her regular updates and told Julianne, "You won't know the place. Please say you'll come to visit us. I would be so honored to thank you personally."

Julianne checked her diary. Something deep inside told her the restoration of the old house would give her a chance to envisage herself as new and useful—not the broken-down heap she felt she was at the moment.

She was due to leave for London the next day.

Paolo stood in the doorway of Julianne's office at the Galleria. He stalked her and turned up at her house, followed her to the office, arrived at the school when he knew she was to collect the girls.

"Let me come with you," he pleaded. "We could spend some time together. I'll be by your side when you go back to the cottage. We have shared history. I was the only one who knew the story of the abuse your father put you through. I need to try to make all of this up to you."

Julianne refused all his entreaties. Paolo, who had absorbed so much of her pain, was patently hurting. And it showed.

Normally he was immaculately dressed in tailored clothes: Gucci loafers with the crispest of white trousers, a crisp white shirt and striped blazer that echoed the height of Roman fashions. Now for the first time ever, Julianne noticed that he was looking just a tiny bit disheveled. He admitted he wasn't sleeping. He promised he would not visit Kira Mae while they tried to resolve the issues that now threatened to undermine all their lives.

Julianne could hardly believe the arrogance of youth that Kira Mae had chosen to refuse to speak to her. As if the secrets she had discovered excused the fact that she had slept with her mother's lover.

Julianne wanted to confide in Paolo, ask his advice, but she had lost that safety net. Now she truly was on her own.

She flew to London and refused to let anyone, apart from Amber, know she was coming. Besides who would she have told?

Certainly not her former best friend Annabelle who had got her entangled in the whole unholy mess in the first place. Annabelle was married to Romero, an international criminal. She too was caught up in the dark world of drug smuggling and money laundering. So far as Julianne knew, Annabelle had been released from the Italian prison where her secret husband, Romero, had been incarcerated and transferred to a British jail.

With his legal connections, Paolo had tracked down Romero, Annabelle and even the small-time crook, Gio Lopez, who was an accomplice and had been jailed with Romero.

Gio was the hit man Julianne entrapped into killing her lover Romero. The hate she had felt for him when he set up her daughter as a murder suspect overrode all the passion and love she had previously felt for him. When her passion turned to revenge, hell opened and she wanted him dead.

For the first few months after Romero was found dead in a remote farmhouse near to her home, Julianne had thought she would be forced to move. She dreaded every creak in the old rustic home and expected every minute of every day to have to pay the price.

Julianne refused to believe she really had gotten away with the perfect crime. Gio had an axe to grind with Romero who had taken him down with him to prison, so Julianne had consoled herself with the fact that many people wanted Romero dead. She had not actually paid to have him killed. Big-time bosses of the Mafia and organized crime syndicates would have paid a hefty price to know what she knew: where Romero was headed after his escape from prison.

Now in an attempt to lay the ghost of Romero to rest, Julianne had come back to the place where her nightmares had begun long ago. Maybe Annabelle would know who had sent the wreath? Maybe Annabelle wanted her old friend dead?

Julianne made a phone call from the airport and screwed up all her courage to accept the invitation of actress Amber Grace to stay in one of the beautifully renovated buildings in the grounds of the new school.

* * *

Julianne dressed for the fete in a floaty mid-length rose

chiffon summer dress with appliqued flowers. The dress, as did all her outfits, had long sleeves. Though the physical scars of her past self-harm and cutting were now faint, the internal scars never totally healed. Julianne hid behind her clothing. She considered, then decided against, wearing a hat, choosing instead to wear her long blonde hair loose. She wished she could feel joy in the annual event that most of her former neighbors looked forward to all year. The village green in the small Devon village where she had grown up backed on to the grounds of the new community house, and tours of the facility were one of the fete's attractions.

Gaily colored bunting had been strung up all around the large communal village green. Once a pastoral land where cows and sheep could graze, now the space was used as the site of cricket club fixtures, the visiting fun fair that arrived like clockwork every bank holiday and the annual county fair that still featured the buying and selling of livestock and attracted record entries in flower and vegetable growing competitions. There were also cake baking contests like those featured in the popular television series, *Great British Bake Off.*

No event was more highly anticipated than the Annual Village Fete. Traditional activities included stalls with games like hula hoop, "catch the fish in the jar," secondhand book stalls, homemade cake stands and "Guess the number of sweets in the bottle."

Julianne had always dreaded the day of the village fete. The Carnival Princess and her handmaidens were chosen and crowned. The Princess was at the head of the parade as she sat center stage in a flower bedecked float. In the year of her reign she would become a local celebrity and attend events as a guest of honor and goodwill ambassador.

Although she was arguably the most beautiful girl in school, Julianne was not the most popular. She was not one of the "in-crowd." Sad circumstances surrounded Julianne's move to the village when her mother died of cancer. She always considered herself an outsider.

Her father saw no value in buying her a pretty, fancy dress to wear just for the one day to join the competition. He did not socialize at such events. At most he might decide to take a trip to the local pub, but he usually preferred to drink alone at home.

Julianne was well aware of the horrible feelings of discomfort that the village fete would provoke, but she also believed she needed to face her fears.

"What doesn't kill you makes you stronger," her mother drilled into her. Unfortunately cancer had killed her mother when Julianne was just thirteen. It had made her stronger, but it had also left a huge well of sadness and fear that threatened constantly to overwhelm Julianne.

She had decided to undergo her own form of aversion therapy by coming back to the village and the painful memories.

Dame Amber, the actress and founder of Hope House project, invited her to stay in one of the new cottages on the facility grounds. The cottage had been so beautifully renovated that even Juliane could not recognize the house as being the gray cheerless place where she had grown up.

The guest room had cheerful furnishings, joyful paintings and photos on the walls, magazines and books and a pretty window that overlooked the pastureland and beyond to the riverbank. During her overnight stay in the cottage, Julianne had not been able to sleep. That was nothing new. To avoid the nightmares that terrorized her sleep, she avoided sleeping altogether. Instead Julianne listened to audio books on her Kindle and even tried to learn Spanish.

She deliberately isolated herself from everyone and everything. She asked herself time and again why she had even accepted the invitation to attend the fete. One major reason came to light at dinner the night when she understood why Dame Amber was so insistent she come to the opening event as her guest.

Julianne had not known, but they shared a history. Amber had been a member of a twelve step recovery program and met Julianne there years before. They knew each other only as the kindred spirits who attended the self-help program to get healed and move on from the traumas of their childhood.

Amber was inspired on one occasion when she heard Julianne share her story at a meeting and she promised herself that she too would take up the challenge to get well.

Now the years had moved on, and, when Amber started the school to help children through their childhood traumas, she vowed that she would personally meet and thank Julianne for the strength she gave her, albeit without her knowledge.

She considered it a gift from God when she learned that the person who owned the cottage she needed to acquire for her expansion plans for the home belonged to none other than her inspiration, Julianne. She was determined to do all she could to make sure that Julianne was there to see the work they had done on the grounds. Hope House was a refuge and sanctuary such as they had all needed back when Julianne first attended meetings in London in her early twenties, over a decade before.

Both women had gone on to achieve remarkable success in their lives. At a private dinner the night before the fete with Dame Amber, Julianne and she acknowledged their joint history with silent understanding but had not gone into details. It was enough to know that they were survivors, and now they were helping other children to survive.

* * *

Julianne had purposefully kept herself to herself when she lived in the Devon village where she grew up. The only person she had really befriended was Annabelle Anstruther, her horse-riding friend who, along with Romero, had later destroyed Julianne's life.

She could think of only one person who might be able to give her up-to-date information about Annabelle. The owner of the local stables had encouraged both girls in their riding ventures and had been very glad of their help to muck out the stables. She had not seen or heard from Mrs. Sadie McQueen for two decades, but now she decided to look her up. Queenie was tough as old boots, and Julianne hoped she was still alive and kicking.

At the stables, Queenie welcomed her warmly. "More tea?" she asked as she reached over to refill Julianne's mug. They sat around the solid kitchen table and ate hot buttered scones fresh from the oven, baked by her daughter Nancy. Queenie looked like she ate lots of hot buttered scones and anything else that would contribute to the considerable pounds of weight she carried. Stout would be a kind word for her sturdy body shape. She was dressed for the outdoors in a heavy black cable knit sweater, beige jodhpurs and black riding boots. Her hair was permanently windswept and her complexion ruddy. She never wore a riding hat though she insisted her staff and young riders protect themselves. She considered it a compliment to be described as "horsey."

Julianne recalled the many times she was so grateful to be in the warmth of the farmhouse kitchen after backbreaking outdoor work feeding, cleaning and washing down the horses early in the morning.

"I think of you and your kitchen often," she told Queenie with affection. "I will never forget how good it felt to warm my hands on outsized mugs of milky sweet tea, eat doorstep-sized sausage and bacon sandwiches and warm my backside on the roaring fire."

Queenie smiled and acknowledged the thanks.

In answer to an unasked question from Julianne she told her, "It was a shock to everyone in the village when we heard that Annabelle had been mixed up in criminal activities in Spain, Mind you, she always was an ambitious girl and very different from you who was always so quiet. Annabelle knew what she wanted and she went after it. Even in competition over rosettes at the horse show, I often felt you didn't fight your corner enough. She was determined to beat you and you let her."

"And when it came to chores around the stables, Annabelle always let you do the lion's share. I think you were intimidated by her and she took advantage of your good nature."

The hierarchy at the stables was such that rich girls paid for full stabling and someone else did their chores for them—they were generally members of the official Pony Club and rode with the hunt. Less well-off ones like Julianne helped out at the stables and took visitors out for rides on the moors.

The tradition of the hunt, where dozens of horses and dogs chased a solitary fox across miles of countryside and then allowed the dogs to tear it apart, had never appealed to Julianne. Now she reflected that Annabelle had often ridden out with the hunt and seemed to enjoy being a member of the elite village set who flocked around the master of the hounds.

Julianne knew that she had been a follower rather than a leader especially in those early days but proudly told Queenie, "In business I learned to be the leader I had always wanted to be."

"Do you know where Annabelle is now?" Julianne asked.

"Well, her aunt still lives in the village. Annabelle's mother moved away and I don't think she ever had much to do with her father. Her Aunt Rosemary still works at the school and she seems to keep in touch. I'm not a particular friend and, you know me, I'm not one to gossip, but people do tell me things. I saw her at the farm store a few weeks ago. She told me that she read in the local paper that the Hope House cottage is to be named after you as the benefactor."

"That's not the case," Julianne said, keen to put the record straight. "I'm just glad to be of service."

Queenie nodded. "I'm impressed. I must say you look wonderful. Designer clothes, huh? Not like us country bumpkins. Mind you, Hope House is not an exclusive facility, it gets funding from the government and that means it includes everyone."

"And what about Annabelle?" Julianne gently reminded her.

"I asked after Annabelle and was told she's serving her sentence in a prison not far from here. Her aunt goes to visit. She keeps her up to date with all the village news. It's almost like a holiday camp, according to her aunt. They've got a library, a gym and even a swimming pool. They also encourage the prisoners to take educational courses. Annabelle is studying for a degree in fashion and fine art. I got the impression," said Queenie knowingly, "that it won't be long before she's released on parole. But I don't think she'd come back here. She's been gone too long."

Queenie offered to find the address where Julianne could write to her one-time friend. She obviously was not aware of what had transpired between the two women. No reason why she should be.

Julianne hugged Queenie and for a moment snuggled into the comforting bulk.

"Thank you for everything," she said warmly.

It had been an emotional visit, and now she was anxious to be on her way home. If she managed to track Annabelle down, maybe one day she would confront her. But that would not happen on this trip.

She called Kira Mae from the car en route to the airport and a return flight to Spain.

She was reluctant to talk to her daughter but did want to check that the girls were OK.

Kira Mae shouted into the phone. "Where have you been? I've been going crazy trying to get a hold of you."

"What's so urgent?"

"What's so urgent is that my daughter has gone missing," screeched Kira Mae.

Her heart racing, Julianne asked her to repeat what she had said. "Missing? What do you mean by missing?"

"Missing as in someone picked her up from nursery school yesterday evening. The person claimed to be Paolo but it wasn't him. They handed over Angel but Isabella was with a different teacher and she was still there waiting for me when I went to pick up both of them."

"Have you called the police?" asked Julianne.

"Of course I have." Kira Mae was almost hysterical. "They keep saying, 'Don't worry, she'll turn up.'"

"Did you get in touch with Paolo?"

"Of course," said Kira. "He flew in from Rome last night. I needed him when I couldn't get you." Clearly she couldn't resist a jibe at her mother. Then in a small voice, she added, "Please, Mother, I need you. You've got to get back here. Straight away."

chapter six

"Suspicion always haunts the guilty mind."
—Shakespeare's *King Henry VI*

The first phone call came as Julianne entered the airport lounge to fly to Valencia. Gio Lopez, the small-time crook and crime syndicate enforcer, introduced himself as someone who had "done work for Julianne before."

"There has been a complication," he explained. "Full payment was not received for the contract we had before. Now my bosses are insisting that I make good the loss."

Julianne said nothing, neither wishing to confirm nor deny her involvement. The two had never spoken before. She gripped her chair and tried to shut out the images of Angel's abduction. She refused to betray herself by crying.

"Did you take my niece Angel?"

"My bill needs to be settled," said Gio. "Only you knew that Romero was at that farmhouse. You are lucky that you were never questioned. Luckily I was given funds to accommodate my rehabilitation." He laughed at his own joke. "Sadly those funds are now gone."

"Have you taken Angel?" she repeated.

"Angel . . . ?" He left the rest of the sentence to hang in midair.

The farmhouse where Julianne had promised to meet Romero for an assignation on the day he escaped from prison was not more than an hour from where she had been living. She too had been surprised that the police had not come knocking. They knew only too well of the connection between Romero and Kira, who had wrongfully served a term in prison for a murder actually committed by Romero.

The police must have had reason to believe that Julianne and her daughter might have something to do with his death but had not questioned her. Sometimes she wondered if they had let her off the hook. The murder wasn't even in the papers. Maybe the police were happy that there was one less criminal to worry about?

"You may like to consider this call as an attempt for us to come to a friendly agreement," he said. "You owe me; I intend to collect. I'll be in touch."

Julianne immediately rang Paolo. He would know what to do.

Paolo completely dismissed any suggestion to pay him off. "He's a blackmailer," he said, "and he won't be content with one payment, however large. We have to call his bluff. Do nothing until we hear from him again."

The call over, Julianne walked through the airport like a ghost, having managed to secure the last seat on the last plane out of Heathrow to Spain that night.

She tried to watch a movie but could not concentrate. Instead she feverishly checked her emails before putting her phone into airplane mode and sent Kira Mae a stream of questions.

Who saw Angel last? Where was Isabella? Why did the nursery school release a young child to someone they did not know? Who authorized them to let her go? What was Angel wearing? Had the Spanish police put out an alert for the child? What were they doing to find her? What was Paolo doing?

Paolo returned her emails and tried to reassure everything possible was being done. "This may all be a misunderstanding. No demands have been received."

By the time her plane landed at Valencia, Julianne was a nervous wreck. She almost forgot her overhead luggage until a fellow passenger handed it to her. She strode through the airport, impatiently showed her passport and exited through the Nothing to Declare channel.

Paolo was waiting for her outside the double doors. He took from her hand the one overnight bag she carried.

His face was a mask of anguish, dark circles rimming his eyes, and the skin looked gray. He ran his hands through his hair. "No news, sorry," he said.

Julianne let rip. "What the hell is going on? Why weren't you there to collect both girls? Who did you send to pick them up? Where is she? Oh my God where is that child? She will be so frightened."

"Julianne believe me, the police are doing everything they can. Kira had thought it was better for me to stay away from her and the girls for a while. We didn't want to cause you any more upset."

She shook her head. "Thanks," she said, her tone dripping ice. "So now all this is my fault."

At Paolo's car in the short-term parking lot, he held the door for her, but she did not acknowledge the gesture. She sat in the passenger seat and stared straight ahead.

"So who was supposed to collect the girls?" she asked as Paolo headed for the highway back to their village.

"Kira was supposed to be there," said Paolo, "but she was held up at work. A message to the nursery school saying she was delayed was not passed on. The assistant who signed Angel out said she thought the person waiting at the school gates was me. She didn't even realize that Angel should be going home with Isabella."

Julianne was so angry and scared that she could not even cry. Instead she told Paolo, "If anything happens to Angel, I will kill myself. After I kill you."

Paolo knew what had happened to the last man who had betrayed her. He did not doubt that Julianne would carry out her threat.

chapter seven

"For where thou art, there is the world itself."

—Shakespeare's *Henry VI*

Kira Mae's home was lit up like a Christmas tree, and inside the villa all lights were blazing. Outside a police patrol car had its headlights trained on the driveway and the entrance porch.

Focused only on the missing Angel, Julianne had not had time to construct her story as to any theories she might have about the disappearance. Paolo assured her he would handle everything and, for the time being, Kira Mae did not need to know about the phone call from Gio. Julianne's role in Romero's death was better buried for everyone's sake.

It was a dangerous strategy. Julianne knew she would never forgive herself if information she had that might lead to the missing child was withheld.

There were just two policemen inside the house, an older guy whose English was not very good and a young policewoman who appeared to be in control of the situation.

Kira Mae was in the large family dining area, making coffee.

"Let me do that," said Julianne, taking the coffeepot from Kira's hands and placing it on the black granite countertop. "Who's having what?"

Kira Mae allowed her mother to take control as she slumped onto the bench at the kitchen table. Half-heartedly she dropped a toy into a large wicker laundry basket and threw a coloring book to the far end of the kitchen table on top of a pile of crayons.

"The nursery school owner has already started an investigation into how Angel was allowed to leave the premises with a stranger. Seems that a new member of staff mistook the guy who collected her for Paolo."

Kira put her elbows on the table, her head in her hands and began to sob.

"If I hadn't been late, this never would have happened," she told her mother, who had left the coffeepot on the stand and was now trying to cradle her unresponsive daughter in her arms.

"Hush now," said Julianne. "It's not about blame, it's about doing all we can to get Angel back home safe and sound. What do the police say? What are they doing?"

Kira Mae raised her head and let her mother wipe away her tears. Julianne managed to hold back her own. Her daughter took several deep breaths, wiped her eyes with her fist and accepted the tissues her mother handed to her.

"The police showed up at the school when the

owner called them. Kids are always going home with some relative or other and everyone panics until the situation is sorted out. When I arrived to pick up the girls and Angel was nowhere to be seen, I lost it. I shouted at the young teacher and the owner. Angel should never have been allowed to leave the building without the proper procedures being followed."

Julianne removed the coffeepot and poured the steaming liquid into mugs on the counter.

"Have you got cream?" she said.

"Milk," said Kira. "No sugar but there are a few sachets of Sweet'N Low; Paolo takes it in his coffee." She had the grace to look embarrassed.

Her mother shook her head. "It's OK," she said. "Getting Angel back is our only priority now."

Paolo stood up as Kira Mae and Julianne entered the living room. Julianne put the tray in the middle of the table and urged the police officers to help themselves.

"The only cookies I could find are animal crackers and Jammie Dodgers," she added, almost apologetically.

As Julianne looked up, she caught Paolo watching her with bemusement. No wonder—the last time they had spoken she had threatened to kill him unless he found Angel.

"Let me bring you up to date," said the young policewoman who insisted they call her Terri, short for Theresa. "The local police headquarters have issued a national alert. That will go to all police stations, newspapers, radio and television stations. We will use the photo you have given us and post it online. Our public information department takes care of that and they will follow up any questions or requests for further information. Any questions so far?"

Kira Mae, Julianne and Paolo shook their heads. The television was already tuned to the local news station and Paolo was monitoring developments on his phone. The police radios were turned down low but were still audible.

"A crime scene unit is on the way," said Terri, "and they'll set up an electronic tap on your landline. Your business number has been routed here."

The family felt reassured. Terri explained, "For a missing adult we have to let 24 hours elapse, so often they turn up of their own volition. With a child, we put all procedures into place with immediate effect. You can be sure that the whole country is now looking for your child."

Unfortunately if that piece of information had been meant to reassure the family, all it did was terrify Kira Mae that her five-year-old daughter was out there somewhere, with person or persons unknown, and all she could do was sit at home helplessly, drinking coffee and watching the television.

Kira Mae began to cry.

Paolo looked as if he was about to go and comfort her but thought better of it.

Julianne went to Kira, sat on the arm of her chair and held her hand. Kira didn't pull away. Everything Julianne tried to say sounded meaningless. She could find no words of reassurance that rang true. The best she could come up with was, "We're all here for you. It will be OK. She'll be fine. You'll see."

Terri asked, "Do you want me to call a doctor?"

Kira Mae reacted badly. "Don't be stupid," she snapped. "My daughter is missing and you think I want to be sedated?"

The police officer looked suitably chastened. "I didn't mean to upset you," she said. "But maybe you should try to get some rest. It could be a while. A family officer has been requested to stay with you, but I suspect it may be morning before he or she arrives."

Rosita, Kira's housekeeper and babysitter, had also been contacted by police, as she sometimes picked the girls up from nursery school, but she knew nothing. This was not a working day for her. Kira or Paolo were supposed to have collected them.

By the early hours of the morning, Isabella had cried herself to sleep because Angel was not there. "Is Angel in trouble?" she had asked Kira Mae when she was being tucked in. "Did she do something wrong?"

"No, darling, she did nothing wrong," said Kira Mae, anxious not to make the situation any worse in Isabella's vulnerable little mind. "There's just been a misunderstanding. It will all be alright soon."

"Mama Mae, don't go away. Stay outside my door and leave the light on."

"Of course, we're keeping the light on for Angel as well," she told her.

Kira Mae sank to the floor outside the girls' bedroom and cried her eyes out. The policewoman could see her from the living room and gestured for her male colleague to let Kira be.

"Let her cry," she told him. "There may be plenty more tears before this is all over."

chapter eight

"Where thou art not, desolation."
—Shakespeare's *Henry VI*

All night long, the police radio relayed messages. At each beep the sad household sprang to alert. Kira Mae insisted on sitting in an armchair in the living room, even though she would keep drifting off to sleep and waking in discomfort when the radio sprang to life or someone in the house went to the bathroom. Julianne had been persuaded to go to bed even though she knew she would not sleep. Paolo stationed himself outside by the pool.

All three were locked in their own misery and could not offer comfort to the others.

Paolo knew that he really should have made full disclosure about the phone call from Gio. You did not need to be a criminal defense lawyer to know that the information was crucial. He had not yet formulated an adequate plan. When the question was asked, "Do you know anyone who might have done this? Is there anyone you know who might want to harm you or your children? Do you have any enemies?" Paolo knew the answer was, "Yes."

It was too much of a coincidence. Gio was a known criminal who worked for the mob.

Gio and Kira had been arrested in the same undercover operation. They had both served sentences and been released back into the community. *Oh what a tangled web we weave when first we practice to deceive.* Paolo could see no way out. He could not endanger Angel any further by concealing what he knew. This was no random abduction.

⋆ ⋆ ⋆

The house was as quiet as a tomb when the phone rang just before dawn. Kira Mae leapt from her chair, and Julianne was pulling a dress over her head as she ran into the room. In the doorway, Paolo took up his position.

"Pick up the phone," signaled the policewoman to Kira.

Her bare feet left moisture imprints on the marble floor as she crossed the room.

"Hello," she said. "This is Kira Mae." Her voice was calm, but her knuckles were white as her hand gripped the receiver.

A woman's voice told her: "Your daughter is safe. We intend her no harm."

"Then why did you take her? Where is she?" Kira Mae's words spilled one over the other. "Please, please," she pleaded. "Bring her home."

Julianne took the phone from her. "Is she there? Can

we speak to her? She's only a child, please don't hurt her. She needs to be here with her family."

Kira Mae grabbed the phone. "If you hurt her, I will, I will… it will be the worst for you." Her voice trailed away, her threat empty. "She's never been away from home before. Please bring her home."

"She's OK," the woman said. "You can take my word for it," in a tone that seemed intended to reassure.

Without warning the phone went dead. "She's hung up." Shocked, Kira Mae shouted at anyone who would listen. "What happens now?"

No one answered. There was nothing to do but continue to wait. Only the police had activity to keep them occupied. A shift change was due and Terri was busy with paperwork. Her male colleague spent most of his time in the car, periodically returning to update the family.

"It was a mobile phone, we are still trying to track the location. The good news is that headquarters think it is local," Terri told them.

Kira Mae and Julianne sat and stared at the phone, willing it to ring again. From the kitchen the smell of freshly brewed coffee and baking told them that, as always, Paolo was making himself useful. He carried a tray into the living room loaded with mugs and chocolate croissants. Though Kira Mae and Julianne at first refused, they were nevertheless temped by the delicious aroma and the fact that neither had eaten for well over twelve hours.

As they ate breakfast, Paolo explained some of the procedures that would be taking place at headquarters.

"It may seem quiet here," Paolo told them, "but the center of operations is at the police station. A nationwide search is ongoing and regular updates will be reported to the media."

As the morning news programs started up, a photo of Angel appeared on each bulletin along with a number to call. A vigil had been held in the local church to pray for Angel's safe return. Kira Mae couldn't take her eyes off the information stream. After a feeble attempt at eating, she agreed to take a shower to freshen up in readiness for what the day might bring.

Paolo tore apart a croissant. It tasted like cardboard but he had to do something to keep his hands occupied. He dreaded the conversation he was about to have with Julianne.

He directed Julianne out to the pool and indicated for her to take a seat at the small table where they had shared hundreds of meals, drinks and confidences. He handed her a wrap but resisted actually settling it around her bare shoulders.

He wasted no time. "We have to tell the police about Gio."

Julianne looked away, embarrassed. "I had hoped to avoid it," she admitted.

Paolo kept his eyes firmly fastened on her. "We could never forgive ourselves," he pointed out, "if something happened."

"I know that, of course, I know that," she replied.

"Part of me hoped that Gio calling and Angel going missing were unconnected. Gio just said he wanted money."

Paolo rarely lost his temper with Julianne—Kira Mae had accused him of being blind to her mother's faults and making too many allowances for what she thought of as her mother's unacceptable behavior—now he lost his cool. "Don't be so naive," he exploded. "It's ridiculous to pretend there is no connection. You might be able to fool yourself but you won't fool anyone else. Certainly not Kira Mae."

Julianne burst into tears, but Paolo refused to let her off the hook. "Her daughter has been kidnapped," he enunciated every word. "And it is more than likely that whoever took her meant to take your daughter, not Kira Mae's. You and I have vital information that could change the whole course of this investigation. I refuse to stay silent any longer. I bitterly regret that I did not admit what I knew straightaway. You and I both know Gio is behind this. The consequences to you or I are of no concern anymore. We have to tell the truth."

She had never seen Paolo so angry. He was always so composed, so focused on the solution. Always the lawyer. Frightened as she was of the demons they were about to release, Julianne nodded. There was no question that Julianne would do the right thing when it came to her family. Julianne had always known that one day she would have to atone for the death of Romero. Of course her punishment would be bound to come wrapped in an agonizing tale of despair and anguish.

Kira Mae appeared in the pool area without warning. "What's all the shouting about?" she demanded.

Paolo took charge. "Your mother and I need to go to the police station. It's complicated, but I'll tell you all about it when we get back. We have information that we believe can help the investigation."

"What do you mean?" said Kira Mae, visibly stunned.

"There is no time to go into it now," he told her.

Paolo often accompanied clients to the police station. Now he turned his back on Kira Mae, appointing himself as Julianne's lawyer.

"Get dressed, Julianne," he said. "I'll call the officer in charge and tell him we are on our way. Take a sweater, it's always cold in the police station and we may be there for a while."

chapter nine

"Now join your hands,
and with your hand your heart."
—Shakespeare's *Henry VI*

Julianne's high heels clicked on the tiled floor as she strode into the local police station. She looked a lot more confident than she felt. Press photographers pushed forward to get a close-up of the tall blonde whose white gauze dress wafted around her tanned legs.

Paolo was by her side just as he had been six years before in Rome when he had acted as Kira Mae's lawyer. The police chief was expecting them but had underestimated the degree of interest the story had already attracted. Missing children were always a top story priority but when the child was the daughter of a high-profile British fashion designer in a small sleepy Spanish town, interest was sky-high.

Camera crews, photographers and reporters who represented national and local media crowded the narrow corridor that led to the reception desk and onward to police cells and administrative offices.

Reporters were anxious for answers. "Do you have

someone under arrest? Where is the mother of the child? Is she under arrest? Have you found the child? Is this a domestic situation? Who was the last person to see the child? Do you have any suspects in mind?"

Paolo was in professional mode as he guided his client firmly but gently through the crowd.

"We have nothing to say," he spoke for Julianne and held up his briefcase as he endeavored to keep the press at bay. Julianne stared straight ahead.

The police chief emerged from his office and escorted Julianne and Paolo to a small waiting room at the back of the building. All nonessential personnel had been instructed to leave the area. He was aware that Julianne had come to the station of her own volition to offer information that hopefully would shed new light on the missing child investigation. She was not a suspect.

"Can I offer you a coffee?" he asked first Julianne, then Paolo. Both shook their heads.

On the short drive from Kira's home to the station, Paolo had instructed his client.

"Let me do all the talking," he told Julianne. "You have done nothing wrong. I will answer questions about what you know and leave the police to decide if it's relevant."

In the car he had held her hand to reassure her, but at the police station, although they sat together on a couch that had seen better days, he maintained a professional distance.

"I will be declaring a personal interest," he told Julianne, "and telling the police that I am a friend of the family. They need not know any more than that for the time being."

Julianne nodded. She did not trust herself to speak. A cold, clammy fear gripped her insides. It felt like Romero's body was about to be exhumed. For years she had buried thoughts of her role in his death. Driven by a hundred forms of self-delusion she told herself that he deserved to die for what he had done to her family, and her only crime was to pass on an address—the farmhouse where he had been hiding out following his escape from prison.

Yes, she had betrayed him, but he had done the same to her and to Kira Mae.

She was not the one who had twisted the knife in his guts. Gio had done that—at her bidding. Still, history was repeating itself. Romero had incriminated Kira Mae as an accessory to the murder of his fiancé, Michella de Jesus Santa Castellana. Julianne and Kira Mae had met the girl once at the restaurant where Romero was hired to entertain the patrons. In a crash on a dangerous stretch of mountain road, Michella's car crashed over the cliff. It was originally thought to be a tragic accident, but later the suspicion fell on Romero as a suspect in her murder. Romero was a career criminal; this was one more murder, one more acquittal.

Now in a bizarre twist, Julianne was to be revealed as an accessory to Romero's murder.

It was as if a hundred evil genies had escaped from the bottle during Romero's reign. His international billion-dollar business was built on murder, drug dealing, gun running and money laundering. Romero showed no mercy to those who crossed him. Julianne knew that his enforcers who still carried out his instructions would show no mercy to her now.

Please God, his slayer and chief enforcer, Gio, would not hurt an innocent child. However, she wouldn't bet on it.

The police chief assured Julianne and Paolo that everything possible was being done to find Angel.

"We have several leads," he informed her, "and my officers are following up everything that might be of interest. Now, I look forward to hearing how you think you can help."

"It is a little complicated," Paolo told the chief, a mature man with decades of exemplary service to Guardia Civil on his service record. A young policewoman sitting nearby took notes. "My client believes that a recent phone conversation she had with a known criminal, not a local one, may have some bearing on this case. You will already know, I am sure, that her daughter, Kira Mae, the mother of the missing child, served a sentence in Italy as an accessory to murder overseen by a criminal mastermind, Romero Rosario, also known as Jesus Santos Floris."

The police chief took up the story. "Oh yes, Romero was legendary," he told them, as if they did not know. "He mostly operated in Italy, his adopted homeland. He had Mafia connections, but he was Spanish by birth. He lived for a while in a neighboring town and, when his fiancée was killed in a road traffic accident on the notorious coast road between here and Altea, on the Costa Blanca in Spain, he was suspected of murdering the poor girl. Michella was a festival queen, La Reina, from a very prominent family. He operated here under the cover of being a respectable flamenco musician, and I understand he was very popular, especially with the ladies, in the local bars and restaurants where he performed."

The young policewoman's pen hovered expectantly over her notepad, poised for the next episode as the soap opera unfolded.

Paolo interrupted, determined to put his own spin on the story.

"Kira Mae was entirely innocent," Paolo was at pains to point out. "She knew nothing of Romero's activities, but we accepted a plea deal and she served a two-year sentence. She was pregnant at the time with the child who was abducted last night."

This was news to the chief and he leaned forward in his chair.

Paolo chose his words carefully. "Romero should have died in jail an old man but subsequently escaped. You know the rest."

Julianne shot him a puzzled look and shifted nervously on the couch. Crossing and uncrossing her legs, she wished she could get up and stretch. Every muscle in her body was rigid and tense.

Paolo then used a tactic common to lawyers in this type of interview session. He offered a crucial piece of information.

"My client received a phone call from one of the crooks who worked for Romero. Since this Gio was released from prison, he has fallen on hard times." Paolo took the chance on making a joke that he hoped the chief would not take as disrespectful. "Things must be quiet in the mafia robbery and extortion business," he said.

The police chief acknowledged the attempt to lighten the tension in the room.

"Go on," he said.

"Gio contacted my client and suggested that he was in need of money. He said he would be in touch."

Quick to see the connection, the chief clarified the situation. "And now Angel is missing?"

"Yes. My client was out of the country, but we cannot help but feel there may be a connection."

"How did he make contact?" he wanted to know. "Phone, email, social media?"

"Julianne is high profile," explained Paolo. "She often appears in celebrity magazines and on television. Mother and daughter are well known in the world of fashion and their Galleria in Villajoyosa is one of the best-known cultural centers in town. Maybe even more famous than our Valor Museum of Chocolate."

"And how did he make contact?" the chief asked again, anxious to gloss over what he obviously considered to be superfluous details.

"Her phone number is made available to the public to allow clients to schedule appointments for fashion fittings."

"Why did you not tell the police officers at your house all this information?" asked the police chief.

"As I am sure you will appreciate, the mother of the child is almost hysterical; she is on the verge of collapse. It seemed better to bring the information direct to you," Paolo explained, "instead of alarming her further."

That answer appeared to satisfy him. Now he excused himself as he signaled for the policewoman to follow him. "I will need the phone on which the call was received. I will be back," he said. "Would you like that coffee now?"

Julianne nodded. "Yes, please," she said with a grateful smile. They were the first words she had said since the interview started. Paolo's airbrushed version of the story had deflected the attention away from Julianne and drawn a picture of a crook fallen on hard times who was desperate for money and ready to try all options.

The coffee arrived and Julianne attempted to make conversation with Paolo. He shook his head.

"Whatever it is, it can wait," he admonished her. "Where's your phone?"

In the waiting room at a police station, there was always a danger that their conversation was being monitored.

Julianne nodded. She felt stupid for not having realized. She reluctantly handed over the phone as she searched her brain for any messages or phone numbers that she would not wish the police to be able to identify. Paolo handed the phone to the young policewoman who had returned to the room. As far as she knew, only the call from Gio could get her into trouble.

The young policewoman accompanied them to the front of the building. "There is still a horde of members of the press outside," she said to Paolo. "Do you want an escort to your car?"

"No thank you," Paolo replied. "It's parked right by the exit."

"Good-bye," said the policewoman as she took her leave of the couple. "If you need anything, just let the officers at the house know. We are doing everything in our power. Your little girl should be back home very soon, safe and sound."

Only a handful of press lurked outside the police building. They had been told to expect a news conference later that afternoon, and this seemed as good a time as any for them to grab a meal break. They already had their pictures of Julianne entering the station, and the implications of that shot were more open to innuendo than her leaving it.

Julianne even risked taking Paolo's arm as they walked the few yards to the car.

"Thank you," she said. "I don't know what I would have done without you."

Paolo gave her a wry smile. "That was the easy part," he said. "Now you have to face Kira Mae and tell her the whole story. Don't worry, I'll be with you. I'm not going anywhere."

chapter ten

"What greater punishment is there than life when you've lost everything that made it worth living?"
—Shakespeare's *Romeo and Juliet*

On the ride home through the arid Spanish countryside, Julianne took the opportunity to question the phone call they had received.

"Is it a good sign that the phone call was from a woman? I mean, a woman is less likely to hurt a child, right?"

"Obviously we are meant to think that," said Paolo, measuring his words, "but it's a ploy to give you a false sense of reassurance. It leaves the kidnappers more room to ramp up the pressure when the next call is from a man. I'm afraid nothing is ever what it seems," he admitted. "It depends on whether the operation was planned or spontaneous."

Much as she wanted to focus on Angel, Julianne could not resist asking, "What do you think will happen to me? Will the police arrest me? What can they charge me with? They only know I took a phone call from a known criminal."

"In theory they could charge you with withholding vital information, or even wasting police time, but I don't think it's likely."

Julianne settled back in the comfort and security of Paolo's SUV with its roomy leather seats. Julianne was glad that Paolo was not still driving his Ferrari Testarossa, the gleaming red Italian sports car he had zoomed around the streets of Rome in when she first met him.

Paolo looked sheepish when she mentioned his choice of vehicle. "The Ferrari still makes an appearance now and then, but most of the time it's stuck in a garage. I drive the SUV; it's more practical for ferrying Kira Mae and the girls around."

Julianne said nothing. Paolo shrugged. He had not meant to introduce a contentious subject, but the fact was that he was a major part of Kira's and the children's lives. And Julianne's when she was in Spain.

She remembered what she heard years before: to instigate an affair, women need a reason, men need an opportunity. That worldview felt cynical even to her, but in her heart of hearts she wanted to believe Paolo's version of events. One drunken night. One mistake.

As they arrived back at the house, a distraught Kira Mae ran through the garden gate into the driveway. Before they got out of the car, she was yelling, "They called again. The people who took Angel called again. Not a woman this time, a man."

Julianne and Paolo exchanged a quick glance as he turned off the engine.

"They want money," said Kira Mae breathlessly, directing her words at Paolo. "They'll phone again and give instructions."

He quickly took charge of the situation. "OK, that's a good sign," he told her. "They're working fast. Their intention is to get money, not to hold on to Angel."

Isabella appeared in her bathing suit. "Mama Mae took me swimming," said Isabella, "but she's not as much fun to play with as Angel. When's Angel coming back?" she demanded.

Having reminded herself that her sister and playmate was not there, she started to wail.

"I want Angel. I want Angel," she said. It soon became a chant.

"We all do darling. She'll be home soon," said Julianne, as she bent down and scooped the crying child into her arms. "Come on, let's go and see if there is any chocolate ice cream in the fridge. I know you are not usually allowed ice cream before lunch but today we'll make an exception."

"What's an exception?" asked Isabella.

Paolo winked at Julianne, who blinked back a tear.

In the living room, two new police officers were keeping vigil. One of the officers suggested turning off the television in the corner of the room, Julianne suspected, so that Angel's beautiful face would not appear on screen every few minutes. Kira seemed to visibly deflate every time the image flashed on TV. The photograph that the news networks were using showed her dressed in pink and holding a doll as she walked into nursery school just two days before. Isabella had been edited out of the photograph.

They also showed a photo of Kira Mae, the very picture of the distraught mother at the nursery school gates having just discovered her daughter was missing. Julianne assumed that this must have been taken by another parent.

"Seems that these days everyone with a cell phone fancies themselves as a photo journalist," she commented to Paolo.

The police had asked Kira Mae to make an on-screen appeal but, Paolo had resisted it for the time being.

"It becomes a side show for the viewers," he explained, "rather than a genuine appeal to the abductors. They know you want your daughter back. We can reconsider later if there are no developments."

Paolo quizzed the police who had been there when the second telephone call came in.

"It was very brief," they told him. "We have trackers on the phone, but we need a little time."

The young fresh-faced policeman consulted his notes. "The caller said, 'There will be a price to pay to have your daughter returned. We'll be in touch.'"

Kira Mae had tried to speak to the caller—"Is she OK? Can I speak to her? Please let me hear my daughter's voice"—before the line went dead.

"He sounded so calm," she said. "Not like the woman who called. I could tell she was nervous. I felt better when I knew Angel was with a woman." Echoing her mother's earlier thoughts, she said, "Isn't a woman less likely to hurt a child?"

Clearly, the phone call had distracted Kira Mae from demanding to know what her mother and Paolo had discussed at the police station, but it would only be a matter of time.

To remove herself from the awkward conversation that Paolo was about to have with Kira Mae, Julianne suggested that she make lunch. "There's probably only chicken nuggets and fish fingers in the fridge," she admitted. "Someone will have to go to the supermarket and pick up supplies. I'll go, and take Isabella with me. I've got my mobile if there are any developments." As an afterthought she added, "And I'll swing by the Galleria too."

"There are police on duty at the Galleria," Paolo told her. "Do you want me to come with you?"

"No, you stay with Kira Mae," she told him. "She needs you more than I do."

Isabella was happy to go on an outing to the shops. Without Angel she had trouble amusing herself, and with all the adults whispering all the time, she knew something was going on.

She just didn't know what. Kira Mae had made up a story that the police were helping her with her work. The word *work* was a turn off to Isabella; she had little interest in it except to know that adults always seemed to be "going to work."

"Are we going to get Angel now?" she asked.

"Maybe later," Julianne answered.

Strapped into the backseat, Isabella played with her iPad. "Mama JoJo, I'm doing school work," she said. "I type in 'Spanish for Kids' and learn a new word every day. 'Hola' is my favorite. I say it to everyone. Then I ask them, 'Comm esta?' That means, 'How are you?'" Her little face screwed up. "I ask everyone, except the new lady at nursery school. She's horrible. I don't like her. Angel doesn't like her either."

Isabella prattled on and instead of Julianne telling her, "Play your game, Mummy needs to concentrate on driving," she asked Isabella, "and why is the new lady so horrible?"

"Because she makes Angel leave me on my own."

Julianne caught her breath. She didn't know what it meant, but she didn't like the sound of it.

"When, baby?" she asked.

"She made me cry. She said Angel had to go away with her. I couldn't go."

"Where was she going?" Julianne pulled the car into the supermarket parking lot in the row closest to the entrance. She turned to Isabella. "Where was she going?" asked Julianne again.

Isabella looked confused and scared. "I don't know," she said. "I didn't do anything wrong."

"Of course you didn't," said Julianne as she unstrapped the child and lifted her out of the car. "Here, keep hold of my hand. I need to make a phone call." Paolo was her go-to man as always. She reached into her handbag and swore. No phone.

Her head in a spin, Julianne didn't know which way

to turn. Isabella did. She wriggled away from Julianne and ran toward the shopping carts. "I want to be a trolley dolly," she called over her shoulder. "I get to sit in the cart."

Julianne followed her and lifted Isabella into the seat. "Stay put while I make this phone call," she said. She ran to the phone booth she had seen inside the door of the supermarket. It was primarily there for shoppers to call taxis, but she was relieved to find it was also good for outside calls. She scrambled in her change purse. She had no idea how much a phone call cost so she fed in all the coins she could lay her hands on. She was all fingers and thumbs and could hardly place the money in the slot. A couple of coins fell on the ground, and she left them there.

Paolo answered immediately, and Julianne relayed the conversation she had just had with Isabella.

"Leave it with me," he said. "We can talk when you get back from the supermarket. Better yet, drive to the nursery school when you've finished shopping and I'll meet you there."

To any staff or shoppers observing her, Julianne must have looked like she was on a manic dash while Isabella called out urgent reminders.

"You passed the pizzas," she yelled. "And the fries."

The drive to the nursery school took less than ten minutes.

Paolo was already there in the small runabout he was driving today; it had seen better days. A vision flashed across her mind of him in the driver's seat of the flame-red Ferrari. He had been the epitome of the super-stylish man about town, a handsome silver fox. Regret ran through her. She and her family had turned him into a gofer who ran around after all of them. Could she ever recover from his betrayal with her own daughter? After all that he knew about her family background? Julianne forced the unhelpful thoughts to one side.

"Now tell me again what Isabella said," he ordered.

He listened as Julianne relayed the child's conversation.

"Let me go in first," he said, "and talk to the owner. She's phoned the house several times asking if there are any developments. You stay here with Isabella."

Isabella unlocked her seat belt. "I'm going to nursery school," she told Julianne.

"No, no," Julianne relocked the belt. "Not now. Later."

Isabella pouted. "Where's Angel? I want Angel."

Julianne could sense that a crying session was about to erupt. She got in the backseat to keep Isabella company.

"Let's have some music on your iPad," she said. "We can sing along."

Isabella brightened.

They were still making music selections when Paolo charged out through the nursery school gates. Despite his usual outward calm demeanor, Julianne could see that he was furious.

Paolo had used his best lawyer interrogation techniques on the owner. He told Julianne what he discovered. "The owner admitted that she didn't do a proper background check on the new classroom assistant. They were short-staffed and the owner took on this friend of a friend. She's been on staff for less than a week and she's not here now. Didn't show up for work today. Won't answer her phone."

"Why the hell didn't she tell the police?" demanded Julianne.

"Didn't want to get in trouble for not following procedure. She knows she could get closed down for it," said Paolo.

"Where does this classroom assistant live?" asked Julianne. "Let's go there. Now."

Paolo shook his head. "We can't take the law into our own hands. We have no idea what we might find if we go round there. Leave it to the police. I've told them about it and they're interviewing the owner on the phone and taking contact details. Just remember she may have nothing to do with Angel's disappearance. It may be a pure coincidence."

"Yes, like Gio turning up out of the blue," said Julianne.

"See you back at the villa," he called over his shoulder as he stomped toward the beat-up old car.

Julianne jumped back into her car. "Who wants ice cream when we get home?" she asked.

"Yeah," shouted Isabella from the backseat, "but we have to leave some for Angel."

chapter eleven

"Tempt not a desperate man."
—Shakespeare's *Romeo & Juliet*

Siesta time threw a blanket of sleepiness over the villa.

Even the police officers seemed to nod off on the couch in Kira Mae's living room. All conversation had been exhausted. Further speculation was futile until some new development advanced the situation.

The arrival of a new police car at the villa gates awoke the whole household. The officers inside the house sprang to attention and made their way outside to greet their colleagues. It was too early for a shift change so their appearance suggested that there had been developments. Significant ones, as the police chief himself emerged from the patrol vehicle, surrounded by his officers. In a navy-blue uniform topped off with a shiny peaked cap, a gun on his hip and multiple badges of honor on his brass-buttoned tunic, he was a commanding presence.

He settled on the couch in the living room and addressed everyone in the room.

"The woman who was employed at the nursery

school is Christina Alvarez. She has no criminal record, but she is known to us. Her husband went to jail a few years ago for fraud and receiving stolen goods. We have not been able to speak with her yet. We visited her home in a small village on the coast close to Altea. A neighbor saw her board the train for Alicante a couple of days before but did not think she had come back. Her cat had been outside the house for a couple of days and the neighbor has been feeding it."

Julianne asked the obvious question. "Did the neighbor say she had a child with her?"

The chief shook his head.

Paolo was anxious to know, "Has she been declared an official 'person of interest'?"

"Yes," Police Chief Xabia assured him. "I came to inform the mother of the child first, but we will release her name to the media as someone we wish to interview. The appeal will be national and international. We understand that this woman lived in Rome before arriving in Spain with her husband about ten years ago."

Julianne bit the inside of her cheek. Kira Mae chewed on her fingernails, a habit she had never been able to break.

"It was her, wasn't it?" she said. "Who phoned me?"

"We can't be sure of that," said Chief Xabia, "but all the pieces of the puzzle seem to be falling into place. We will of course keep you informed of any developments."

At that he took his leave and a strange easing of tension replaced the desperation of uncertainty.

Progress was being made. The police were on the case. There was a suspect in the frame.

Endless cups of coffee fueled the endless questions.

Where is Angel? Is she safe? Why haven't her abductors contacted us again to demand their payment?

Kira Mae constantly checked her mobile and stared at the landline phone willing it to ring. She was in the bathroom with Isabella when the phone did ring. Julianne had gone to the Galleria, and Paolo was totally absorbed in his laptop. He had no immediate intention of returning to his office at the British Embassy in Rome, but he did have work to be getting on with and documents to prepare.

A new policewoman picked up the phone and held it out to Kira Mae. She took it and listened, her heart beating hard.

The male voice that Kira Mae recognized from the previous call started barking orders at her. "Tomorrow you will have the money ready. Fifty thousand euros, cash. You will receive further instructions. Be ready. If you bring the police, the deal is off."

"What about Angel? What about my daughter?" asked Kira, desperate to have confirmation before he hung up the phone.

"She is fine. She is being taken care of. You will get her back when we get our money."

The call ended as abruptly as before. Paolo took the handset from Kira Mae's hand and replaced it. "I'll go see your bank manager," he said. "He can't fail to know what has happened with all the publicity. Leave it with me. The company account will have to be used as security. As soon as your mother gets home we will sit down and work it all out."

The policewoman was already on her phone, and it was obvious that she felt the police chief needed an input at this stage.

"What about the police?" whispered Kira Mae when the policewoman was out of earshot. "Will they try to stop us delivering the money?"

"Give me some thinking time, please," he told Kira Mae. "I need to work this out."

Kira Mae had not fully understood the implications of the phone call her mother had received from Gio. This was neither the time nor place to have to reveal dangerous details about the connections to Romero. Paolo had offered her no insight into the possibility of a direct link between Romero's death and Angel's abduction.

Though she was exhausted, Kira Mae had not slept. Her body refused to relax enough even to let her lie down for more than a few minutes. Eyes closed she would see the beautiful face of her darling Angel. On one occasion, when she had drifted into a state somewhere between waking and sleeping, she thought she heard Angel cry out for her. "Mama Mae, where are you?" Kira blamed herself for everything. If she hadn't seduced Paolo, he would not have distanced himself from the family. If she had left work when she was supposed to, she would have collected her daughter and none of this would have happened.

She told herself she was a lousy mother.

Mentally she beat herself with obsessive thoughts.

What if they hurt her daughter? What if she never saw her again? Why was she late to pick her up? How dare the nursery school let her leave with a stranger?

Kira Mae looked outside. A television satellite van was stationed at the bottom of the lane and as much as the police tried to prevent it, enterprising reporters had still found their way to the bougainvillea-draped driveway of the villa. She and the girls had loved the villa on first sight. The mountain range dominated the backdrop of the whitewashed property with its blue shutters. It was very close to town but still secluded. It didn't feel secluded anymore.

"One day I am going to climb that mountain," Kira had told the girls. But she never did. She was too busy working. She should have spent more time with her beloved daughter, she reflected now. When she came back, then they would climb the mountain. Together.

In her aimless wandering through the marble-floored villa, Kira picked up and put down items belonging to Angel. A large pile of photographs she had looked through for the media took up most of the dining-room table. Angel holding her favorite doll, Angel with a friendly dog, Angel on the beach, Angel on her bike, Angel sitting in a giant box of toys, Angel on a theme park ride. Angel giving her mother a huge hug.

She pored over the photographs, praying. Kira Mae sensed there was a missing component in the abduction, but she couldn't put her finger on it. She didn't know where to look for the missing piece of the jigsaw.

"Please, God, bring Angel home safe. I promise I will be a good mother. I will put her first. I'll give up work. I'll become a stay-at-home mum. I promise I'll never, ever let her out of my sight again."

Kira Mae did not know what was worse, being alone in the house with non–English speaking police officers for company while her mother and Paolo went about their business, or being treated like a child.

The phone rang and Kira answered it, her hands clammy. She was relieved to find it was Paolo calling to say that the visit to the bank had gone off without a hitch. Their friendly local bank manager had promised to take care of everything. As soon as instructions for the delivery of the money was received, he would have the funds to hand. The bank had promised to be at their service 24/7.

* * *

Paolo and Julianne sat in the hard-backed chairs at the police station across the desk from Police Chief Xabia. The meeting was cordial but it was obvious that both sides had different agendas. Paolo's instinct had been right. The chief cautioned him against paying the ransom, at pains to point out that kidnappers were not honorable. Meeting their demands did not ensure the safe return of the victim. Family photographs on the chief's desk showed smiling grandchildren—at least they indicated that he would understand the dilemma of a parent missing their beloved child.

What parent would not pay to have their child returned?

On their way to the meeting at the police station, Paolo had assured Julianne that the police could not actually prevent them from handing over ransom money to the kidnappers. However, they could threaten to withdraw police protection or more likely suggest that going alone, as per the kidnapper's instructions, was not sensible or safe.

"I urge you to let us deal with this," said the chief. "Let me send one of my men. We will contain the situation and endeavor to have the child returned, as well as arrest the perpetrators."

Paolo thought, *Good luck with that,* and only smiled. He did not want to antagonize the chief or frighten Julianne further. They needed Chief Xabia on their side. They were law-abiding citizens, doing everything they could to assist the police force.

Paolo said, "When the next phone call comes in, I plan to offer to deliver the ransom money. I do *not* want police back-up."

The chief opened a buff-colored file that lay on the top of his desk.

"Now, let's talk about Gio Lopez," he said. "A career criminal. Recently released from prison after serving yet another sentence. He can't seem to stay out of trouble for more than a few months. Many members of the criminal organizations he likes to boast he works for have already discarded him. My colleagues in Rome judge that he has become increasingly more desperate. This may be a last-ditch attempt to set himself up financially. They formed the opinion that he is working alone. Although he may have an accomplice. A woman."

Julianne gasped. "Is it the woman from the nursery school?"

"Too early to tell," admitted the police chief. "Gio was living in a run-down part of town, but we no longer have an address for him. A police informant claimed that he had recently acquired a new girlfriend. Not a local."

Julianne and Paolo started to fire questions at the same time, and Chief Xabia held up his hand, urging patience.

"Gio is now under surveillance. If the woman turns up, she will be too. We are in the process of obtaining a search warrant for her property."

Paola pushed back his chair, allowing it to scrape on the worn wooden floor, and stood up. Instinctively he held out a steadying hand to Julianne as she rose from her chair and gathered up her purse from the desk.

"Please, do not do anything foolish," the chief cautioned. "You will be the first to know of any developments," he added, stating the obvious as the house phone was already linked to the police system. Not that they had had any success with tracing the incoming calls so far. Mobile phones were not easy to track. Their signals move between receiving towers and it is easy to change phone numbers and dispose of devices.

Forty-eight hours after Angel disappeared, a system had been established. Press conferences were held twice a day. The news bulletins led with the photograph of the woman employed at the nursery school now named as Christina Alvarez. Police identified her as someone they were anxious to interview, a "person of interest."

News broadcasts were supplemented with film of the nursery school, shots of the family home and footage of Paolo and Julianne at the police station. No one had yet managed to update photographs of the mother of the child, Kira Mae, since the kidnap. Instead the media relied on the one shot of her, distraught, leaving the nursery school on the day she discovered Angel was missing.

Most stations also carried a brief interview with the owner of the nursery school who described her missing pupil as "a real-life Angel." She continued to refuse to answer questions about the woman she had employed to take care of her precious charges. Several parents had already withdrawn their children from the nursery.

* * *

At the house, the hours dragged by—every minute felt like an hour. The digital counters on the clock seemed to stay still. Paolo sent out for pizza for everyone.

Kira Mae was in the bedroom reading Isabella a story while Julianne reviewed some new designs on her laptop. Well, that was the idea. Except Julianne couldn't concentrate and instead found herself staring off into space, trying to fathom how this nightmare situation had befallen her family.

She surreptitiously googled websites about kidnapping. How long till the victim was usually released? What were the reasons for and against paying a ransom? How often were kidnappers caught and brought to justice? How did child abductions tend to differ from one another?

If only she had a contact number for Gio. She held an improbable and irrational belief that, if only she could talk to him, she could convince him to let Angel return home unharmed. Julianne was conducting a spirited conversation in her head with Gio when the phone rang. Though he initially called Julianne on her cell, he now used the landline at Kira Mae's villa to make contact but never stayed on the line long knowing police would have a phone tap on the call.

Kira Mae nodded to indicate to Julianne that she should take the call. Taken by surprise, Julianne mouthed, "Call Paolo."

Kira Mae shook her head. "No, you do it." She handed her mother a pen and notebook.

Julianne grabbed the receiver. A man addressed her. "Who's this?" he asked.

"I'm Angel's grandmother," said Julianne.

"You're all over the news," he told her. "Going in and out of the police station with that lawyer friend of yours. You make a handsome couple." His voice was almost friendly. Now he adopted a menacing tone. "Listen to me. Write this down. Just you. You will deliver the money tomorrow. Be at the Plaza de Toros at one. *Alone,"* he restated. "Bring the money. Fifty thousand euros. In small notes. Await further instructions."

"Please, listen to me," Julianne spoke fast in an effort to get her plea across before he hung up. "The girl, can we talk to her? Please. Please, her mother needs to know she is safe."

"She's safe," he said, and ended the call.

Paolo returned from outside and listened to the recording of the exchange on the speaker phone.

"You're not going," he said. "It's too dangerous."

Julianne gave him an icy stare. "I can assure you, I am going," she said. "They said 'just you.' They didn't say no police, but I think that is what they meant."

Kira Mae nodded. "They asked for her. Let her go. We'll figure it out," she said, without meeting her mother's glance. "All I care about is that we get Angel back unharmed."

The implication of her words escaped no one.

The family conference was interrupted by the young on-duty policeman. "I need to inform the chief immediately and see what he plans to do."

"Don't worry, I'll tell him what we plan to do," said Paolo. "Exactly as we have been instructed."

chapter twelve

"For now they kill me with a living death."
—Shakespeare's *Richard III*

Loudspeakers blared out marching music as the crowds headed toward the Plaza de Toros.

Julianne walked briskly and looked about her anxiously. Perverse it certainly was, but she now wished that she had agreed to police back-up. She had the bitter taste of fear in her mouth. Desperate to run, but scared to show outward signs of agitation.

Every person who came near made her jump. She dared not look at anyone for fear of attracting attention, yet she didn't want to lose her acute sense of her surroundings. Were Paolo and the police tracking her on GPS? She kept her phone in her pocket as she waited for the slightest vibration.

The outdoor stadium looked old and shabby, as the once proud national pastime of bullfighting had rapidly lost public appeal. Small bullrings all over Spain had been closed and awaited demolition or a change of use, Julianne reflected. In other cities, older members of the community still came out to watch the sport but increasingly the young declined to join them. Family members were sometimes coerced to accompany the seniors but the millennials rarely attended. In countries like Portugal where the sport had been popular, new regulations meant that the bulls were no longer killed in the ring.

Instead the focus was on the color and artistry of the spectacle. Julianne would never have imagined that she would ever attend a bullfight. The closer she got to the bullring, the closer her footsteps fell into a rhythm with her unspoken mantra. "Dear God, keep Angel safe. Dear God, keep Angel safe. Dear God, keep Angel safe."

Julianne followed the crowd. At the first entrance gate she tried to present her ticket but was refused entry. The ticket Julianne had bought was "in sun"—10 euros cheaper than a shaded position. The gnarled old Spanish gentlemen who took her ticket spoke no English but pointed Julianne to the opposite side of the stadium. She walked around the concrete edifice past a small ticket office and there she entered the bullring.

A colorful poster displayed names and photographs of that day's matadors. The stadium depicted on the poster conveyed the impression of a gigantic venue, but in reality the Plaza de Toros was more like a local football stadium. The painted decorations of blue rosettes were faded, especially in the sunny areas. The seats were concrete tiers. Most people had the foresight to bring a blanket. A small bar at the top of the stadium was the only place with shade—under a solitary tree. A few old men stood around drinking beer and talking loudly.

Perhaps they were discussing the relative merits of the afternoon's players. Man against beast.

The marching and toreador music continued inside the stadium and a sedate level of anticipation began to build up. Julianne checked her watch. She hardly knew what she was supposed to be doing there.

The bullfight was to start at 2 p.m.—she had an hour to wait. She walked around the stadium not knowing where she should be stationed. Was this where the exchange would take place? Should she be outside or inside?

Julianne suddenly noticed that uniformed officers were stationed strategically all around the stadium! Had Xabia ignored the family's instructions? What the hell was going on? Her question was answered almost immediately when she heard shouting coming from one of the entrances. Protestors: activists protesting the bullfights. Police moved into place and after repeated warnings, the protestors were moved along. The police appeared to resume their lookout positions.

Julianne prayed that their presence would not scupper the meeting she was dreading. What if Angel's abductors refused to release her?

She tried to reassure herself that all was well and, after she had settled down, looked around her. The arriving audience were mostly families: grandparents, parents and children. The families had come well prepared for a family day out. They arrived in processions with young mothers carrying babies and toddlers, older children carrying blankets and cushions to soften the effects of the concrete seating, and dads with overladen bags and ice boxes. Grandparents brought up the rear as they leaned on the arms of younger family members who held parasols to keep the sun off the older ladies. Later the umbrellas might be used to ward off the threatening rain.

Julianne caught a glimpse of the Puig Campana Mountain that overlooked the stadium. Local legend had it that the wife of the giant Roldan was dying. Mad with grief, her heartbroken husband commanded his workers to carve a deep gorge into the mountain pass to prolong the moment when the sun would set and his wife would die.

Julianne had given Kira Mae her promise that Angel would be home safe and sound before the sun had gone down behind the mountain.

She scanned every face, suspected everyone and finally chose a place on the top row where she could see the whole parade ground. The Spanish flag flew proudly over the stadium atop a small observation tower and sound booth from which powerful patriotic music played. The booth was empty, she noted.

Julianne felt like a cat on a hot tin roof. She stood up, she sat down and she walked around a little trying to keep a distance between herself and the police. She imagined herself under constant surveillance. She searched every face. Saw kidnappers in every person who glanced her way.

She thought she had identified a definite criminal type: a fat man in a black leather jacket, a black fedora and steel-rimmed glasses. He stood on the very top level of seating, a powerful character who observed all he surveyed.

Then Julianne found herself watch a woman feed a child an orange. She tried to stop him running away—neither seemed to realize that the child was only able to go as far as the extent of his reins.

The stadium began to fill up. Julianne placed the bag that contained the money between her feet and checked out the stadium. It reminded her of the gymkhana rings where she had participated in horse-riding competitions as a child growing up in England with Annabelle.

The sound of pounding hooves and disturbing thoughts of Annabelle provoked a terrifying reflection: what if she was involved in the abduction?

Around the outer edges of the ring, numbered red painted boxes hugged the inner wall. Anticipation built and the music got more gladiatorial. The last of the audience took their seats and settled down for their afternoon of bloody entertainment.

Two musicians, a mandolin player and a flamenco guitarist, walked around the upper concourse carrying their instruments and stationed themselves by the observation tower. The younger of the two tossed his head, ran his fingers through his hair and for a heartbreaking moment, Julianne was reminded of Romero the flamenco guitarist. She recalled a conversation she once had with him about bullfighting. He had explained that it was a highly ritualized art form deeply embedded in Hispanic culture, not a barbaric blood sport as she claimed.

"The matador seeks inspiration for his art from the bull and makes an emotional connection," he told her. "The bull is not a victim but a worthy opponent. It is not unknown for the matador to spare the life of an animal who has fought with special courage."

"And if his life is spared, what happens then?" Julianne had asked. "He lives only to be killed in the next fight."

"No," said Romero, laughing. "The bull is honored and returned to his farm to live out his days as a stud. Not a bad life, eh?"

Her attention returned to the day's events. Perhaps today's bull would be spared.

Heavy storm clouds hanging in the air above the mountain appeared to herald a celestial signal that the show was about to start. The crowd cheered wildly and proudly as the names of bullfighters were announced.

At the high-pitched sound of a single bugle, the bright parade was led by a horseman waving a banner on a chestnut stallion, who galloped into the ring. The horse performed choreographed dance steps in the center of the ring.

The main attractions and the stars of the show were the matadors in their golden suits of lights, followed by their entourage, banderilleros in silver suits wearing jewel-encrusted white sombreros.

More horses—their shanks protected with padding to prevent gores from the bull's horns—were ridden by picadors who carried lances.

The parade stopped to salute the presiding dignitary.

All around the stadium, men removed their hats and the crowd stood for the playing of the Spanish national anthem.

Julianne watched the clean-up men with their shovels entering sedately in their high-visibility red jackets, leading a donkey who pulled a wooden trap. The trap, she knew, had a central part to play later in the proceedings.

The matadors, the only ones allowed to kill the bull, took up their positions in the center of the ring and quickly won the approval of the onlookers, flashing and twirling their traditional magenta and gold satin capes that have been worn for centuries.

The bugler signaled the start of the first of five scheduled bullfights. Julianne sensed the audience hold its collective breath as the first bull entered the ring. This one was small and was immediately engaged by one of the bullfighters who flashed his cape before the bull reached him.

The matador jumped the fence and threw his cape over the top, leaving the bull to stare at an inert cape while he sheltered in safety.

The bull seemed less than aggressive and wandered off. Not for long. As round two got underway, a picador on horseback with a lance entered the ring and banderillos antagonized the bull by sticking barbed sticks into him. Julianne, who was continuing to scan the crowds for sign of an approach, could barely watch. The dejected bull looked more confused than intimidating—until the cheer of the crowd signaled the arrival of the horsemen. Their horses' flanks protected from the sharp horns of the bull, they threw their spears into the bull's back.

The matadors taunted the bull as he clawed aggressively at the ground, bleeding. Anyone could see he had no chance, cornered by the matador's entourage and a handful of horsemen. It was desperately unfair, a battle weighted against the bull. Julianne couldn't help comparing Angel's plight to that of the bull.

She scanned the crowd unobserved, trying to hold back her tears. They were absorbed in Tercio Tres, the third stage of death, indicated by the reentry of the matador into the ring carrying a red cape and sword. Julianne remembered Romero claiming that the red cape is not "a red rag to a bull" but the best color to hide the animal's bloodstains. But the bull didn't give up without a fight. The bull was snorting and steaming, charging, now enraged, clawing at the floor, following first one, then another bullfighter.

The man was an expert at playing to the crowd and turned his back to walk away from the bull. Arrogant and superior, Julianne noted. Proud to have won in a fight with a wounded animal. Blood from the spikes flowed onto the parade ground.

The matador prepared for the final act. With his back to the bull, he unsheathed his sword.

Julianne could watch no more. She covered her eyes with her hands. She felt as if the blood of the bull was being released from her own heart; the pain and frustration suffered by the bull struck at her very core.

She rose from her comfortless seat and started toward the restroom, certain she would throw up. The adrenalin that was pumping through her and the spectacle of the blood sport had sickened her to her core. As the crowd yelled "Bravo!" and "Ole!" and cheered the bullfighter who was carried on the shoulders of his fellow fighters, she observed that children ran freely in the stadium oblivious to the drama that was being played out in the ring. Julianne could not fathom how their mothers allowed it.

Julianne gratefully rested her forehead again the cool tiles by the basin. The nausea passed as she splashed her face with cold water. She entered an empty stall holding firmly onto the brown leather bag that contained the ransom money.

From the next stall she heard a woman's voice. "Give me the bag," she said. "Push it under the partition."

Julianne could not believe her ears. She peered under the door and saw a buggy obstructed her stall.

"Where's Angel?" she said. "I want Angel before you get the money."

"She's safe," said the woman. "Give me the money and you will find her waiting for you outside."

Julianne knew she sounded frantic. "How do I know I can trust you?"

The woman laughed, seeming to enjoy her part in the drama.

"We want the money. Not your daughter," she said. "If you don't give me the bag, we can take your daughter with us and you will have to start all over again."

"Please, I beg you. Promise me," said Julianne. She sat on the toilet seat lid and passed the bag under the divider. The woman took it. Julianne felt the rush of air as she passed Julianne's stall.

As the stranger rushed from the restroom, Julianne heard the taunt, "Tell Isabella, 'Hola' from me."

Furious, she pushed her way out of the stall, past the buggy, but there was no child to be seen. She spotted the woman and tried to catch up, but her progress was slowed by a dozen policemen running en masse toward the gate-crashing activists at the exit.

Julianne looked around in despair, trying to remember how the woman had looked. Protestors held up posters of dead bulls—Julianne turned from the gory sight only to be confronted with an even worse one. A bull being carted away on a small cart. He lay pitifully dead and displayed for all to see.

Julianne ran in to the stadium, frantically looking for a sign that Angel was about to be returned. She heard police sirens in the distance and officers harassing and arresting protesters. At the approach of a posse of motorcycle cops, they scattered.

Julianne stood helpless by an entrance. What next? A motorcycle cop approached her.

Without removing his helmet, he stretched out a gauntlet-clad hand and pointed up to the sound booth and commentary tower where the two musicians had earlier established themselves.

His voice was muffled, but the words could not have been more distinct to Julianne.

"Look, over there. The child," he said, then walked away.

As she lifted her hand to shield her eyes and stare toward the booth, Julianne heard the crowd cheer and shout even louder. The dead bull was being paraded around the bullring.

Julianne had a different cause to cheer. A small figure was running toward her, waving. Paolo looked on.

"Angel will be home before sunset," she said under her breath. She threw her arms wide open and Angel leapt into them and the two cried and held onto each other as if for dear life.

"Mama JoJo I had an adventure," said Angel, "I missed you. Where's Isabella?" God had answered her prayers. Angel had indeed made it home before the sun set behind the mountain.

Julianne remembered that Romero had told her every bullring had a small chapel where the matador could pray before the fight. She guessed his prayers had been answered that day.

chapter thirteen

"Love is a smoke raised with the fume of sighs."
—Shakespeare's *Romeo & Juliet*

Julianne had a million questions for Paolo, but none of them seemed important now that their darling girl had been returned. She would hear all the details later but now, before they left the stadium, the most important call of all.

"Does Kira Mae know? Has she spoken to her daughter?"

"That's the next thing on the agenda," said Paolo, his grin so wide he looked like he would burst with happiness.

"We need to call her immediately."

He dialed the number and changed the setting to loudspeaker as he handed the phone to Julianne.

"A little girl wants to say hello to her mummy," she told Kira Mae.

Kira Mae was already in tears after having been informed that the whole operation was racing toward a conclusion.

"Mama," shouted Angel with glee. "I had an adventure and everyone says I was a very brave girl."

Julianne heard Kira Mae's sobs as she struggled to speak through her tears, giant tears of joy.

"I love you, Angel," she said over and over again. "Mama JoJo and Paolo will bring you home straight away. Blow me a big kiss."

To Julianne she said, "How does she look? Is she OK?"

Julianne laughed, "A little grubby in two-day old clothes and her hair could do with a good wash and brush up, but she looks gorgeous."

Paolo indicated that he needed to speak to Kira Mae. "Stay put," he said, "we can be there in half an hour. Chief Xabia thinks it will be better for you to be reunited with Angel at home rather than at the police station. Do you agree?"

Julianne did and Kira Mae agreed. "I can get some food ready and make myself look a little presentable. Isabella can't wait to see her. She is doing a little dance here round my feet. Put Angel back on the phone, please?"

Julianne still held Angel in her arms. She felt like she would never let her go.

Angel and Isabella babbled a mile a minute, each wanting to tell the other what they had been doing and to find out the news from their sister.

"I had an adventure," Angel repeated over and over again, as she sensed that this won her lots of brownie points. Isabella had her war stories of policemen staying at her house and the new Spanish words she had learned.

"OK, you two, there will be plenty of time to catch up on all your news when you see each other." Julianne spoke into the speaker.

Kira Mae had one crucial question for Angel. "What do you want to eat?"

Angel didn't need to be asked twice. "Spaghetti hoops and ketchup," she said.

Not to be left out, Isabella shouted from the background, "And ice cream. I have ice cream every day for my dinner," she boasted.

The approach of Chief Xabia brought the phone call to a close. Now that communication between the family members had been established, he was anxious to move all parties out of the bullring and on to the next stage of the operation.

"There's a police escort and a patrol car waiting outside to take you home," he told Paolo and Julianne.

"So far the press and media have not been informed. I'll call a conference for later this evening and, once the child is home with her mother, we can decide on the next step. Obviously we need to allow opportunities for the reunion photographs," he explained, "but that doesn't have to be tonight. We'll schedule it for tomorrow at the police station."

Julianne hugged the police chief, who had a huge grin all over his face. She did not know what had taken place but whatever had happened—it was successful. Angel was home.

As the little family of Julianne, Paolo and Angel walked the few yards across the concourse and outside to the waiting police car, the crowd rose to their feet, cheered wildly and called "Bravo" and "Ole." Julianne realized the bullfight was still in progress in the bullring below them.

Angel reacted to the word "Ole" and Julianne quickly turned her back to the crowd as they increased their pace toward the entrance.

"Isabella says 'Hola' to everyone," said Angel. "She learned it on 'Spanish for Kids' on the computer."

Julianne and Paolo exchanged a knowing look and a nervous laugh. "Thank God, she doesn't say it to everyone," Julianne said under her breath. "But that's another story."

They would all retell their parts in Angel's adventure in good time, for the moment they just needed to get home as quickly as possible. The driver did not put his siren on. He did not want to attract attention to his precious cargo, but he certainly pressed his foot on the gas pedal on the highway between Benidorm and the villa.

Paolo cautioned Julianne. "Little ears, we don't know what she knows," he mouthed to Julianne as she settled into the backseat of the police cruiser with Angel close beside her. He took the seat up beside the police driver in the front. He needn't have worried. Angel's constant chatter stopped as the car pulled onto the highway. She slept all the way home.

Paolo and Julianne acknowledged the iconic landmark—Puig Gap. As they passed, tears cascaded down

Julianne's face. Paolo reached between the seats and held her hand all the way home.

They shared one thought. The promise was true. "Before the sun sets behind the mountain, Angel will be home safe and sound."

chapter fourteen

"Can one desire too much of a good thing?"
—Shakespeare's *As You Like It*

The atmosphere at the villa was more joyful than Christmas and ten birthdays all rolled into one. Laughter and energy again filled the home. The girls raced from room to room and chased each other as they talked a mile a minute, so glad to have their playmate back again. Angel was in no hurry to discuss what had happened and her mother and grandmother did not pressure her. She didn't seem to have been hurt in any way.

They knew there would need to be a full scale debriefing with the police over the next few days. Chief Xabia had already intimated that there might need to be medical examinations and psychological tests to evaluate Angel's mental and physical state. So far she seemed to be taking everything in her stride. She said little about where she had been or what had happened to her, except that it had been an adventure.

Media waiting outside the villa had been promised a press conference first thing the next day.

The adults shared their joy of the reunion, and over dinner and a few glasses of wine they laughed and chatted in a way they had not experienced for a long time. Divisions were forgotten.

"Thank you both," said Kira Mae, "when the chips are down, you can always count on family. I couldn't have gotten through it without you two. I love you."

Kira Mae had given Angel a soothing hot bubble bath and hair wash and Isabella had insisted she share the bath. One at either end, as usual. They looked like twins in their matching pajamas with their long, dark hair brushed and shining.

The girls did not argue about bedtime tonight. Both, though they would never admit it, were exhausted. They chose to sleep in the same bed, arms around each other. Kira Mae wound up the music box with the twirling ballerina and lit a small bedside light.

"Love you millions," she told the girls and kissed them good night.

"Love you more," they chorused.

★ ★ ★

For the first time in days, the family had the house to themselves. The onsite police presence was over—at least inside the house.

A feeling of calm settled over the family, disturbed only by the sound of chirping crickets from the garden. Through the open French windows that led out to the pool, the smell of night-time jasmine wafted indoors.

Julianne stretched out on the couch and Kira Mae did the same. *Bookends facing each other,* Julianne thought, just like it used to be many years ago before Romero had disrupted all their lives. Tensions between the three disappeared as they shared their relief in having Angel home.

Paolo refilled their wine glasses and settled back in his chair. Peace and harmony restored.

"Julianne was never out of my sight for a minute," Paolo admitted. "Except when she went to the ladies room."

They all laughed.

Julianne gave Paolo a stern look. "I told you I could handle it by myself," she said.

"And you did," he said, "with just a little help from me. And about twenty policemen. The chief insisted and they were all very well trained. He brought them in from some of the nearby cities, and the undercover cops worked like a relay, maintaining surveillance."

"I thought the guy on the train I took to Altea reading his newspaper—or more like not reading it—looked suspicious," said Julianne.

"What about the conductor?" asked Paolo. "He was the one who directed you to the bullring. He was undercover too. The order was to observe and follow. We had our eye on the mother with the child from the moment she appeared on the station platform."

Julianne was relieved at how well it had all turned out but wanted to know what was going to happen to the kidnappers. Were they to be allowed to get away with kidnapping an innocent child? Just who else had been involved?

"The motorcycle cops were all over her," said Paolo, "and as soon as Angel was returned and the woman tried to disappear into the crowd of protestors, she was picked up. She's at the police station now being questioned, though according to the last update I had from Chief Xabia, she denies that she knew anything about a kidnapping.

"She claims her only job was to follow you and get you to hand over the bag with the money. Christina, the nursery school assistant, was also detained and says she was told there was a domestic dispute between the mother and father and the child was to be 'removed' from the nursery for a couple of days. She was vague about the details but eventually admitted that she handed Angel over at the nursery school to a man she knew to be a criminal, her new boyfriend, Gio Lopez. She wanted to please him. Seems that your daughter was kept at an apartment with another woman who looked after her well enough. They insist there was never any intention to harm her, getting the money was their only concern."

"I don't even care about the money," said Julianne, "it's a small price to pay to get Angel back. Of course I'm sure the police chief wants to charge them, but all I care about is that Angel is home."

Julianne glanced at Paolo. She knew he was reading her, as usual. If Gio was charged, he would put her name in the frame over Romero's death. She also had a lurking dread that her former friend Annabelle somehow played a part in the abduction.

"Let's put all worries about what happens next to one side," said Paolo. "Tonight we only need to be grateful that Angel is asleep in her own bed."

"And that's where her mother needs to be," said Julianne.

Paolo followed her gaze and looked with compassion on Kira Mae, who had finally fallen asleep after so many sleepless nights. For the first time he seemed to lose his composure.

She nodded and dreaded the thought of the next day when she would find out what Gio had told the police. Would Gio tell the police that she hired him to kill her former lover?

Julianne checked on the two little ones. When she returned, Paolo was sitting outside. Julianne noticed that in the reflected light that illuminated the swimming pool, he looked much older. Careworn. She knew that he had borne a great deal of the worry of the whole abduction and, despite everything that had happened, he still saw it as his duty to protect all his girls, Julianne, Kira Mae, Angel and Isabella.

Julianne sat down on the edge of the pool, close to Paolo. She was barefoot, and now she lifted her flimsy skirt above her knees and dangled her legs in the water.

"What happens now?" she asked.

Paolo shook his head. "There's a whole media circus

to deal with tomorrow at the press conference. This story is far from over. Angel seems to be fine, but we have to be sure. She may have some delayed reaction."

"Paolo," said Julianne quietly. "I can't go to jail. Please promise me that you will do everything in your power to ensure that I don't have to face that. Kira Mae is stronger than me, though she doesn't know that yet. When she went to jail, she coped. I just know I would fall apart. Please tell me what I need to do to escape that fate."

Paolo left his chair and sat beside her at the pool. He reached out and put an arm around her shoulders.

"I promise," he said. "I will ensure that you are advised by one of the best legal minds in the country."

"Oh thank you," she said, as relief flooded through her, then laughter as she realized what he was saying.

"You are the finest legal mind?"

"Of course," he said.

"Perhaps I should get a second opinion."

"You are in safe hands, I promise you. We'll face it together."

chapter fifteen

"Doubt time to be a liar,
but never doubt thy love."
—Shakespeare's *Hamlet*

Julianne went to bed with a smile on her face. She awoke in a cold sweat, staring into the eyes of Romero as he gripped her throat and strangled her. Filled with fear, she attempted to push him off her. His whole body covered hers. He forced the very breath out of her. Romero was powerful and mad as hell. Julianne had no doubt that Romero wouldn't rest until she had paid for what she had done to him. She reminded herself what she had always suspected—that you can't kill gangsters and get away with it. Why had she ever thought she could?

Dawn broke and Julianne sat on the side of her bed. She stared out of the bedroom window and contemplated her future.

Her whole body was in turmoil. She felt sick and scared, wanted to cry and scream and rage against the pain that filled her heart. And yet she also wanted to beat her body into submission until it stopped feeling. Until it stopped making her crave a man she had never really known. Like a drug addict, she did not care about consequences. She wanted what she wanted and she wanted it now. Despite the fear she still felt toward Romero, she still wanted him to hold her, to feel that all-encompassing passion that had driven her into his arms.

A huge hole had opened up in her solar plexus. She had hated Romero with all her heart, and now she was surprised to find that she loved him again. The image of him. His maleness and his strength seemed to override his cruelty. Julianne felt like a wounded butterfly who dreamt of living for one more day.

An abusive childhood had surely set her up, had ensured that a kind, gentle love was never going to satisfy her as an adult. She wanted to be possessed, she was sick of being nice, sick of settling for vanilla; surely life had to hold more richness, more meaning and more excitement?

Paolo had been understanding when Romero had left her mentally and emotionally battered and bruised. Paolo was the man who held her close, assured her, protected her, whereas Romero had shaken and stirred her and taught her how to feel like a woman, not a vulnerable child.

When Kira Mae had gone to prison, pregnant with Romero's child, Julianne—also pregnant—had cursed the man who had betrayed her. Alone in her small cottage with a new baby, she swore vengeance on the man who had manipulated and enticed both women into his web. Like a demented witch, she googled spells and prayed he would die. Then she took fate into her own hands and hired Gio to kill Romero. At the time she had been proud of herself.

There had been no consequences for more than five years. The girls had grown up in the joint care of Julianne and Kira. Then Kira took over most of the motherly duties while Julianne returned to the career she had loved before her life had been shattered, traveling the world as a fashion consultant working first for a global fashion house and then under her own brand.

Fashion had always been the substitute in her life for true passion. Exotic trips abroad and the delight of discovering new fabrics, designs and colors had consumed her senses.

During this time, Julianne felt too terrified to open herself up to someone. She wouldn't allow her heart to unfreeze for fear of the havoc she could cause if she ever fell in love again. What kind of woman orders her lover to be killed, what kind of woman rejoices in having avenged her devastating pain and loneliness?

She wished now that she had told Paolo about the wreath, but she had held back. To be secretive was in her nature. To trust was not.

Julianne fought the desire to self-harm, to make her own blood flow. She craved the release it gave her, to take away the unbearable thoughts from the inside and feel the mutilation on the outside. Cutting herself had always been her way to relieve the pain she felt as a child—until she gave birth to Isabella and vowed not to give in to the destructive behavior.

Now the desire to scar and mark her body rushed to the surface again and her inner demons screamed at her to do it. She sat on her bed and cried for the woman who thought that the only way to make herself feel better was through pain. Now, after the kidnapping of Angel, which she knew to her shame was ultimately all her fault, she felt the overwhelming desire to do it again.

She would have loved to turn to Paolo who had so often soothed her pain, but now she dared not make that choice. Although he had promised that his one-night stand with Kira Mae was just that, Julianne feared arousing more jealousy in her daughter. Kira Mae deserved some respite from all the worry she had suffered. Julianne would do anything to protect her daughter, and if that meant giving up Paolo, then so be it.

If it wasn't for the pain it would inflict on Kira Mae, Isabella and Angel, Julianne knew that she had the potential to take her self-abuse one step further. In her dreams and nightmares, Romero wanted to kill her. But not as badly as she sometimes wanted to kill herself. She wished she could start all over again, without the mistakes this time—but who on this earth was lucky enough to get a second chance?

Dead men can't commit murder, she reminded herself. But spiritually dead women are still capable of what many in Spain considered to be the worst crime of all.

chapter sixteen

"Love all, trust a few, do wrong to none."
—Shakespeare's *All's Well That Ends Well*

As the household slept, Julianne slipped into her bathing suit to take an energizing early morning swim. She crept through the villa, conscious that she did not want to wake any of the others. Fortunately it was sectioned into two wings, each with its own bathrooms. Kira Mae and the girls slept in the bedrooms adjacent to the kitchen, they couldn't see the pool from their windows.

Julianne and Paolo used to share a section at the back of the house closest to the pool when they stayed over. Now Julianne stayed there alone.

Paolo suggested a swim before Julianne retired for the night.

"Join me?" he asked

Though tempted, she refused. "I'll pass, thank you."

No way did she wish to invoke happy memories of midnight dips, flirting, teasing and kissing in the warm waters of the pool. She shook the memories of happier times with Paolo from her head as she prepared for her early morning dip. A swim would help her to prepare for the media circus Paolo had warned her the family would face later that day.

The prospect of the press and their prying questions terrified Julianne but she knew that she would arouse more suspicion if she left Kira Mae to face the cameras alone. Her plan was to stay in the background as much as possible and pray that the reporters would not start to look too closely below the surface. A press investigation was the last thing she needed right now.

Her head full of possible scenarios and suggestions as she searched for a resolution, Julianne seriously contemplated that the whole family should move not just from the area but to another country. Another wild plan was to find Gio and see how much money he would accept to be paid off once and for all. Certainly as long as they stayed where they were, the threat from him was not over.

Julianne walked slowly and breathed deeply; she forced herself to take notice of her surroundings. Endeavoring to practice mindfulness and meditation, she heard the sounds of the birds and animals waking up, smelled the fresh dew and acknowledged the early dawn heralding a new day.

In the uncertain light she could see another bather already in the pool. It could only be Paolo. She was about to turn and make the return trip to her room but stopped in her tracks. He was drifting silently, casting not a ripple in the water. His dressing gown ballooned out around him like a sail. He was face down in the water.

A chill ran through Julianne's body.

She slipped into the pool and swam toward Paolo.

His body was lifeless. He had stopped breathing. Using the buoyancy of the water, Julianne attempted to turn him over, but he kept slipping back facedown in the water. Not knowing what else to do she maneuvered him closer to the side of the pool but was horrified when he drifted back toward the center. She tried to roll him over onto his back, but he literally felt like a dead weight. Driven by panic, Julianne tried to remember how long a person could survive without oxygen. Was it three minutes or longer? How long had Paolo been lying face-down?

With an enormous effort she turned him over to hopefully allow him to breathe. She was fighting a losing battle. She needed help and climbed out of the pool on autopilot, aware that she felt utterly numb. She ran toward Kira Mae's room. Wishing she didn't have to, nevertheless, she shook her awake. She could not risk having failed to take all the action necessary.

Kira was alert in seconds and seeing her mother's stricken face, she looked scared.

"What happened? What is it? What's wrong?"

Julianne soothed her. "Shush, don't wake the children. I need you to phone an ambulance. Paolo has had an accident in the swimming pool."

Kira Mae was now fully awake and pulling on her jeans. "Is he alright? What can I do to help? What happened?"

"Phone the ambulance," said Julianne, avoiding her daughter's searching look. "I'll wait with him at the pool. You need to stay with the children. Don't let them come out to the pool. Text when the ambulance is coming."

"OK, but . . ."

"Just do it please, Kira," she said.

Julianne rushed back to the pool and watched in horror as Paolo continued to drift. He looked dead, she had to admit. What had Paolo been drinking last night? He had never been one for sedatives. Now that the full awful reality of the situation was impacting her, she had another, dreadful thought. Maybe this wasn't an accident. She scanned the garden, scared of what she might pick out in the early morning gloom, but there was nothing.

She prayed that the ambulance would arrive quickly. Her phone beeped, making her jump. Ambulance on its way. Is Paolo OK? texted Kira Mae.

"Too soon to say," Julianne texted back. "Just need those paramedics to get here."

Julianne knew that if she allowed Kira Mae to come to the pool she would fall apart. The ambulance arrived in minutes, even faster than Julianne dared hope. From her position at the pool, she could see a blue flashing light making its way up the narrow lane, but there were thankfully no sirens, it being so early in the morning.

She ran to the gate which led to the front of the house and the police car and ambulance. A paramedic made his way to Julianne.

"Quickly," she called. "We may still be in time. I don't know if he is breathing."

"Please lead the way," he said.

The paramedic and the policeman followed Julianne to the pool. "Wait here," they told Julianne as they approached Paolo.

Julianne watched the men wading into the pool and dragging her ex-partner out of it. They laid him out on the grass and she closed her eyes. She almost couldn't stand the sound of them performing CPR.

She did not have to wait long for a verdict.

"We're going to take him to the hospital," said the paramedic.

"So he's alive?" she said, hardly daring to hope.

The man didn't answer and Julianne said nothing. She felt gripped by a feeling of such unreality that she had to pinch herself to be sure that this wasn't another bad dream.

His colleague appeared in the gateway and the first paramedic signaled that a stretcher was needed. While it was being brought around the small patio area by the pool, the paramedic continued to try to perform lifesaving maneuvers. All to no avail, it seemed.

Julianne wondered whether Kira was even aware of the terrible scene unfolding before her eyes. She hoped and prayed that she would stay away until Paolo had been removed.

After the body was loaded on to the collapsible stretcher and taken out to the ambulance, the paramedic resumed his questioning of Julianne.

"What happened? How long has he been in the water? Was anyone else with him? Does he have any known medical conditions that could have caused heart failure?"

Julianne answered to the best of her ability but did not know the answer to most of the questions.

"Can I go to the hospital with him?" Julianne asked.

"Sorry, it's too late for that," said the paramedic quietly. "Are you the next of kin?"

Julianne found she couldn't speak. She had expected to ride in the ambulance with Paolo and hold his hand. To reassure him that she was there for him.

Instead there was nothing. It was already all over.

Her phone beeped and she looked at it, unable to compute what Kira Mae was asking her. Her daughter wanted to know what was going on and was not happy that her mother had told her to stay with the children.

Above all else, she didn't want Kira or the girls to see the dead body.

"Situation contained," she heard one of the policemen say into his radio. Everything had happened so efficiently. Julianne sat by the pool and cried.

What now? Paolo was her right-hand man, the one who knew all her secrets. How could she go on without him? She looked around the villa. It would have been so easy for someone to sneak in, undetected. Were they safe? She needed to ensure that the police had checked the grounds.

She texted Kira Mae. Bad news. We need to talk and decide what to tell the girls. I'm on my way.

She met her daughter in the kitchen near to her bedroom. Kira Mae, who knew nothing of what had been going on except that Paolo had had an accident, was frantic.

"What's happened?" she cried.

Julianne sat her down at the kitchen table and asked Kira to make them both tea before she told her the story.

Kira Mae broke down and could only say, "Oh, my God. Oh, my God. Please tell me this isn't true. And just after Angel's abduction too. What does it mean? What's going on?"

Julianne's whole body shook as she reached out to stroke her daughter's hand.

"We've got to be strong," she said. "We have to have to work through this together."

"But how did he die?" said Kira. "He was a good swimmer."

"I don't know yet," said Julianne. "The police will have to investigate."

She said nothing of her fears about whether Paolo's death had been an accident.

The two women sat enveloped in a cloud of doom, trying to process the news. Not sure what to do next. Not believing what had just happened.

The policewoman called Terri, who they had come to know during the long ordeal of Angel's kidnapping, appeared in the kitchen doorway.

"Sorry to disturb you," she said. "I just wanted to know what I can do to help."

Kira Mae and her mother looked at each other and shook their heads.

"Nothing, nothing thank you. We're just trying to work out what to tell the girls. Right on top of the kidnapping we don't want to scare them," said Julianne.

"Would it help if I stayed here and made them breakfast while you ladies get ready to go downtown?"

"Downtown?" said Julianne, as if she had never heard of such a place.

"You will need to see the chief, answer some questions and the press conference is still scheduled for this morning. Everyone wants to see Angel home safe and sound." Terri looked sympathetic.

"What time is it now?" asked Julianne in a daze.

"It's already eight o'clock and I've been asked to bring you to the station around ten. The chief personally wants to debrief you before the press conference, which is scheduled for noon."

"And what will he tell the press about Paolo?" Julianne wanted to know.

"That will be part of your discussion with him. Best plan is probably that you go to the station with me when you're ready. As I understand it, they need a statement about what happened yesterday at the bullring. A little later we will send an escort for Miss Kira and the children. We'll try to keep their time at the police station as short as possible."

Julianne felt a cold shiver run through her body. Her teeth were chattering and her head pounded.

Much as she tried to avoid taking painkillers because she knew they were dangerous for her, maybe this was a time to make an exception.

A sudden thought occurred to her.

"Where are the children?" she asked. "They're unusually quiet. They're normally up before now even when they've had a late night."

Kira nodded. "I took chocolate milk and cookies in to them and told them it was a treat to stay in bed and watch television."

"OK," said Julianne. She mustn't lose her head at a time like this. "How is Angel?"

"She seems to be just fine," said Kira. "Children, they are so resilient. We need to talk and get the full story but I don't think there is any benefit in pushing her. Let her take her time to adjust to being home."

Julianne sat in a daze at the kitchen table while Kira fussed around the room getting breakfast ready.

"I can do all that," said the policewoman.

"Thank you," said Kira, sitting down. "I need to keep occupied." She turned to her mother. "Tell me what we are going to say to the girls about Paolo."

"The less said the better," Julianne told her as she massaged her temples. "We could say that Paolo is not feeling well and has gone away to recuperate. They don't need to know more than that. He's always coming and going."

"But what about the press conference? They might hear things that will worry them."

"That's something I need to talk to Chief Xabia about," said Julianne. "Let me get ready and we can start to deal with all of these matters."

Julianne went to the girls' room to say good morning

and then continued to her own bedroom to get dressed.

She chose her press conference outfit with care: a tailored navy shirt dress and black high heels accessorized with a large silver ornamental necklace. She wore her flowing blonde hair loose.

Accepting the offer of a police escort to the station, Julianne agreed that she was far too distracted to drive. Her head pounded and her thoughts tortured her. This was all her fault. She had Romero murdered, and now her whole family was under attack. Guilt tormented her and fear threatened to make her throw up. Where would this all end?

Without Paolo by her side as friend, protector and legal adviser, she felt she was being thrown to the lions. She was rushed through the waiting reporters by her police escort and taken straight to Chief Xabia's office.

The chief could not have been more kind or concerned. He started by commiserating with her on the death of Paolo, then continued to talk about the kidnapping.

"You did a great job yesterday," he congratulated her. "We could not have pulled off the operation so successfully without you."

Julianne smiled wanly and waited for the follow up. She knew there was more to come and she was terrified of what it might be. More than anything she needed to know if they had arrested Gio and if he had named her.

"The woman from the bullring is still in custody," Xabia told her. "She's a tough cookie and is not giving us much information, but we will continue to work on her. She refuses to name her accomplices, and even when we suggest names, she refuses to answer. We have little to go on as she had no money on her when she was detained."

Julianne looked puzzled.

"Seems an accomplice had already whisked the money away before she even left the stadium. We recovered a plastic bag full of women's clothes in an empty buggy. A decoy."

She shrugged: the truth was, she didn't care about the money. Only that Angel had not been harmed. "What happens now?"

"We will pursue our lines of inquiry, but chances are she'll be released later today," said Chief Xabia. "If she is to be believed—and I am sure she is not—then her story is only that she was paid to follow you. Going to the restroom was a perfect opportunity for her to be alone with you and ask for the bag that contained the money. She insists she didn't know the plan, only that she was texted instructions. That she carried out orders."

Julianne was scared to ask the next question but scared not to. "What do you know of her accomplices?"

The chief tapped his fingers on the desk. He looked to his assistant, the policewoman who usually took notes for him.

"Very little. When the motive is only money—not personal—it is harder to make connections. The nursery school assistant and the woman at the bullring are probably known to each other, but it could be that there is no other connection."

Julianne could hardly believe her ears.

"These woman may have targeted you because of jealousy about your lifestyle," he continued. "You and your daughter have very high profiles. You live an enviable life. It's easy to want to think that this is some huge kidnapping conspiracy, but it may just be a spontaneous plan carried out by a person who already had criminal inclinations. The intention never seemed to be to hurt the child."

Julianne leaned back in her wooden chair. She felt relief begin to flow through her.

"Angel can fill in the gaps for us," said the chief. "Where was she held during the abduction? Who looked after her? Of course the investigation is ongoing but I am not inclined to rush matters. We already have a successful outcome. The press will be happy. The wheels of our legal system move very slowly and it may be up to a year before she is brought to justice. Even then we cannot depend on the courts to lock them up. Our prisons are already overflowing."

Julianne could hardly contain herself. She wanted to get out of the chief's office as quickly as possible, certainly while her name was not in the frame for a serious crime.

"May I say again how sorry I am about the death of Mr. Paolo?" continued the chief. "He was a good man and a great lawyer. I think we should keep his passing a separate matter from the press conference where we present your darling little girl.

"We can issue a statement later today, keep everything low key. Just a statement of the fact that your lawyer passed away earlier today. No cause of death has yet been established."

"I can't thank you enough," said Julianne, standing.

He beamed. It was not every day that he had such a high-profile case in his small local police precinct. The child had been returned safe and sound. It would make a beautiful picture on the national evening news, the heroic police chief alongside the beautiful mother and the adorable child.

A police officer appeared in the doorway to confirm that Kira Mae and the children had arrived. She had tried to explain to Isabella that this really was all about Angel, but it was clear that the two were inseparable. Angel was not going anywhere without Isabella, especially when they knew there were to be television cameras and photographs. Today the girls were dressed in matching pink frilly party dresses, their choice.

Julianne joined her family on the steps outside the police station. The police press department had endeavored to manage the media without much success. A scramble worthy of any red carpet event threatened to get out of hand. This was a feel-good story, plus a success for the local police. Win-win all round.

The hundreds of questions to which the press wanted answers were mostly deflected by the police press officer. Prepared answers were provided in a statement.

Angel played her part on the steps and when she was asked how she felt, she repeated the answer that had been instilled in her, presumably by her captors.

"I had an adventure," she repeated in an excited voice, adding, "and I am a very brave girl."

Angel had claimed her own sound bite. A true little star. The media loved her.

The press conference ended and the police chief thanked Kira and Julianne for their co-operation.

"Are we free to go?" Julianne asked.

"Of course," said the police chief. "My officer will take you home." He laughed. "We know where you live."

At home, the girls were happy to take off their party dresses. They had been promised that there would be a special treat later in the day and they'd go out for an early dinner. They were not to be allowed to use the pool, as it was still a crime scene, but didn't question the police tape around the pool. They had become well used to following instructions and not asking too many questions.

Kira was happy to babysit and spend time with the children while Julianne followed up on phone calls pertaining to Paolo and his sudden death.

Julianne found that she just could not process the sudden turn of events. It seemed unbelievable that he had gone. She stared at a photograph on the lounge wall of the whole family, happy, laughing at a celebration lunch round the pool where he had died. He brandished a grilling fork from the barbecue and the girls giggled.

The telephone rang and she answered it in a monotone.

It was the hospital morgue. "When will you come to identify the body?" they needed to know. "His wife has requested that we arrange for someone locally to confirm the identity of the body."

Julianne wondered if she had heard properly.

"His wife?" she asked slowly. "Are you sure?"

"Yes, I am sure," said the young man at the other end of the line. "I just spoke to her. She is in ill health and will not be able to travel from Rome. She has asked us to arrange for the identification of the body locally. Presuming that the corpse is identified as her husband, she intends to take the body back to Rome for burial."

"Let me get back to you," she said and hung up.

Julianne sank back into her chair and as Kira Mae walked into the room she passed on the message.

"Paolo's wife wants his body shipped back to Rome."

Kira stared at her mother. "Paolo's wife? Please tell me this is not true."

chapter seventeen

"The stroke of death is as a lover's pinch, which hurts and is desired."

—Shakespeare's *Anthony* & *Cleopatra*

Julianne packed up Paolo's belongings, ready to hand them over when the body was shipped home to Rome.

Clothes and books and music formed a neat pile on the bed in his room at Kira's villa, with official documentation, including his driver's licence. Periodically Julianne would go to the room and just look at how little was left of a relationship she had once thought was destined to last a lifetime. The devastating revelation that Paolo had a wife was almost the final blow on top of the anxiety about Angel and the fears of Gio betraying her to the authorities.

Julianne sat on the bed fingering a fine silk shirt, pale blue with navy piping on the cuffs and collar. She had bought it for him on one of their romantic weekend trips to Paris. Julianne rubbed the soft shirt to her cheek.

Love for Paolo filled her, then rage that he had left her so suddenly. She dried her eyes and marched to the kitchen. Still, she held the shirt. In the utensil drawer she pushed the implements around till she found what she was looking for—the largest pair of kitchen scissors she could find.

Attacking the delicate material, she allowed her fury to drive her untamed energy as she cut the shirt into ever smaller pieces. Her task finished, she stuffed the remains of the shirt into the trash can and returned to the bedroom to find other items of clothing to inflict damage on.

Free from the need to be seen doing the right thing, she grabbed a handful of his ties, cut them into pieces and threw them on the floor at her feet.

A beautiful lightly checked Armani jacket was the next to fall victim to her demonic fury. She cut off the sleeves and sliced through the back of the jacket. As if reversing the tailoring process of piecing together the jacket, she dismantled the entire thing and scattered the remains on the floor.

A sense of relief flooded through her, but she wasn't finished yet. Every item of his beautiful designer clothing fell victim, one by one, as Julianne wielded her scissors through his wardrobe.

"He's not going to need his clothes anymore," she reasoned, making a small apology to herself for her furious behavior. Deep down she knew that the wounds she inflicted on the clothes acted as a satisfying substitute for the wounds she wanted to inflict on herself.

To finish off the indignities she had wrought on his wardrobe, Julianne stamped them underfoot like a child having a tantrum. All the pain and agony of the past weeks burst out of her. To have been betrayed by Paolo, followed by there not being enough time for a reconciliation, felt like a cruelty she did not deserve. He was the only man who had ever really loved her. He was the one who solved her problems, who knew all her secrets. Without him she feared that she would again drown in the sea of helplessness that before Paolo had always led to self-harm.

Rage quickly turned to self-pity. Julianne sank to the floor surrounded by the wreckage of her wild rampage.

The front door opened. Julianne listened. She could hear the sounds of Angel and Isabella following Kira into the house as they returned from a shopping trip with their Rosita. Quickly, Julianne began to throw the ripped clothing into a big bag. She didn't want anyone to see her like this, especially her adult daughter.

She could hear Kira Mae giving the girls a job to do. "Go help Rosita with the shopping bags," she instructed them.

It wouldn't be long before they came looking for her. Julianne looked at the remaining debris at her feet. Now that the storm was over, she felt embarrassed and ashamed. These high emotions were old feelings that she had struggled for so many years to overcome. To deny the feelings that were so much a part of her life didn't help. When the inferno was finally released, the consequences tended to be dramatic.

As Julianne stuffed the remains of Paolo's clothes into the bag, she wished that her feelings and doubts and fears could be consigned to the rubbish as well.

It seemed there was to be no real closure for Julianne or Kira. No burial, or memorial, no service at which to say prayers and sing hymns and send Paolo's body onward to the next stage of the journey.

Communication with his newly discovered family in Rome had been polite but uncomfortable. From the time that they had informed his wife, police had acted as go-betweens. According to their information, Paolo had separated from his wife many years before—a not uncommon situation in a Catholic country where divorce was still frowned upon. He wasn't registered as living at her address, but she was still next of kin.

There were two grown-up children who still lived at home. The eldest son was in charge of arrangements and as soon as Paolo's body was officially released, he would have it transported to Rome. Julianne dreaded that he might want to visit and ask questions about the family and their relationship with his father. She decided to ask the police if they would accept Paolo's belongings, those that she had not destroyed, and pass them on to his family. That way neither she nor her daughter would need to become entangled in a potentially fraught situation.

They only needed now to wait for the postmortem result that would confirm how Paolo had died.

Kira Mae offered to call the police station. By now she was on first-name terms with all the officers.

"No results yet," said a friendly, young female policewoman. "There have been complications and we need your mother to come down to the station and answer some questions to help us build up a complete picture, as she was the one who found the body. It needs to be sooner rather than later," she explained when Kira Mae asked for a postponement. "But if it helps, we can send someone to you rather than your mother having to come here."

"Yes, thank you," said Kira. "I appreciate that."

Julianne, who had gone to bed with a sleeping pill, woke a couple of hours later and it was as if the whole mad incident had never occurred. She dismissed Kira Mae's suggestion that she see a doctor.

"No need for that," she said. "I feel fine. I've been suffering from insomnia, that's all."

Kira Mae told her mother about the conversation with the police station. Julianne said nothing. Privately she dreaded how she would react to police questioning. Perhaps they could delay the process for a couple of days to allow her to regain some of her mental strength.

* * *

"It's just a formality," said the officer who had come to talk to Julianne. She had returned to her cottage for the first time since Angel was abducted and it was lovely to be home. Was it really just a week ago since Angel had gone missing and Paolo had died?

Julianne had been surprised to answer the door to a detective, along with the young policewoman she had gotten to know from the long hours at the villa.

Detective Arturo Hernandez immediately took the

initiative. In the small living room of her home, his presence seemed huge.

"I just need to ask you a few questions, Miss Gordon," he said, refusing to call her Julianne as did all the other officers she had spoken to.

"The medical examiner is considering the possibility that Mr. Paolo had a heart attack. However, he had no medical record of heart problems and hadn't to our knowledge seen a doctor in the past six months. Can you tell me what he had been drinking the night before you found him?"

"We were celebrating," Julianne said. "We were massively relieved. Our little girl had been returned to us. We all drank more than usual, but not excessively."

"What about his drug taking?" asked the detective. "We found high levels of cocaine in his system."

Julianne stared at the officers. "I've never known Paolo to use drugs. In fact, as far as I know, he was completely against them. In his professional life he saw so many people whose lives were destroyed by illegal substances—including legal ones in the form of alcohol and prescribed pain medication."

"Did you know that his licence to practice law was suspended because of a drug conviction?" said the detective.

It was the first time Julianne had heard of it. She shook her head wordlessly.

"He lost his position at the British Embassy's legal department because of the conviction and was working as a paralegal in a lawyer's office on the outskirts of Rome."

Julianne was shell-shocked. Surely they were talking about a different person. Paolo was a model of sobriety and respectability. She had never even known him to have a speeding fine. Well, maybe a speeding fine—he did drive a Ferrari.

"I'm sorry this is all a complete revelation to me. I have no knowledge of any of this," she reiterated. "As far as I knew Paolo worked at the British embassy. He never told me any different. I don't think I can help you at all. Obviously my information is out of date."

"Do you know where he got the drugs?" asked the detective. He was doing all the talking while the police-woman said little. Now Julianne followed her gaze around the room and wondered if they were contemplating searching her home.

Julianne shook her head again. She was out of her depth. Recreational drugs had never been part of her life. Like many other people she knew, she considered prescription drugs in a different category. Yes, she used painkillers, when necessary. To relieve her pain.

The police officer now consulted his notes and asked, "What is your connection to Gio Lopez?"

Julianne tried to react, but the words felt like she had taken a body blow. Gio. What the hell did he have to do with any of this?

Without being asked, the policeman answered her question.

"He is a known drug dealer," he told her. "Have you ever bought drugs from him?"

"Of course not," said Julianne as she struggled to

keep the righteous indignation out of her voice. "I don't take drugs, I told you."

"Well, your boyfriend did," he said. "And we have reason to believe that the batch of drugs he bought from Gio just a few days ago may have contributed to his death."

chapter eighteen

"Love is a familiar; Love is a devil: there is no evil angel but Love."

—Shakespeare's *Love's Labors Lost*

The silence in the room was deafening. Julianne did not trust herself to speak while her whole world crashed around her. She stared at the detective and willed herself to come up with an appropriate response.

Her head spun and she thought she might faint. She had no option but to ask the young police officer to get her some water while she searched frantically for an answer.

The detective waited, then asked again, "I believe you know Gio Lopez? I understand that he was connected to the abduction of your granddaughter Angel."

Julianne could not formulate one straight response. "I don't know him personally," was her feeble reply. She calculated that she really needed time to digest this information. Paolo would never have allowed her to answer leading questions without knowing where they were headed.

She didn't need to be a lawyer to know that she was in dangerous territory, whatever she said. "This has all been a terrible shock," she said in an unsteady voice. She sipped the water and tried to buy thinking time. "Forgive me but I don't think I can continue. After all the strain of my granddaughter's kidnap, and now this, I have a massive migraine and I really need to lie down. Would you be kind enough to allow me to take a break and come back to this discussion when I'm more able to concentrate?"

Julianne felt like the walls were closing in on her, and she didn't know what else to do. She watched the detective considering his options. In the circumstances she judged that he would comply with her request. He would be aware that the police chief had developed a special relationship with the family. Julianne and Kira Mae had the public sympathy through the huge media interest in Angel's case and the detective would not want to jeopardize his relationship with Xabia. Julianne could almost see his thought processes. She had known the beautiful ones always get away with more. And anxious as he was to get answers to his questions, she also knew that he wanted to please Julianne.

He nodded to the police officer. "Let's leave Miss Gordon to deal with her headache. We can continue this discussion at a later stage. Next time perhaps we can ask you to come down to the station."

"Yes, of course, thank you. You're very kind," Julianne gave him the benefit of her best smile.

She showed the two of them out and leaned against

the back of the door as if she feared they would suddenly return.

Julianne poured herself a whisky in her living room as she considered the two primary responses. Fight or flight?

She was shocked rigid to learn that Paolo was a drug user. She had never seen any indications of it. How was she to process the information when she felt like they were talking about a man who was totally unknown to her?

Paolo was a rock, a pillar of the establishment.

When her lover Romero had been revealed as an international drug smuggler, Paolo was the man who had done everything in his power to have him convicted. The fact that he had dragged her daughter Kira Mae into his evil web made Paolo all the more determined.

Kira Mae was not the first or even the last foreign national he had represented who found herself in trouble as a result of unwise connections with criminals, but Paolo very quickly developed a special relationship with Kira Mae and her mother.

It would not need six degrees of separation for the detective to connect her with Gio as the known accomplice of Romero Rosario. When Gio went to prison and Romero did nothing to help him, Gio had sworn revenge.

Julianne lay on the couch and closed her eyes. She did not trust her legs to carry her up the narrow staircase to her bedroom. She was enveloped in sweat as if she had a fever, and her senses felt out of control. Her limbs felt leaden as if she had no energy and yet her body shook. She was sure she was going to throw up.

Julianne was scared. She had felt this way before. Almost an out of body experience. She tried to remember what she had learned years ago when she still suffered flashbacks from the night-time terrors her father had put her through.

"Breathe. Breathe," she told herself. "Stay present. It won't kill you. This too shall pass."

Julianne heard someone crying. Huge wracking sobs. It was her. She felt trapped and scared for her life; she had no idea what to do.

Had Gio been arrested by now? If so, how long before her name came up? It would not take long before the police started to put pieces of the jigsaw together.

The woman at the nursery school who handed Angel over to a stranger was a girlfriend of Gio's. Paolo was a drug-buying customer of Gio's. Julianne considered the facts. He had not told her he had a wife, he had not told her he had lost his job, he had slept with her daughter, he had omitted to mention his crucial connection with Gio Lopez. Why?

Think, Julianne, think.

What would Paolo do?

Look for the common denominator, she realized.

Paolo was the lynchpin. He was party to all the latest information from the police and he was also an insider at the house. He was aware of every phone call, every instruction, plus he had collected the money from the bank.

Had Gio and Paolo been in this together? She did not even want to contemplate that Paolo could have had anything to do with Angel's kidnapping.

But, she now reflected, he could have orchestrated the whole thing every step of the way.

She reviewed the facts. Paolo had admitted on the night Angel was returned that he had been the prime mover and shaker in organizing the trip Julianne took to the bullring, and he was there when Angel was released.

God forbid he had arranged the whole thing. But why?

Was money the objective? Did he need to pay Gio off? He was the only one besides Julianne who knew about the first phone call from Gio and the crime Gio that had carried out for her. Was she being blind? She could not believe her darling Paolo was some kind of Jekyll and Hyde character. When had it all started? How long had he been a drug addict? Was cocaine really what had killed him?

Julianne did not have answers, and she did not want to be asked questions. Not by the police, not by Paolo's family. Not by Kira Mae who had been shielded from the part that Julianne had played in the death of Romero. Julianne felt forced to take drastic action before the police began to make difficult connections. She would not stay and answer their questions if she could avoid it.

There was only one thing for it. When there was nothing with which to fight—it had to be flight. While she still had her passport and no one accused her of anything, Julianne decided to disappear. With her out of the way, she reasoned her daughters and granddaughter would be safer.

The threatened panic attack passed. They always did, but who knew when they would return? Julianne took advantage of the respite and climbed the stairs to her bedroom and the bathroom. There she located the pills that she used to calm herself at times of crisis. Two was the recommended dose, she took four. It crossed her mind that she too was a drug addict but her pills were prescription—not illegal. She began to feel calm almost immediately.

She needed to think—and quickly.

Where to go? That was the question. She knew she had to act fast. Now. Straightaway. Don't give the police a chance to arrive on the doorstep again.

If she could have a breather somewhere new, she would be able to face the world again, whatever it might throw at her.

Delay could be fatal, she thought, as she packed a small suitcase. She was an expert in making a small amount of clothes go a long way. She always looked immaculate when she traveled, although that was the least of her worries now.

She needed to get to the airport. There she would buy a ticket to any place she judged was far enough away from the jurisdiction of the Spanish police.

Her mind raced. She had not been accused of anything, she was free to go wherever she chose. From the airport she would call Kira Mae. She did not want to have to offer explanations or to give Kira any opportunity to stop her. Nor would she tell her the real reason for running away. Once she was safely out of the country, she would explain everything and no doubt the police would tell Kira about the drug connection Paolo had with Gio.

Julianne kept telling herself that she could be more useful from a distance. She chose her favorite Louis Vuitton travel bag and carried it downstairs. Her car was in the driveway. She quickly locked up the house and put her bag on the backseat. Feeling like a criminal she checked that no one was watching the house.

The drive to the airport took just half an hour. On the way, she considered her options.

She tried to convince herself she was going on one of her regular work trips. Kira Mae would look after the children and the business as usual. She would call her from the airport and say good-bye to the children.

In the main concourse, she checked the departures board. In just over an hour an Iberia flight was headed to Madrid, which sounded like a good bet. She handed over her frequent traveler platinum American Express card.

"Do you have a business class seat on the next flight?" she asked.

"Let me check," said the desk clerk. "You're traveling alone?"

Julianne nodded. "Yes, we have availability, a window seat," the desk clerk said with a smile. "Any luggage to check?"

"No thank you," said Julianne. "This will go in the overhead," she indicated her LV bag.

"If you care to wait in the executive lounge, we'll call you when your flight is ready to board," said the clerk.

Julianne thanked her and walked briskly to the lounge.

She telephoned Kira Mae and was relieved to reach voice mail. "Darling. I'm at the airport. You know how upsetting this situation with Paolo has been for me; I need to get away before his son arrives in town. I have some unfinished business in Bali so I'm headed back there. I knew you wouldn't mind now that we have Rosita to help out. I'll call you when I land and we can have a long chat. Give the girls a kiss for me. Lots of love."

Julianne turned off her mobile phone. She certainly did not intend to have a long chat with her daughter if she could help it.

chapter nineteen

"Whoever loved that loved not at first sight?"
—Shakespeare's *As You Like It*

Julianne felt as if she was underwater, as if she could not hear or see properly. Zombie-like, she walked through the airport, fearful every minute that the police would stop her. She had never envisioned herself as a criminal on the run, but her current actions could be considered as indicators of guilt.

Voices in her head were the main accusers. They screamed at her that she was wicked, stupid, uncaring, unfeeling, selfish and unworthy. She bit the inside of her cheek to deflect the searing emotional pain and dug her long red fingernails into the palms of her hands.

So desperate did she feel that she wanted to sit right down in the middle of the airport lounge and wail. She wanted to have a tantrum and demand that someone come and take care of everything for her. Paolo had been her go-to man for that support and reassurance.

As usual, heads turned and several fellow travelers turned to look at the beautiful, elegant blonde whose long legs carried her confidently across the concourse.

No one would guess the turmoil she suffered. Julianne knew that humans, like icebergs, reveal only one eighth of their mass to the world. The other seven-eighths are hidden under the water, ready to damage and capsize anyone or anything that comes too close.

To give herself brief respite from the constant pacing from the lounge to the ladies room, from the ladies room to duty-free, from duty-free to the bookstore, she sat down and briefly observed her fellow travelers, wondering what inner conflicts other individuals might be experiencing. Again, she returned to the ladies room, a refuge where she could splash her face with cold water and reapply makeup.

Emerging from the restroom, she was horrified to discover that the flight had been delayed. Just what she did not need. She approached the ticket counter, trying not to draw attention to herself.

The friendly young airline representative reassured her. "Not long, maybe 20 to 30 minutes. Business-class passengers will board as soon as we get authorization."

Julianne prayed. Dear God, please get me out of this situation. I can't stand the strain. I don't know what I will do. Please don't let me scream, cry or have a meltdown right here on the floor.

"You could go back to the VIP lounge," said the clerk in an effort to be helpful. "They'll inform you when the flight is ready to embark."

Julianne indicated her carry-on bag. "It's too far for me to walk. No, don't worry. I'll stay here."

By the time the announcement came to board,

Julianne was a nervous wreck. She hid behind her sunglasses and checked out every single person who entered or left the waiting area. She tied her long hair into a bun at the back of her head hoping that might make her look less noticeable.

A security guard in uniform was engaged in a deep conversation with the ticket clerk, and Julianne became convinced he was talking about her. Was he glancing at her or wasn't he?

She had nearly shredded the tissue in her hand when the announcement came over the loudspeaker.

"Business-class passengers are now free to board."

Julianne tried not to look as if she was in too much of a hurry. Thankfully she joined the short line and was grateful for the gentleman who let her go in front of him.

"You are very kind," she told him and gave him the benefit of a first class smile.

She handed her ticket and ID to the staff at the desk and set off through the security door, down a short passageway and finally onto the plane.

She made a valiant effort to return the smile of the flight attendant who guarded the entry door as she turned right into business class. The one-hour flight to Madrid was going to be fraught with danger—or so Julianne was imagining.

Every passenger who walked down the aisle, every flight attendant who interrupted her with questions—did she want a newspaper or drinks or a snack? Announcements over the speaker system put her into a panic. The seat next to her was empty. Was that a good or bad sign? She feared that the police were pursuing her and would suddenly appear to make her go back and face the music: "We need to ask you a few questions about your accomplice Gio Lopez." Gio wasn't her accomplice; he had never been connected with her. There was no proof; it was his word against hers.

The flight continued without incident, and she closed her eyes as she tried to calm her breathing. Maybe she had gotten away with it so far. Or had she?

Justifying her actions, she reminded herself that it was her own fault her family failed to depend on her. She would hardly be missed. A consequence of her constant absences. Sure, Kira Mae probably deserved support at this time after all she had endured, but Julianne doubted her own ability to be the person to offer that support. When she felt in danger of falling apart—she chose to remove herself from those she loved. As she began to question her ability to truly love, she offered a sharp rebuke, *"Don't even go there."*

Disembarking in Madrid, she began to relax, to feel the safety of distance. Now she would be able to think straight. She checked the departure board. Bali? It was still midafternoon, but this was no time to be starting the multiflight 18- to 20-hour journey to Indonesia.

Casablanca? That sounded like a place a fugitive on the run would go.

She did have business connections in the city though. Casablanca was only an hour and a half away from Madrid and a whole world away on the African continent. She hurried to the ticket counter and booked a ticket. She had promised herself years ago, after a particularly uncomfortable transatlantic flight that all her air travel from then on would be in first class.

"I take it for granted to turn left when I get on the plane, toward the first class cabin," she liked to say, only half joking.

Now she boarded the Royal Air Maroc plane and turned right toward a window seat numbered A1. Before she could stow her bag, the zealous attendant whisked it out of her hands and deposited it in the luggage storage. Next she relieved Julianne of her red leather jacket (worn today with black pants and a handmade black lace blouse) and hung it up in the small wardrobe by the cockpit.

Julianne settled herself in the super-comfortable seat, located the headphones in the pocket and turned up the volume. Then she became immersed in the in-flight magazine and successfully shut out the outside world. Her nerves were still shot, and she almost leapt out of her seat when the flight attendant leaned over and asked, "Would you like a glass of champagne before we take off?"

Julianne said "No" automatically and then thought better of it. "Yes, I will please," she said, "but you can add some orange juice and make it a Buck's Fizz."

She stuck her head back in the magazine and was not happy to have her attention further distracted by a man who boarded and was claiming the seat next to her. She much preferred the arrangement on some airlines where passengers traveled in their own private little first-class pod with no stranger up close and personal. Ignore him, she told herself. Don't smile, it might encourage him.

The flight attendant returned with her drink and the man leaned back to let her take it from the tray.

"I'll have one of those too, please," he told the attendant.

Julianne stayed hidden behind her sunglasses, headphones, the magazine and the drink. She stared out of the window and observed that the steps had been removed from the front of the plane and the luggage truck was making its way back across the tarmac to the airport buildings.

Feeling like a prisoner and a hostage, glued to her chair, unable to move or make any decisions that would hasten her departure, Julianne took a large gulp and drained the glass. All she desired was to be out of this country and safely on her way to the exotic delights of Casablanca, Morocco.

"We're closing the cabin doors," said the flight attendant over the loudspeaker system, and Julianne let out a sigh of relief. Once airborne she would be safe.

As she did on all her flights, Julianne prayed until the plane was safely in the air. Hands clasped in her lap, she repeated her novenas over and over again.

God keep me safe. Guard my family. Take me home to them.

"Would it disturb you if I asked you to close the window blind, as the sun is in my eyes?" said the man beside her.

Without turning toward him, Julianne pulled it down halfway with a shiver of irritation. Why did she have to be sitting next to a lily-livered chatty type who couldn't handle a bit of sunlight? Under her breath she mouthed, "Baby." It was barely audible, or so she thought.

There was a beat, and then the male voice replied, almost as an aside, "Thank you, darling."

Julianne laughed out loud, partly from nerves, partly from sheer adrenalin. She turned to face him. As she wondered how to respond, she looked him over: The eyes that had been so sensitive to the light were velvet-brown with flashing gold flecks. His hair was dark and curly, long on top, squared off with a neat line at the back. A strong, square jaw gave him the appearance of a superhero, and he sported a light brush of designer stubble.

"I wasn't calling you 'Baby,'" she said.

"I know," he said, "but at least I got a reaction from you."

He wore a snow-white dress shirt, his strong muscles visible through the smooth fabric, black trousers and silver trainers. He certainly knew how to attract attention. His long legs were stretched out and crossed at the ankle. He looked like a man at ease with himself. And there was something else.

Julianne was fascinated by the black leather gloves he wore. They seemed strangely out of place on the plane. He noticed her puzzled expression.

"Forgive the dramatic black leather gloves," he said, "but I have to keep my hands protected."

Julianne couldn't help rolling her eyes. Sensitive eyes and sensitive hands.

He smiled and a huge grin spread across his face, revealing a full set of perfect white teeth.

"May I introduce myself," he said. Julianne detected an accent. He sounded European but with a veneer of American.

"Dominic," he said. "Like the Dominican monks. Though I don't have too much in common with them."

Here was a man with a sense of humor who obviously did not take himself too seriously. Except when it came to his sensitive eyes and delicate hands.

"Julianne," she said. "Pleased to meet you."

Julianne and Dominic exchanged small talk until the attendant came round with hot towels for them to wash their hands before lunch.

Dominic laughed loudly when the attendant held the silver tray out to him, little white rolls of towel all neatly arranged.

"I'll pass," he said.

The attendant noticed the gloves and gave him a quizzical look.

"There is a perfectly logical explanation," he said to Julianne. "Maybe I will tell you one day. Now that's a secret to be revealed."

Julianne shivered. She too had a secret, more like a Pandora's box of secrets, and the last thing she wanted was for them to be revealed to this handsome stranger. Still, he was a great distraction from her deepening worries.

Choices for lunch were all Moroccan-based. Julianne was pleased to note that Dominic selected the vegetarian option. They selected the same salad, the same dressing and even chose the same sparkling white wine to accompany their meal.

On the short flight they shared tasty morsels of personal information as they ate and drank. Smiling at each other from time to time, enjoying this passing flirtation.

Dominic was an engaging companion. "I seem to spend more time traveling between countries than being in them," he told Julianne. "As a professional singer I go where the work is and often that means crossing the globe for an engagement of just one or maybe two nights. I promised myself that one day I will settle down but I think the gypsy in my soul will always keep me on the move."

Julianne was quick to question him. "Are you a gypsy?" she asked.

Dominic laughed. "No, it's just an expression but now I feel bad because you are looking at me as if you've seen a ghost."

"Sorry," she said, "it's just that I had a bad experience with a gypsy once. He was also a musician. I'll tell you about it one day. But not today. Another secret to be revealed."

They both laughed at what had already become a private joke about secrets to be revealed.

Julianne couldn't believe how much she had relaxed. Of course they were 5000 miles up in the sky and no one and nothing could shatter their cocoon of comfort and seclusion. She had already adopted the professional mask behind which she usually hid, coping mechanisms firmly in place.

Dominic wore no jewelry, Julianne observed, although his marital status was really no business of hers. With all the current problems piled on her shoulders she was certainly not looking for romance, and definitely not with a stranger on a plane. Romance was exactly what had gotten her into her terrible predicament in the first place.

After dinner, he had coffee, she had tea, and conversation waned. They settled back into their own personal space. From the large red leather tote bag by her feet, Julianne pulled out a fashion magazine. She intended to lose herself in the world of *Vogue.* The last time she had visited Casablanca it had been for the Casa Fashion Show, now an annual event that attracted fashionistas and media from all over the world. Generally the events showcased the wonderful array of Moroccan leather and top-quality wool items that are a tradition of Casablanca and one of the reasons why she made regular trips to the region. As well of course as the bustling, colorful, treasure-filled bazaars and souks.

Surreptitiously Julianne observed Dominic as he leveraged himself out of his seat, an impressive figure of a man, over six feet and powerfully built. An athlete, maybe? From a briefcase in the overhead locker, he pulled a copy of *Music Today,* a classical magazine, in Italian.

To outward appearances, so comfortable in each other's company and engrossed in magazines that revealed different but complementary passions, music and fashion, they made a beautiful couple.

Julianne's stolen glance at Dominic did not go unnoticed. He glanced down at her and smiled. "Hello, lovely lady," he said.

chapter twenty

"Love looks not with the eyes but with the mind.
And therefore is winged Cupid painted blind."
—Shakespeare's *Midsummer Night's Dream*

Julianne pretended to be engrossed in her magazine, but she could not settle. On the one hand she wanted to keep her head down and not be forced to reveal anything about herself. On the other hand she wanted to find out more about Dominic.

Sparks of sexual chemistry passed between the two and when their arms touched across the dividing seat, the reaction was electric. At the same moment, they lowered their magazines.

Dominic asked Julianne, "So, madam, what is the real purpose of your visit to Casablanca? A potentially dangerous choice for a beautiful lady like you. You could easily be whisked off into the white slave trade. In fact, I might contemplate capturing you myself."

And he had a sense of humor.

"I have business there," she said.

"You didn't tell me what kind of business," he said.

"Fashion business," she replied. "I buy and sell luxury clothing for an art and fashion galleria in southern Spain. We call it Wear 4 Art Thou?"

"Sounds fascinating," said Dominic. "But tell me, is we you and a husband, or you and a boyfriend?"

"Daughter," Julianne admitted, although she had promised herself that she would give as few details to this stranger as possible. "Kira is a designer, mainly evening gowns and special occasion dresses. She's very talented and has an excellent reputation. I'm very proud of her."

"And do you also design?" asked Dominic.

"No, that's not my area of expertise. I'm the business person. Administrator and organizer and chief buyer. That's the reason for my trip to Casablanca."

Julianne realized that she was talking more than she had intended. A common fault when she was nervous.

"I have many suppliers in the city and it's always good to have face-to-face meetings with clients," she continued, feeling that she was babbling now. "You get a better level of service when you can put a face to a name. I like my suppliers to know who I am. Of course Arab businessmen will talk for hours negotiating a deal, offering hospitality and fine food and it's considered an insult to refuse the meal and to rush negotiations. They don't only sell themselves or their businesses, they also establish a relationship. Very different from the way we Westerners have started to do business, all rush and no community, fly in fly out, even having airport meetings. I like to take my time and visit the factories and even the homes of the owners . . ."

Julianne stopped herself in midflow, embarrassed. Dominic looked amused and interested. He never took his eyes from her face.

"Enough about me," she said. "You probably already know everything I am telling you."

"No," he said, "actually this is my first visit. I'm here for a friend's wedding in Marrakesh, staying overnight in Casablanca and then traveling to Marrakesh tomorrow. The wedding feast is going on for several days, though the actual ceremony is not till the weekend."

In a matter of fact tone—although she sensed some pride behind the revelation—Dominic told her, "I'm the strolling troubadour, a lyric tenor. I guess that means I sing for my supper. Add a touch of operatic class to the proceedings. It's a good way to get on the guest list for weddings in exotic locations. I was even part of the entertainment team for George Clooney's wedding to Amal in Italy. Impressed?"

"I'm definitely impressed," said Julianne.

Time and miles flew past, and the conversation continued to flow. Dominic explained that, as well as being a classical singer, he played piano and guitar. That was the reason for the protective gloves.

He told her that he was to stay at the Art Palace Suites and Spa in Casablanca.

"Sounds like just your cup of tea," he said mimicking her English accent. "Where are you staying?" he asked.

Julianne hesitated. Should she admit that she had no hotel booked? She had planned to call from the airport before leaving and make a reservation but hadn't.

"This whole trip was very last minute," she eventually admitted. "I usually stay at the Four Seasons, but I haven't actually made a reservation this time."

"Do you want me to see if there's a room available at the Art Palace?" he asked. "It might be fun for you. See how other companies complement their regular business with culture and art."

Julianne was indeed interested to check out the famous hotel, even though she would not normally accept an invitation on the recommendation of a complete stranger. She hesitated, trying to decide on the best course of action. Was it wise to accept Dominic's invitation, or should she politely refuse and lie low? He was just a passing stranger, after all. Or was he?

"That would be lovely," she said finally.

On their arrival at Casablanca airport, Dominic wasted no time in making a reservation for her.

"Do you want the Marilyn, the Elvis or Arabian Nights room?" he asked.

"Surprise me," she told him.

Neither had checked baggage, the sign of the experienced business traveler. They knew the frustration of missing luggage and long waits at the baggage claim.

Dominic guided her into the taxi line and gave the driver the address of the Art Palace. "Do you have plans for this evening?" he asked. "It's not even 7 p.m. We could explore the city together. Will you join me?"

"I'd love to," said Julianne.

She was checked into a contemporary modern art room, all geometric carpets and splashes of unrecognizable shapes in the furnishings and artwork. Dominic was handed the tasseled key to the Sultan's Den.

"Meet me here in the lobby," said Dominic. "Will nine o'clock give you enough time to unpack and get ready?"

As they parted at the elevator each to go to their separate rooms, he blew her a kiss. "Missing you already," he said, with a wink.

Part of her screamed out that her behavior was completely inappropriate but that willful part that usually got what it wanted insisted. *I have nothing to lose,* she told herself defiantly.

Julianne unpacked and hung up the contents of her small case. She always carried an outfit or two that could be glammed up with accessories if she was invited out unexpectedly. However, she struggled a little on this occasion, having packed in such a frantic rush. Julianne made a quick executive decision. She needed a new dress, and she needed it now.

She rushed from the hotel and ducked and dived through the narrow streets, grateful for her familiarity with the city's alleyways, until she came to one of the small souk market places. There she selected a full-length vibrant blue silk dress with silver decorations and a striking off the shoulder neckline.

Clever bargaining bought her a veritable treasure trove of intricate filigree silver jewelry: necklaces, earrings and an armful of bangles. She drew the line at ankle bracelets but did purchase a shiny decoration for her hair.

She rushed back to the hotel and was delighted to find there was plenty of time for a long soak in the bathtub before it was time to get ready.

Submerged in bubbles in a deep tiled square bath, with perfumed and exotic bath spices, Julianne took a moment to reflect. Her spontaneity surprised and alarmed her sometimes and though she chose to categorize it as daring, bold, exciting, she knew that really it was self-will out of control. She wanted what she wanted when she wanted it.

That might be OK when it came to buying a new outfit, but was it appropriate for an assignation with a fellow traveler on a plane to a place that she shouldn't even have been going? She could not deny that when she woke up that morning she had no intention of flying to Casablanca.

She could not avoid the fact that these flights of fantasy were as much about the need to run away from herself as about the situations in which she found herself. Truth was that for all her business success, she was a mass of insecurities.

Now Julianne admitted to herself that fear had driven her to neglect her responsibilities.

Kira Mae deserved a phone call to know the whereabouts of her mother, but Julianne wasn't prepared to make the phone call there and then. She accepted that Kira Mae would be angry, and rightly so, but she did not want an argument with her daughter to take the shine off her date with Dominic.

It might have been an unwise decision, just a meaningless fantasy, but at that very moment Julianne chose to believe that the meeting with Dominic was destiny. Their stars had aligned and real life was to be left far behind, to be dealt with later.

Seize the day. Isn't that what all the self-help gurus tell you to do?

chapter twenty-one

"No sooner met but they looked: No sooner looked but they loved."

—Shakespeare's *As You Like It*

"Wow, you came prepared," said Dominic when he met up with Julianne in the lobby of the Art Palace. "You look absolutely gorgeous."

Julianne smiled. The effect of her hastily purchased outfit was spectacular—as she knew it would be. Her years as a fashion consultant meant that she knew exactly how to make an impact. The cobalt blue and scarlet colors suited her perfectly. Silver ornaments flashed in her long blonde curls. In a land of dark-haired beauties—well, blondes did look more fun.

She resisted saying, "You look pretty damn gorgeous yourself," even though he did. He wore white trousers with a black silk shirt and he carried a white jacket. He still wore silver sneakers but now his socks were sky-blue. His hands were bare and she found herself admiring their shape and his long fingers. The opulent tiled lobby was crowded with people all dressed up and heading out for the evening, although it was still early by

Arabic standards. Many restaurants did not really come to life till midnight.

Dominic stood head and shoulders above everyone else and drew admiring glances from men and women. The hotel staff swarmed around him and offered assistance.

"We're fine. We know where we're going," he said giving Julianne another wink.

He took her by the arm and guided her through the crowded lobby into the frantic activity of the Casablanca nighttime. A black luxury sedan awaited them and the fez-wearing driver had a smile as big as the open car door. Julianne had not asked where they were going, but she had made an educated guess.

Dominic described it in the lobby as "a classic scene of romance and intrigue." She had been there once before with clients, but she resisted telling Dominic—so much better to have this shared experience.

Julianne could not decide whether she was reckless or adventurous, driving off into the Arabian night with a complete stranger. Life is too short, she reminded herself, as she made a silent vow to call Kira Mae tomorrow. All her very real problems back at home could wait till then. Tonight she was ready to abandon herself to the moment.

The gates of an exotic garden came into view and confirmed her expectations of their destination. Stepping from the car, the heady evening perfume of blossoms permeated the air and the sight of millions of stars in the sky took Julianne's breath away.

Dominic and Julianne were shown to their table by the American owner, a one-time US Embassy staff member who after 9/11 had decided to do something meaningful with her life. She could think of no higher vision than to open an iconic bar in Casablanca dedicated to the memory of Rick and his lost love, Elsa.

She helped them choose from the traditional menu and it was a source of great amusement when again they both chose the same—goat cheese salad with figs and pastry with pistachio, dates and cinnamon cream.

Dominic looked at Julianne. "I'm so glad you get to play my Ingrid Bergman. I was determined to come here but I really would have felt a little silly saying to myself, 'Of all the gin joints in all the world, you have to walk into mine.'"

Over dinner, Dominic and Julianne talked about their careers, their passions, their visions and their dreams. Both had achieved much success in their professional lives, but they were still looking for the next mountain to climb.

Dominic made a proposal. "Let tonight be about us," he said. "I want to get to know you by what I see and feel and observe. And that's how I want you to know me. Too much revelation too early on when two people meet is damaging in my opinion. Do you agree?"

Julianne thought over the question. She did not want to appear too keen to avoid revelations about herself, but she also wondered what secrets Dominic was keeping.

He read her mind. "Do you give us permission to

each keep some secrets?" he said. "I promise I will not knowingly hurt you, but nor do I give body and soul to anyone without being very sure that I am serious about my future intentions."

Julianne nodded. "Suits me perfectly," she said. "If this is our only night together, let us just be. Let's make a beautiful memory."

Dominic reached out and took Julianne's hand across the table.

"You are my kind of lady, Miss Julianne, and I am very glad that of all the gin joints . . ."

"No, please, not again," she laughed.

At closing time, Dominic left a large tip and apologized to the waiter for keeping him so late.

"We didn't want to leave," Julianne explained. "We were so comfortable. Thank you. I hope we can come again."

In the car back to the hotel, Dominic and Julianne held hands as if it were the most natural thing in the world.

"I have a suggestion," said Dominic. "I'll show you when we arrive."

She hoped it would not be that they go to his room—even for a nightcap. Apart from Paolo, she had not slept with anyone since Romero, and wasn't sure that she was ready to.

Instead, Dominic invited her up to the roof of the hotel. As she stepped out of the elevator, Julianne was speechless. Ahead of her was a scene straight out of *One Thousand and One Arabian Nights*. A shelter was draped with black velvet and white damask and huge purple cushions were arranged close to the scented flames. Red rose petals covered the carpeted floor. A fire pit gave out warmth and the smell of sweet burning wood wafted across the rooftops.

"Take off your shoes," said Dominic. Julianne did as she was told, and an attendant appeared to bathe and towel dry their feet in perfumed water before helping the pair into silken slippers.

For those so inclined the attendant indicated a hookah pipe in the corner, and off to the side a small brass trolley held drinks and ice water. He bowed as he discreetly left the couple to their privacy. "Ring the bell if you require anything. If it is your wish, I will not return till morning."

Dominic thanked him and slipped a tip into his hand.

Plumping up the huge pile of silky tasseled pillows, Dominic patted the place beside him for Julianne to sit down. As they gazed up at the twinkling stars, he told her, "This is your Scheherazade moment. As long as you keep telling me stories to beguile and bewitch and enchant me, I will not ravish you."

Julianne laughed nervously.

"I'm serious," he said. "You don't really think the sultan was going to kill that gorgeous young maiden, Scheherazade? No, he was in love with her. She was too young, too pure and too holy. He wanted to keep her close by and gaze on her beauty, be enchanted by her storytelling."

Julianne lay beside him on the cushions. They might

not have a thousand days but there were a thousand stars glittering above.

Who is this amazing man? she wondered.

A poet, a romantic, an artist. He stirred her soul and made her believe in herself and all that was good and right. Lost in wonder, she lay perfectly at peace. Dominic reached for her. He enfolded her in his arms.

"You waited too long to start the story," he said. "I did warn you what would happen."

He pressed his lips to hers and she exhaled with delight. Dominic's tongue gently explored her mouth. Julianne felt her own resistance, and, sensing it, he took her face in his hands and assured her, "Nothing is going to happen that you don't want. What's your story, Julianne?"

Julianne wanted to scream, "Don't stop. I'm just a slow starter. Don't give up on me."

Summoning up all her courage she looked directly into his eyes and admitted, "The story is that I did not think I would survive the heartbreak the last time I allowed myself to be seduced. I called it love. That's not what it was for him."

Dominic sat up, and they faced each other, holding hands.

"Women are not the only ones who can die of the pain of heartbreak," he told her. "Don't tell me the ending of the story. Don't let out the secret. Not yet. Let me take you in my arms and make love to you. I don't make any promises, only that from the moment I saw you, I felt a deep and powerful connection. Our souls talked to each other. Don't deny that. Allow us both this one night of ecstasy. If you believe in romance and love and truth, abandon yourself to me. Join me on my magic carpet ride, high above the sky, far away from doubts, fears and pain."

Julianne gazed at the vastness of the midnight universe above. The sky, the stars, the moon. She saw the towering minarets, she heard the calls to prayer and gave herself permission to let go. Without expectations, maybe she would at last experience pure unconditional love, even if it was for just one night.

It sounded like a song, never mind a story.

Julianne leaned forward, lips parted, ready to abandon herself to the passion of the moment.

"Yes, please, Dominic, take me on your magic carpet ride," she said.

chapter twenty-two

"Hear my soul speak. The very instant that I
saw you did my heart fly to your service."
—Shakespeare's *The Tempest*

"Every woman deserves to be taken on a magic carpet ride," Dominic whispered in Julianne's ear. "Trust me and hold on tight. We could be in for a bumpy ride."

Once she had signaled her willingness to allow their intimacy to develop, Dominic took control. He unzipped Julianne's sleek blue silk dress and handed her the light robe. He removed his own clothes and, as she reclined on the cushion-strewn platform, he stood before her wearing just a pair of black jockey shorts that he covered with his own robe.

"Let's take this nice and easy," he told her. "Lie beside me. Let me feel your body align with mine, top to toe."

Julianne felt as if she was being prepared for a divine ritual.

"Do you meditate?" he asked her, "because if you do, you may have heard about the tantric tradition."

She shook her head. "I've tried to meditate, but I

can never close down all my thoughts enough to get really comfortable. But I do yoga. Does that count?"

"We can work with that," he told her. "I'll guide you. In the tantric tradition, the connection we make is through our breath and inner being. In the silence, in the place between our thoughts, we will come together. Gradually, naturally, at a refined pace. When the connection is particularly powerful, we may not even make it to the physical part of our connection. The souls align deep inside the body and produce all the benefits of a pure and beautiful love. But, personally," he added, "I like it when it gets physical."

Julianne reached out and stroked his face. She aligned her body with his. "Kiss me," she said.

Dominic pressed his lips to hers and held the embrace, long and with passion, for what felt like an eternity. He stroked her face and planted kisses on her eyes, her cheeks and her nose.

Hypnotizing her, he looked deep into her eyes and her soul.

In a heightened state of awareness, Julianne succumbed and breathed in his essence, his masculine aroma. Rhythmically her breath rose and fell with his; even their heartbeats aligned. Carried on the air, the celestial music of nature filled their senses. The soft breeze transmitted the sounds of the earth over the rooftop. Brilliant stars continued to bathe the earth in a silver glow.

Julianne was mesmerized and enchanted. She'd never experienced anything like this before.

As much as she wished to resist comparisons, Julianne could not stop her mind from returning to the frantic passion she had shared with Romero. He had been wild, demanding and passionate. Only later did Julianne learn that he really was a man in a hurry. One who was also making love to her daughter and possibly several other woman, including his wife, but probably not his virginal fiancée.

Julianne shivered and Dominic paused.

"No, no, go ahead," said Julianne. To show her willingness, she sat up and allowed him to remove her bra. When he linked his strong hands inside her pants, she resisted momentarily before abandoning herself to all the delights that the night had to offer.

"Ready to step on board the magic carpet?' he asked with a slow grin. "Let me take you up above the stars."

Julianne had never been more ready to immerse herself totally in the joy of lovemaking. Every fiber of her being cried out for him to overpower her, consume her. She longed to lose herself in him, body and soul. The two came together, and for the first time in years, Julianne really did feel the earth move. She was naked in mind and spirit, and it felt so good

Later, she stirred from a blissful relaxation. She opened her eyes and there Dominic lay beside her. He was asleep and looked peaceful. At some point in the night he had covered them with one of the sumptuous purple tasseled throws. He still held her hand.

Julianne felt as if she were under the influence of a love spell. She had no recollection of drinking a potion, but she knew that her whole level of consciousness had been altered. She wondered how long this amazing feeling would last.

Dominic awoke and smiled at her. "Did you enjoy the ride?" he asked with a wicked grin.

"Wherever did you learn to do that?" Julianne asked with a smile to match his. "No, don't tell me."

Minarets all over the city signaled dawn. The magic of the night gave way to daybreak.

Dominic and Julianne dressed and reluctantly left the oasis of the rooftop.

It was time to return to their separate rooms. Later that morning they arranged a date to tour the city.

"What do you have planned for the rest of the trip?" Dominic enquired.

Julianne indicated she had to make some appointments, see clients and only then she would have a better idea of her itinerary. She had no intention of telling him that she had nothing on her agenda.

Back in her room, bathed and dressed, reality started to impose itself on her dream state. The world outside her hotel window didn't seem so alluring in daylight. Feeling her mood begin to plummet, she proceeded to formulate a plan. She could put off no longer the call to Kira Mae. Guilt reared its ugly head when she considered that she had abandoned her daughters at such a desperate time. Now she must face the music and call Kira.

More important, what did she think she had been doing by leaving her daughters alone? Her granddaughter had been abducted; her lover had died. Were they safe in the villa? What had she been thinking, taking off like that?

Her hand shook as she dialed the number. To prevent the call being traced, she used the hotel landline, not her mobile phone. Julianne realized that she actually felt safer knowing that she couldn't be contacted. She may have felt less threatened , but how did her daughters feel?

She placed a call from her room but asked the hotel receptionist not to reveal her whereabouts. Julianne both hoped and dreaded that the call would go to voice mail, hating herself for her cowardice. However, she accepted that she must be brave and find out what was happening back in Spain. She felt dreadful that she had not even called to say good night to the girls.

The old familiar critical inner voice that told her she was a lousy mother sounded in her head. Her mind raced back to the time when Kira Mae was just a toddler and, at the invitation of their darling grandmother, Mama Mitchell, Julianne had left Kira Mae with her in Scotland and moved to London to pursue her career.

You always put yourself first, said her accusing inner voice. *What Julianne wants, Julianne gets and to hell with the consequences. No wonder Kira Mae and Paolo turned to each other for loving companionship, while you traveled the world, all in the name of business. Now you've done the same thing again. How could you run out on your daughter—again? Now you are so obsessed by a handsome young man you barely know, you've left her to deal with all of your problems.*

"Shut up, please shut up," Julianne told the voice. "I know you're right. Just give me a break while I try to sort this out."

The bedroom phone rang and Julianne braced herself.

"Where the hell are you?" shouted Kira Mae. "I've been out of my mind with worry. Though why it should be such a surprise when you are always running off and leaving us, I don't know. Why didn't you answer my phone calls or my texts?"

Julianne took a deep breath and tried to will her heart to stop thumping. She knew she had no reasonable explanation, and the one she had come up with sounded feeble even to her. "I lost my phone at the airport," she began, horrified by how easily she could lie to her own daughter. "Maybe it was stolen. But whoever has it can't use it because it's locked with a passcode. I needed to get an upgrade so I'll do that now."

"Mother," Kira Mae's voice was still raised. "You could have still called me. You knew I would be frantic. Where the hell are you?" she demanded again.

"I had some business to deal with," Julianne told her, keeping her voice low in an attempt to take the drama and confrontation out of the situation. "Give me a day or two and I'll be home. I'll tell you all about it then. How are the girls? Make sure the nanny moves in and stays with you till I get back. Just tell me you are OK."

"Oh, yes, I'm great," said Kira Mae. "My daughter was kidnapped but now she's back. My best friend and the only father figure I have ever known died suddenly. He also happened to be my lawyer. And now my mother and business partner has gone missing. As usual, never around when she's needed. If this is meant to punish me for what happened between Paolo and me, you win."

The last remark struck gold, and, while Julianne was desperate to deny the accusation, she had no defense against the truth. She just did not have the mental stability to deal with difficult situations. *Seems she always fell apart,* she told herself.

"By the way," Kira Mae added as if an afterthought, "the police still want to talk to you. They say you left the country without permission when they were in the process of pursuing an investigation."

"Kira, darling," said Julianne, "the line is really bad. Give the girls a kiss for me. And I'll make sure I deal with everything when I get home. Maybe tomorrow—or the day after. Don't bother trying to call as I don't suppose my phone will be found. I'll phone you. Love you."

Kira Mae did not reply or if she did, Julianne didn't hear it. She had already hung up the phone.

Julianne sat on the bed and made a resolution. She would call Dominic and tell him the sightseeing was off. She had to fly home now, today.

The phone rang again.

"What time shall I book the car for the tour?" asked Dominic. "And I've got another suggestion. Do you want to come to Marrakesh with me? We could leave straight after the sightseeing tour. Get the same driver to take us all the way. It's about a three-hour journey. Julianne?"

"Yes, I'm listening," she said. Ignoring all her good intentions and the angry voice in her head, Julianne heard herself saying, "I'd love to. Count me in. But do we need a car and driver. Haven't you got a magic carpet?"

She heard him smile at the other end of the phone.

"Behave yourself," Dominic replied.

"OK. I'll be good," said Julianne, pushing unwelcome thoughts away. "Give me a couple of hours to sort out some things, answer a few emails. Don't you have any obligations?"

"Most of the people I know from the wedding party don't arrive till tomorrow," he explained. "It will get pretty frantic after that, but until then, no problem. I always planned some time alone to explore this fantastic city. Now I get to be alone with you. Make it noon. See you in the lobby."

She ordered mint tea from room service and lay on the bed, alternately napping and planning her outfits. For the sightseeing tour and drive across country, she chose a white linen suit, channeling Ingrid Bergman. She knew in her heart of hearts that avoiding real life would come with a price, but the temptation to live in the moment was too great.

Julianne had a moment of clarity as she lay soaking in a hot bath. How did this happen? *Here I am a woman on the run from the police about to drive across the African dessert with the most beautiful and amazing man I have ever met.* She consoled herself. *I'll enjoy one more night of freedom. Tomorrow I'll go home and face the music.*

chapter twenty-three

"Go to your bosom; Knock there,
and ask your heart what it doth know."
—Shakespeare's *Measure for Measure*

Casablanca was as noisy, chaotic and vibrant as Julianne remembered. The driver of the sleek black limousine assured them that he had the city covered. He would show them all the sights. Julianne and Dominic settled back on the plush cream leather seats. They declined the offer of champagne but accepted coffee.

Their tour started at the magnificent Cathedrale du Sacre Coeur. The driver fast-tracked them to the front of the long lines of waiting tourists and pilgrims, and they marveled at the opulence of the gold- and jewel-encrusted statues and religious artifacts.

Believing that most visitors to the city were more interested in shopping than praying, the driver quickly moved on to Casablanca's main market, the Marche Central.

"Here," he told them, "you can buy everything from a cinnamon pod to a camel."

The bustling market overflowed with stalls selling

rare spices, vintage goods, home décor and sumptuous fabrics. Delighting in the visual feast and cacophony of different sounds, Julianne took time to reacquaint herself with some of the vendors, all of whom were eager to share their bolts of silks and satins in every shade of the rainbow.

"This is the basis of our evening-wear collection," Julianne told Dominic. "These fabrics are encrusted with borders of fine jewels and we make them into exquisite gowns and, for some of our more adventurous clientele, saris."

Stallholders waved at Julianne and rushed out of their stores to welcome her. Even those who didn't know Julianne were happy to make a new friend and customer of the beautiful English lady.

"Come, come, I have something special for you," they entreated. Bargaining was the order of the day. The more vocal of the expert salesmen voiced their disappointment when Julianne refused to go inside their small shacks, which were piled floor to ceiling with fabrics. Many remembered her sitting with them, cross-legged on the floor, drinking mint tea as they haggled over the best price for her latest order.

Across from the market Dominic spotted the iconic Hotel Transatlantique, built back in the 1920s and popular with famous singers such as Edith Piaf and Josephine Baker. Glad to be out of the sun, Dominic and Julianne strolled hand in hand through the lobby of the hotel and admired old black and white photographs of a bygone era. Julianne realized they were seamlessly combining their twin passions, fashion and music.

From Marche Central, their driver promised to show them the number one tourist attraction in Casablanca, Hassan II Mosque, completed in 1993, which overlooks the Atlantic Ocean. "Awesome," they agreed.

The driver played a game with the couple as he tried to hide the identity of the next destination on their tour. "You have to guess," he said. "It's a very famous place and a very famous man."

Exchanging glances, they decided not to tell the driver that they had already been to Rick's Place. Later Julianne and Dominic allowed romance to prevail and pleased their chauffeur by posing for photographs by the piano. They had missed that treat the previous evening. Today they were happy to play tourists.

"The photograph will help us remember our first date," said Dominic.

"I'm not likely to forget that," said Julianne as she felt a sadness touch her heart. How long could this fantasy last? Her real-life situation was almost as tragic as Ingrid Bergman's character. She too was desperate for an exit strategy.

The visit to Rick's brought on a melancholic mood, and Julianne and Dominic were quiet in the car as they headed to their next scheduled stop, the Old Medina of Casablanca, an ancient maze of alleys and buildings. "This is a dangerous part of town," their driver warned them, "and you must not go here without a local guide, especially after dark."

Next came one of the city landmarks that Julianne was able to claim she knew well: Musée Abderrahman Slaoui. She was always entranced by the museum and its art deco building. Dominic listened as she told him about some of the design inspirations that she had taken back to her workshop and turned into pieces of contemporary jewelry, to be sold in the Galleria.

Julianne worried that she was overwhelming Dominic with sightseeing and talk of fashion and art, but he showed no signs of losing enthusiasm. "I am an artist," he reminded her as he took her hand between both of his. "Your enthusiasm and knowledge excites and inspires me. You are a woman of rare taste and experience, darling Julianne," he told her as they settled in the back of the limousine on the journey to Marrakesh.

The journey through the desert weaved a magical spell and, lost in its wonder, they sat in the air-conditioned luxury of the car and stared out of the dark-tinted windows as the mysterious landscape flew by. The desert dunes passed before their eyes, and they were transfixed. The journey was a meditation, a deeply reflective time in which neither spoke much but both had a sense that this was a once in a lifetime journey. Julianne knew she would never forget the sense of majesty the desert inspired.

At journey's end in Marrakesh over 150 miles from Casablanca, Dominic invited Julianne to his room in the hotel. The two wasted no time in climbing into bed and making sensuous, dreamy love while they claimed to be planning to take a nap before dinner.

Dominic had a treat in store for them that evening. With advance planning, he had made arrangements to go to one of the most amazing spectaculars in Morocco. This time Julianne wore a red silk dress and piled her hair high on her head. Long chandelier earrings offset the whole outfit, which included her favorite Jimmy Choo silver sandals and a small evening clutch.

Dominic emerged from the bathroom and saw her leaning into the mirror fixing the last earring. "You take my breath away," he said. "You look like a goddess. You would certainly be the sultan's favorite wife."

"As long as I am your favorite date," she said and smiled at him. How likely was it, she reflected, that this gorgeous man did not already have a wife or partner or even a girlfriend?

Surely one day she would be deserving of a man who would dedicate himself to her. A true soul mate. Forever lover. A one woman man. Her.

Dominic could have attracted a harem of beautiful concubines, she concluded. He wore a scarlet dress shirt and black tailored trousers with a Gucci belt. A few wisps of dark curly hair escaped from his open neckline. He carried his trademark white Armani jacket.

He explained to her that the world of classical music was very conservative, and he always ensured he was dressed appropriately in case he ran into any of his patrons. Dominic lived the life of an international musician, traveling from city to city, country to country, giving concerts. He might be in a city for just one evening or for a whole opera season.

After the short Moroccan vacation where he was both a guest and an entertainer at his friend's wedding, Dominic was to return to America where he spent at least half his year performing. New York would be his first port of call, followed by California.

On his iPhone in the car, he had showed Julianne a couple of YouTube videos of himself in concert. But as much as she claimed she wanted to know all about him, Julianne was resistant to know too much.

"We're ships that pass in the night," she told him. "Let's just be glad we have this time to spend together. No promises. No regrets. No expectations."

"My philosophy exactly," said Dominic, as they made their way down the grand staircase at the Kasbah Tamadot, a luxury hotel owned by the British bilionaire businessman Sir Richard Branson. Julianne noticed people staring at them. *We look like movie stars tonight,* she thought. How amazing it would be to live like this all the time.

It was clear that Dominic's lifestyle was one of privilege and celebrity. On exiting a hotel he always expected an executive car or limousine on hand to take him to his next engagement. Tonight he had VIP tickets for an entertainment tour de force.

The chauffeur drove through the streets of Marrakesh and pointed out the few landmarks. Ever deeper into the desert they were driven until, like a mirage, out of the star-splashed night rose what looked like a palace and a plant-lined entranceway lit with flaming torches and saber-wielding turbaned guards.

"Tonight you will be truly transported to heaven and back. Buckle up. The ride is about to begin again," Dominic whispered in Julianne's ear.

They stepped out of the limousine. He stopped to press her tightly to him and kiss her passionately as they walked down the fairy-tale driveway, a location straight out of a film set. Under the spell of the exotic perfumes of musk and patchouli, Julianne's senses reeled and she admitted to her innermost self that she was already falling in love with Dominic.

No man had ever made her feel so special. His whole world was enchanted, and she had been invited to share it. Should she reveal what was in her heart? She shook off this latest conundrum. Whatever was she thinking? Kira Mae and Isabella and Angel needed her, relied on her. What was she doing out here with this stranger? And what if Paolo had been murdered by Gio—was she next on the list?

"Welcome to Fantasia," said a greeter in the full Moroccan costume of pantaloons, jacket and turban. Men in costume lined the entrance to the grand ballroom beyond him. "Come this way, the show is about to begin."

The couple were escorted to a picturesque palm grove and settled inside a cushion-strewn Berber tent to enjoy a succulent Moroccan dinner serenaded by exotic singers, musicians and belly dancers. Afterward, they watched electrifying displays of tribal horsemanship, fire-eating, acrobatics and dancing. Cocooned in a palm grove, the seven-course dinner, eaten seated on cushions at a low table, was a feast of traditional Moroccan dishes.

Later, Dominic and Julianne stretched out on sumptuous pillows and watched as entertainers reenacted scenes from *One Thousand and One Arabian Nights*. The highlight of the evening was the sensational tableau when the sultan and his favorite wife flew off over the heads of the audience out into the star-filled desert night on a magic carpet. Julianne and Dominic smiled at each other. They knew all about that.

Dominic spooned into Julianne's mouth a sticky perfumed desert. "I would not have missed this opportunity for the world," he told her. "Believe me when I say that I am genuinely overwhelmed that we met and connected in time to enjoy this once-in-a-lifetime event together."

He gazed at Julianne and she sensed he felt genuinely sad. Their time together was coming to an end. Should she dare to ask him if he was married or single? She chose not to risk it, suspecting that she would not like the answer.

That night they slept under the stars in a tented camp on the edge of the desert. In the light of a roaring fire, the couple enjoyed the luxury of a private bathroom with hot showers. They made love and again climbed aboard the magic carpet ride. But just past the magical world beyond the stars, Julianne knew all too well, reality awaited.

On the ride back to the hotel Dominic turned to her

and said, quite casually: "Vacation time is over for me now. I rehearse with the orchestra tomorrow in preparation for the wedding night concert. I arranged a car to take you back to Casablanca. Is that OK?"

Julianne nodded. She wanted to pretend she was grown up and sophisticated and hide the fact that her heart had broken in that moment. She honestly could not say what she had thought would happen. She could not just walk away from her own life and impose herself into Dominic's, but she had not expected the end to come so suddenly.

"Yes, I have business to deal with too," she said, "before I leave and return to Spain."

Dominic reached out and tenderly touched her hand, putting her fingers to his lips. "Don't forget. Some people are in our lives for a reason, some for a season and some for a lifetime. It can take a lifetime to figure out the part each person plays. You are very special to me, Julianne. I don't know if or when we will ever meet again. We agreed. No promises. No expectations."

He hummed under his breath the music from "As Time Goes By." "Kiss me, Julianne. Fate brought us together. I think it was for a reason."

Julianne turned away, finding their parting hard to process. The tears fell and mocked her avowed intention to accept that this was always meant to be a brief encounter. He had promised nothing.

"Listen to me," he told her, "you need to go home. You need to heal the deep sadness that I sense is inside you. I hope it helped to know that you can fall in love again. That you can love and be loved. Learn the lesson and hold it deep in your heart."

So Dominic had felt it too, she thought. Their foreheads touched. The blackness of the desert flashed by, unremitting. Julianne's heart and soul ached.

Back in their room at the hotel, Dominic took her in his arms and held her. Caressed her face, her hair, her bare arms. Then he tenderly undressed her and lay her on the bed.

"Breathe with me," he said. "Look into my eyes. Let my soul touch yours. Don't be sad. It's only pain. It doesn't kill you. We know there was a reason for our meeting. We were blessed to experience a wonderful, spontaneous love affair in one of the most exotic locations on earth."

Julianne could not hold back the tears any longer. She began to cry.

"Will I ever see you again?" she asked.

"Don't ask about the future," he replied. "It is veiled from us by the hand of God. You know what they say in this country. *Ishballah.* If God is willing."

Outside the hotel, Dominic kissed Julianne one more time before her car left for Casablanca. As she pulled away, she could not resist the temptation to turn around for one more look at Dominic.

She was shocked by what she saw. Assured as ever, he stood on the steps embracing a glamorous red-headed woman. Julianne immediately concluded that this was his wife, despite the lack of any evidence to support that belief.

Julianne told the story to herself that clearly the love of his life had arrived at the hotel earlier than expected to join him for their friend's wedding. They probably could not bear to be apart a moment longer. Julianne gave her heart permission to break.

Dominic did not wave good-bye to Julianne, but she dared to blow a sad kiss to him.

chapter twenty-four

"The course of true love never did run smooth."
—Shakespeare's *The Tempest*

Every mile of the journey from Marrakesh to Casablanca increased Julianne's anxiety. The desert trail that had seemed so magical now looked bereft, featureless, uninspiring. She felt such a fool. How could she have fantasized that a one- or even two-night stand was destined to become a long-term relationship? Dominic had not deceived her; he had been perfectly truthful from the beginning. He was his own man, an adult, a seasoned player in the seduction game.

It was not him she was angry with, it was her. She was an obsessed teenager in the body of a forty-two-year-old woman. Hadn't she learnt by now that a real relationship wasn't built on fantasy? As a straight-talking teacher used to tell her, "If you can't keep up, you might as well give up, because the rest of the world is not going to wait around for you."

Julianne wrapped a comforting blanket around herself in the back of the limousine and took out her phone.

She called Kira Mae and left a message on her voice mail, trying to sound upbeat.

"I'm on my way to the airport. I'll be home later today. I love you."

As luck would have it, Air Maroc had one direct flight to Valencia that afternoon and an available seat. "I'll take it," said Julianne. She kept her fingers crossed that the seat next to her would be empty.

At the airport she bought generous and exotic gifts for Kira Mae and the girls. Julianne was sure Kira Mae would love the hand-embroidered gown and jewel-encrusted slippers. The children would enjoy the musical boxes that featured a snake and its charmer and an acrobat.

In the executive lounge, she ate a leisurely lunch and drank mint tea while she watched an Arabic news program. It wasn't distracting enough. Her head continued to play out various scenarios, each more alarming than the last.

Sure the police wanted to talk to her but what had she actually done? She had never bought drugs from Gio; she had never even met Gio.

Julianne persuaded herself that she needed to keep calm and refuse to divulge any information that might incriminate her. To the question of why she had left the country so suddenly? Well, she did not want to risk running into Paolo's wife or son. It was a matter of the heart.

She gratefully accepted the executive lounge offer of a relaxing massage while she waited for her flight and calculated that she even had time for a super-fast manicure and pedicure. A little bit of self-care would help her to relax.

During the flight she refused to engage with anyone. The seat next to her remained empty and she allowed herself the luxury of a nap. She had been a little short of her beauty sleep the last couple of nights. Don't even think about Dominic, she told herself.

From the airport she took a car directly to the villa. She could not avoid the disapproval of her daughter any longer. Kira Mae had been friendly enough when Julianne called her, though she did say with a slight edge, "So you managed to find your phone?"

"The girls are excited to see you," said Kira Mae as she opened the door to her mother. "I've made dinner."

Julianne had her story prepared. As she and Kira ate a simple meal at the small table in the kitchen, she chatted away about her trip to Casablanca and described details of a nonexistent contract with a wonderful new nonexistent manufacturer.

She did not mention Marrakesh, or Dominic. Luckily, Kira Mae was keen to talk business, having been fully occupied at the Galleria since Julianne left. "They say it's an ill wind that blows no good, but the interest in the Galleria since all the publicity about Angel's disappearance has been amazing. We have more clients than ever. I've even agreed to do an interview with one of the glossy magazines. They promise to be sensitive to my ordeal and say they will give me an opportunity to thank everyone in the community who supported us."

Julianne was delighted that her daughter, resilient and

practical as always, was getting on with what needed to be done. "I did as you suggested," she told her mother. "Rosita is living with us now and taking care of the children when I am at the Galleria."

Kira Mae called the children in to share dessert with their mothers.

The girls insisted on sitting one on either side of Julianne.

"You look beautiful, mama," said Isabella.

"Not as beautiful as you, darling," Julianne told her, stroking her hair.

"I wish I had blonde hair, like you, Mama JoJo," said Angel.

"I would not change one single thing about either of you," said Julianne. She turned to her daughter Kira Mae and said, "Nor would I change a thing about you, my lovely."

"Thanks, but I don't think that can be true," said Kira Mae, "I'm not sure how to make it up to you, but please believe I am genuinely sorry for what happened between Paolo and me. It was all my fault. You must believe that he always loved you. He was a good man but, like the rest of us, deeply flawed. We're only human. And you know what they say, you always hurt the one you love. Please forgive me."

Julianne reached out to stroke her hand and assure her daughter of her forgiveness.

Without warning, Angel piped up with a question that had obviously been on her mind. "Why haven't I got a daddy?" she asked.

Julianne and Kira Mae froze.

"I want one too," said Isabella.

"When I was on my adventure, the lady made me cry. She told me, 'You don't have a daddy. Even the puppy has a daddy.'"

Kira Mae swallowed. "You do have a daddy," she told her. "He's in heaven looking down on you."

"What about me?" Isabella demanded.

"Your daddy is in heaven too," Julianne answered. "He loves you very much and is always looking out for you."

Isabella had an idea. "Perhaps he found Angel for us. He could see her from heaven."

Kira Mae was anxious to move on from the dangerous subject. The girls were too young to be told the story of their parentage, and hopefully they could be spared the pain of ever having to know the full tragic story. This was one bedtime story that neither she nor Julianne planned to share with them. With a mock stern tone, she asked, "Excuse me but are you two going to talk or eat?"

To bring the subject to a close, she turned to her mother and resumed a conversation they had begun earlier. "I'm not prepared to send Angel, or Isabella, back to the preschool. Give it a little time. They are fine here, and at nursery they only play; they don't learn anything. They will go to proper school soon. Between the three of us, we can keep an eye on them till then. I'd like for us all, as a family, to go traveling. It will be good for all of us.'

Julianne could not fault her daughter's logic and suggested that they could all go away together a little later in the summer. "Yeah," shouted the girls and, on the wave of their excitement, Julianne brought out their gifts.

Kira Mae was delighted with her robe and slippers and seemed to readily accept her mother's explanation that her trip to Casablanca would benefit the business.

Reluctant to rush away again, Julianne agreed to stay the night at the villa. After the girls had left the room, Kira Mae had a message for her mother. "Sorry I should have told you earlier. I promised the police I would get you to call them as soon as you were back. They haven't released Paolo's body to his family yet. They refuse to say why there is a holdup."

"Really?" said Julianne, turning away so that Kira couldn't see the look of uncertainty on her face. If the police hadn't told Kira about Paolo's drug habit, then she had no intention of telling her. On the other hand, why hadn't they told her? "Too late now, I'll do it first thing in the morning."

"Tomorrow is another day," she told herself, settling under the covers. She was determined not to show any signs of anxiety to her family. "I need a good night's sleep. I should count my blessings that we are all home safe and sound under the same roof. Not sleeping out under the stars somewhere with a married man."

chapter twenty-five

"These words are razors to my wounded heart."
—Shakespeare's *Othello*

Paolo would have known what she should and should not say to the police. Best to say nothing at all, he would probably have told her. Now Julianne had to trust her own judgment.

Once again she denied that she knew Gio personally.

"At the time that my daughter was wrongfully arrested, I did hear his name. I was grateful to him as he disputed Romero's claim that Kira Mae had been connected with his crimes. Presumably he wanted to do the right thing knowing that he too had been framed by his former boss, Romero. As far as I was told, he was a crook but Romero tried to implicate him in activities other than his actual involvement. Romero cared only about saving his own skin."

The memories flooded back as Julianne relived the ordeal of sitting in a dark, damp interrogation room in Rome as Paolo, whom she had just met, told her that her daughter was to be charged with accessory to murder. The men involved were Romero and his accomplice Gio. Later they would also question and charge her childhood friend and the owner of the villa where Julianne and Kira were living in Spain, Annabelle Anstruther.

At least the living room of her cottage was more comfortable than the police station. The detective and the uniformed officer who had called on her previously now resumed their line of questioning. "What is your relationship with Gio Lopez?" the detective asked again.

"I have none. I've told you, I don't know him. Well, only by name," she repeated.

The detective leaned forward in the armchair. "So would you object if we searched your home? Or do we need to get a search warrant?"

Julianne weighed the question. If she allowed the search now, she had no idea what might turn up. Paolo stayed at her home regularly enough to have left incriminating evidence of his alleged drug taking. But if she refused, the search would take place anyway with a warrant and then she might not look quite so like the cooperating witness and innocent party she wanted to project. However, refusing a search would at least buy her some time.

If only Paolo were here to give her the right advice. She did not want to antagonize the police but she did not want to be a sitting duck. Perhaps with them out of the way, she could do a search of her own and identify items she may not want offered up for scrutiny.

"I would rather you obtain a warrant," she said finally. "I resent the implication that I am a guilty party."

The policeman nodded. "We will be back," he said. "Please be aware that you are now a person of interest, helping us with our inquiries. You are not free to leave the country again without permission."

Julianne started to protest, but the need to attend to important business commitments sounded weak even to her ears.

For the time being they did not threaten to confiscate her passport, just warned her that she was not free to travel. Not about to be rushed, the detective settled farther back into the comfort of Julianne's favorite armchair.

"You told us you had no knowledge that Mr. Paolo was a drug addict," said the detective in a tone that clearly signaled he did not believe her. "What if I told you that he and Gio Lopez worked as a team? That they are suspected of the abduction of your daughter? Has this crossed your own mind, I wonder?"

"Granddaughter," Julianne corrected him, trying to process this new information. So she hadn't jumped to a wild conclusion.

"And," he continued as if he hadn't heard her, "they're members of a gang who operate under the control of their leader Jesus Floris."

Julianne looked at the detective as if he were mad. Or maybe she was.

Jesus Floris, she knew that name alright. Surely she had heard wrong. There must be some mistake. Jesus. It was as if his very being was invoked in the room. She looked at the places he had once inhabited. The walls and the doors and the furniture and the stairs they had climbed to go to the upstairs bedroom. The places they made love. The places she had vowed everlasting vengeance on him. His very essence permeated her whole home. She was never really free of his presence, his memory. The daughter she had borne him.

Jesus. Her Romero.

Julianne opened and closed her mouth. No sound came out. Her mouth and brain and whole body were on high alert. "You know this man?" asked the uniformed policeman.

"No," said Julianne.

As if on a silent command, the two officers of the law stood up and walked toward the front door.

"We'll be back with the search warrant," said the detective.

"I'll be here," said Julianne in her best upright citizen voice.

As soon as they left, Julianne raced upstairs and started to pull the contents out of drawers and cupboards. She didn't know what she was looking for but might know if she found it.

Romero, Romero, Romero. She said the name out loud and questioned over and over again what it meant. Romero was dead. She ordered his execution. She hired Gio to kill the man she had loved. The call at the time of the murder that told her *"The roses have been delivered"* and the wreath she received at her cottage with the RIP card confirmed the deed was done.

In a court of law, Julianne might be able to prove the

order to kill Romero had come from his mafia rivals, but she was responsible for supplying the information they needed to carry out the contract.

Julianne was in a spin. She literally didn't know which way to turn. She continued to pull out drawers where Paolo might have left some indication of his new secret life. In the bathroom cabinet she checked all the medicine bottles, nothing seemed untoward.

On a window ledge she found a small pile of Paolo's papers. They appeared to be legal documents, but the police told her that he was dismissed from his position at the British Embassy.

How could Paolo and Gio have been working for Romero? He was a dead man.

Julianne frantically searched until she remembered what she was looking for. A photograph of Romero hidden at the very bottom of a box. So many times over the years she had promised herself she would throw it away. Wrapped inside a letter he had sent her from prison while she played the game of persuading him she still loved him, the photograph showed him in a promotional flyer advertising the restaurant where he performed as a flamenco guitarist. He stood tall and proud in his black beaded matador jacket and slim-fitting trousers. His curly black hair flicked up from the collar of the jacket. His eyes seemed to bore into her and his wicked lips enticed her.

She knew why she had not thrown the photograph away. Her love for Romero refused to die. What she had never even in her wildest dreams considered was that not only would the love live on, but so would Romero. Twisted as it was, Romero personified her only experience of love.

Julianne visited the grave with Kira Mae and they each threw a blood red rose onto the varnished black coffin with gold handles. Ecstatic that he was finally out of their lives forever, they danced beside the grave. There were no other mourners. Paolo told her that it was Romero's grave. She had no reason to doubt it.

The hurt and pain and betrayal he had inflicted on the family was so desperate that Julianne and Kira Mae, accompanied by their two young daughters, had joined the ritual to rejoice at his passing. They ripped off their veiled mourning hats, threw them on top of the coffin and whispered, "Adios, gypsy boy. Not a tear will we shed." Julianne took responsibility for conspiring to bring about his death. Kira Mae knew only that he had been avenged by his crooked associates.

How could he still be alive?

And in a moment of sudden clarity, Julianne knew. Like the tumblers of a locked safe clicking into place, the door swung open. It was obvious. The common denominator. Paolo. Her loyal friend, the lawyer who had defended Kira Mae against Romero and his international criminal organization.

She did not know the exact moment or time when Paolo had turned his allegiance from prosecuting the international criminal to befriending him, but it was the only scenario that made sense.

Paolo had orchestrated the Romero story all along.

It was Paolo who had conscientiously followed Romero through the prison system. He knew when and where he was going as the authorities moved him round the country, always trying to minimize his influence within the prison system and make it more difficult for him to arrange his escape.

Paolo had encouraged Julianne to write to Romero, to persuade him that she wanted to see him and that she would be waiting for him when he was released. Julianne had used all her creative and seductive powers.

Paolo encouraged her to contact Gio and to reveal the whereabouts of Romero after his planned escape. And it was Paolo who had driven her to a graveyard in Italy where she watched a priest intone the words of the funeral service and throw dirt on top of an open grave.

For Julianne there was no reason to doubt that the grave contained the body of the man that Paolo had told her had been stabbed and left for dead on a bare wooden floor in an empty cottage in the Spanish hills, not too far from her cottage.

Desperate to distance herself from any repercussions, Julianne had never double-checked whether the body had been found. Certainly no one had ever come to her door to make enquiries. She had seen no reports of dead bodies in the local paper. Paolo had told her that Romero was dead, he had taken her to an open grave, and she believed him.

How could she have been so naive? She had never doubted one word Paolo told her. He was her Mr. Fix

It. Her rock. Now he was gone and her whole life was unraveling.

Why had Paolo done this? Was Julianne such a threat to Romero, such a loose cannon?

She had not found anything incriminating in the cottage except the photograph. She could think of only one way of removing the evidence of her association with Romero. After all these years of refusing to let it go, she now prepared a ritual at the small shrine on her dressing table. She arranged the candles, incense, oils and crystals, tore the photograph into tiny pieces, and placed it in her brass praying bowl, then set fire to it.

Flames leapt into the air as if trying to escape their fate and were reflected in the vanity mirror. Julianne used the wooden end of an incense stick to ensure that every tiny piece of photograph burned. The smell of jasmine filled the room and she lit the myriad of candles of every color and perfume on the altar. Smoke and mirrors. The religious artifacts of a good Catholic girl.

She was so engrossed in her ritual, she did not hear the first few rings of her front door bell. No matter. Should they ask, she intended to tell the visiting police officers that she had taken advantage of their absence to meditate. Tantric meditation was good for the soul, she would tell them. It seemed a lifetime ago that Dominic had introduced her to the joys of tantric meditation. She had a crazy thought. Perhaps the power she and Dominic had invoked had conjured up Romero. The genie was out of the bottle and she did not relish the day that he would find her. And yet, strangely, she admitted to herself that she was excited. Romero always did have an unnatural effect upon her. The devil incarnate, the lover divine.

chapter twenty-six

"Love goes toward love."

—Shakespeare's *Romeo & Juliet*

Julianne held back the lace curtains and peered out of the bedroom window. Kira Mae was knocking at the door. The two girls were in the car. They saw Julianne at the window and waved.

"We're going to the beach," said Kira Mae. "Want to come with us? We can grab a pizza at one of the beach cafes."

"Sure," said Julianne. "Give me two minutes to grab my purse and I'll be with you."

Her favorite large red tote was sitting in the middle of the dining table. She threw in her mobile phone and charger, made sure she had her wallet. She never left home without her passport, not even to go to the beach.

Lipstick, perfume, brush. Julianne was good to go.

As ever, Kira Mae had come prepared. The children wore swimsuits under shorts and T-shirts and she had a bikini under her sundress. Julianne had no intention of swimming. She dressed quickly in light casual trousers and a loose-fitting blouse. Her long blonde hair was tied in a ponytail.

Between the four of them, they managed to carry all their baggage to the beach in one trip. The children were keen to get straight into the inviting blue water, but Kira Mae insisted they help claim their spot on the beach. They soon staked out their territory with blankets, towels, dry clothes, hats, sunscreen, iPads, books, and an ice box and cooler stocked with drinks and snacks. They had enough stuff for a small army to camp out for more than a month. They were close enough to the ocean's edge so that Kira Mae could supervise while they were in the water alone—up to their knees was the rule—or played on the sand.

Finally they were ready to launch themselves into the sea. Kira Mae ran toward the water with the two girls who raced behind and competed to see who would be first. None of the three seemed to notice that the water was not quite the temperature of a tepid bath, more a melting ice bucket. The girls screamed with delight and immediately began to splash each other. Kira Mae laughed as she got caught in the crossfire.

Julianne watched from the shore and a lump formed in her throat as she watched her beloved girls together having fun. She loved them so much. Now that Paolo was gone, there was no one apart from Julianne who knew the real truth about the family.

Julianne was just sixteen when she had given birth to Kira Mae. Her own mother, Martha, had died of cancer the previous year.

When she became pregnant, her father banished her to live with a relative 500 miles away in a small village in Scotland.

Mummy Mitchell turned out to be the sweetest lady imaginable, and she poured unconditional love on Julianne and Kira Mae. "It was as if she had been put on this earth just to love us," Julianne believed.

Julianne constantly told Kira Mae, "You are the beloved child. I will kill anyone who ever harms a hair on your head."

Kira Mae led an idyllic, charmed existence, adored by Julianne and her honorary grandmother. Kira Mae had no inkling of the depth of her totally unconventional background. Mummy Mitchell passed on and Kira Mae, not yet twenty years old, was forced to grow up fast.

A violent and traumatic event forced both mother and daughter to relocate from England to Spain to live in Annabelle's villa. She pretended to be a friend but was actually a leading player in a very dangerous and criminal game. Money had always been her God.

The devil in disguise was waiting for them in Spain. Romero, a gypsy flamenco guitarist and long-term member of the criminal fraternity, exploded into their hearts and their lives. He played a game of passion and deceit with mother and daughter. Handsome, cruel Romero. A romancer, seducer, murderer and gangster.

A horrifying thought now struck Julianne. With the help of his sidekick Gio Lopez, had Romero tried to kidnap Angel? Why hadn't she considered this before?

Romero knew Angel was his daughter but when given the chance by a bewildered Kira Mae to be a part of their lives—he wanted nothing to do with either of them.

Instinctively Julianne looked out to the water's edge where Kira Mae, Angel and Isabella had been paddling. Now they were nowhere to be seen. Surely it had only been a few minutes ago that they were laughing and playing in the waves.

Julianne ran along the water's edge, scanned every face. They were nowhere to be seen. She asked other bathers, mothers with children, if they had seen two little girls, twins dressed in pink swimsuits and their mother, a tall blonde in a black and white polka-dot bikini?

One man did remember seeing them walk away. He pointed and Julianne turned away from him, frantic. Running across the beach toward their encampment were the girls, Kira Mae strolling behind. Without remembering to acknowledge the man's help, Julianne sped the full length of the beach toward them.

"Where were you?" Julianne asked in an angrier voice than she had intended. "I looked everywhere for you."

Kira Mae at first reacted with her own anger. "I took the girls to the bathroom. It's miles away." Her tone softened as she realized how distraught Julianne must have been. "I'm sorry," she said. "You know what they are like, when they want to go, they want to go now. No hanging about."

Her mother smiled. "My fault. I panicked."

"Of course, I should have realized you'd wonder where we'd gone," said Kira Mae. "Sit down, let me get you a cup of tea. I brought a flask. I know you get withdrawal symptoms if you don't have your tea."

Silence reigned as mother and daughter drank their tea. The girls slurped on neon-red tropical juice and plonked on their headphones. They were glued to one of their favorite YouTube shows, *What's Inside?*

"So tell me about the psychologist," said Julianne, trying to recover from her latest panic.

"Not much to tell," replied Kira Mae. "Angel is very matter of fact about the whole thing and no one wants to go digging for problems that aren't there. She still calls it her 'adventure.' From everything she says, she was treated well and made to feel that she was on vacation. Only thing she didn't like was that Isabella wasn't with her, but then she got the idea that poor Isabella had to go to school and she didn't."

"But where exactly was she for two days?" asked Julianne.

"All she could tell us was that she went on a train. A man took her from the school on a train. At his house there were some chickens and a sweet little puppy dog and the dog's mother. She didn't like the food the man's wife gave her so they gave her biscuits and milk. They let her watch television, and the dogs slept beside her on the pull-out couch. She liked that. She also liked the fact that she didn't have to have a bath. That's kids for you."

The women didn't notice that Angel had taken off her headphones and was listening to the conversation.

"They couldn't speak English very well and they didn't know that I can speak Spanish," she said. "The woman said she would teach me to count up to ten in Spanish. But I already know because I go to school."

Julianne and Kira Mae looked at each other. "Did you understand anything that they said to each other?" asked Kira Mae.

Angel looked uncertain. "No, I mustn't tell anything because I'll get her into trouble and she won't be allowed to come to our school anymore. And she won't let me see the puppy. Or his mummy."

"Did you ask to come home?" Kira Mae wanted to know.

"Yes, but she said 'Mummy wants you to be a good, brave girl. She will come for you soon.'"

Julianne waited. When Angel said nothing more she asked: "Is there anything else we should know that you are not telling us?"

Angel shook her head. "Just that I should have a daddy. Even the puppy's got a daddy."

Kira Mae and Julianne exchanged horrified looks. *What the hell was the daddy business all about?*

"Why didn't you tell me before what the woman said?" asked Kira Mae.

"I don't want to get into trouble," she said. "Because I was a good girl and the woman said I can go again and play with the little puppy."

To try to minimize the importance of the conversation they had just had, Kira Mae suggested they have one more swim and after that they would all go to eat at their favorite sidewalk café where the chef let the girls help make the pizza. If there was anything to tell, maybe they would tease it out of Angel at the cafe.

"I better stop by the police station on my way home and tell them what Angel has just said," said Kira Mae. "Unless you want to do it?"

Julianne shook her head. "I've seen enough of the police to last me a lifetime. Besides they did say they were going to come by the house again to ask me more questions."

"By the way, did you know that Chief Xabia races pack mules up in the mountains? Did you ever hear anything so weird? I never knew pack mules raced," said Kira Mae.

Julianne's phone rang and she sighed as she saw the caller ID. It was the detective in charge of the case. *It can wait,* she thought and let the call go to voice mail. Let me get lunch first and then I'll see what he has to say for himself.

They packed up and left the beach chatting and laughing.

"We look like pack mules," Kira joked. "I just hope no one asks me to race. I can hardly walk with all these bags. And once I've eaten pizza—well, forget it."

Julianne delighted in the lovely day they had spent together and the closeness she now felt to her daughter. This was how she always dreamed it would be. Their whole lives were enmeshed. Mothers and friends and business partners, and joint mothers to their two daughters.

She dared to voice to Kira Mae the thought that had just struck her.

"Perhaps I have not been quite such a lousy mother. You've turned out pretty well?"

Thanks, she knew, were due as always to Mummy Mitchell and she offered up a special prayer to the lovely lady whom she believed looked over them from above. What would she make of the huge mess that was swirling around the family now?

Please God, Julianne prayed, someday soon let their lives return to normal.

She had withheld from Kira Mae the troubling information the police had passed on about Paolo's betrayal and the uncertainty surrounding Romero. She hoped against hope that there had been some mistake about Paolo's involvement. Perhaps there was a perfectly reasonable explanation and the police had simply jumped to conclusions.

Lunch was almost over at the pizza restaurant when Julianne decided to return the call to the detective.

"Sorry, I didn't get back to you earlier," she started to explain, but he cut her off.

"You need to come back to your house immediately," he told her. It was a command, not a request.

"Yes, I know," she said. "I'm on way, it will take me . . ."

He cut her off again. "There's been a fire," he said. "Your house is in flames."

chapter twenty-seven

"Come not between the dragon and his wrath."
—Shakespeare's *King Lear*

Stuck behind a slow-moving farm vehicle, Julianne had a crazy urge to roll down the car window and shout, "Get out of the way, my house is on fire!"

She envisioned Romero's face in the flames, laughing at the thought that she could set fire to his photograph and be rid of him, just like that.

A childhood song ran through her head. "Ladybird, ladybird fly away home, your house is on fire and your children are gone."

No one ever gave her a reasonable explanation for why the ladybird was so tormented if her children were safe. But *were* her children all gone? Wasn't there one who stayed in the house under a pan?

In her mind's eyes she saw the candles on her dressing table. They were all shapes and sizes. She saw the spark of one rogue flame leap onto the ribbon she had draped over the mirror for decoration. When had the fire started? The detective hadn't given her any details.

She completed the journey home in record time,

driving way too fast into the narrow main street that led to her home. On the skyline above the houses she saw black clouds of smoke. Her home, her life, in flames.

Outside her house a small crowd had gathered, and Julianne made her way through, trying not to draw attention to herself. The upstairs bedroom window at the front of the house where she slept was blown out and her pretty voile curtains hung in tatters. Once snow white, they were now black.

One of the town's two fire engines was there, but the small village crew were already rolling away the water jets. This was a fire that had already peaked.

Julianne's heart broke as she observed the damage to her sweet little cottage. This place had offered her a way to fulfill her dreams and make a brand-new start.

She remembered as if it were yesterday, Romero bringing her to the hilltop cottage. Picture book perfect, covered in purple and white wisteria it would become her home, her sanctuary.

Her heart had pounded with joy and fear at being so close to him in the small, intimate cottage.

No man ever produced such an effect on her, before or since.

Romero was more handsome than any man had a right to be. He resembled the silent movie star Valentino. His chiseled features were undoubtedly masculine but softened by the smoothness of his skin, almond shaped eyes and sculpted jet black eyebrows, Black untamed curly hair fell below the collar of his shirt.

She well remembered the mesmerizing effect of those

coal black eyes with long lashes and his full lipped cruel mouth. Julianne trembled at the memory of her lost love.

She aimed to compose herself as she saw the detective approach in the distance.

"The fire is out," the detective informed her, "'but it will be a couple of days before you can go inside. The property is badly damaged by smoke. Is there somewhere you can stay until then?"

"Can I go and rescue some personal items?"

"No, it's still too dangerous," the detective told her.

He called over a fireman who was about to climb into the cab of the fire truck. "Habla usted inglés?" he asked him. The eager young fireman nodded.

"Please confirm that Señora Gordon will not be able to enter her premises until you give the all clear," instructed the detective.

"Certainly, sir," he nodded his head. "Senora, I have been inside the house," he said. "It is not pretty. Everything went up in flames, and what was not taken by the blaze is blackened with smoke. The old wooden window frames gave the fire a place to take hold. Furniture, bedding, furnishings, they are all destroyed. Unfortunately the water we used to put out the flames also adds to the damage. Think yourself lucky that you were not inside."

Julianne let the information sink in. "Who called the fire department?" she asked.

"One of your neighbors, I think, but it may have been the police. They were here when I arrived."

"Thank you," she said. Julianne turned to face the detective. "And what do you have to add?"

He shrugged. "Obviously we will investigate to find out exactly what happened," said the detective. "My colleague and I came back with the search warrant and you were gone. We were worried at first that you were still inside."

The two stood yards away from her home. The crowd thinned out, and Julianne realized she did not need to torture herself with the sight of her ruined home any longer. She turned her back on the charred cottage.

Now she could think straight and offer the explanation for her absence.

"My daughter arrived unexpectedly and I went to the beach with her and the children," Julianne said with as much conviction as she could muster.

"I know what you're thinking," she added, unable to resist answering his unanswered question, "but I didn't set fire to my own home. It must have been an accident," she said. "I think I left candles burning."

"Is that so?" said the detective as he raised his eyebrows and looked straight at her.

Julianne wanted to slap him. Of course it was unthinkable that she would burn down her own home! The only secret she had harbored, her relationship with Romero, was long gone. Up in flames.

"Please make sure we know where to find you if we have further questions as part of our investigations," said the detective breaking into her thoughts.

"I'll be at my daughter's, you have the address, or at the Galleria in Villajoyosa."

"Then I will leave you in peace," said the detective, his voice softening. "I'm sorry about your home."

"Thank you," said Julianne. "Fortunately there was nothing of value here. All my stock is at the Galleria. It's going to cost the owner's insurance company a fortune to restore and rebuild the place."

"Or the owner," said the detective. "Insurance is not always a priority where property has been in families for generations." He shrugged and made as if to walk away.

Julianne could not make out whether he was being deliberately malicious. Would she now be facing a massive financial claim on top of everything else?

"Thank you for adding one more worry to my perfect day," she told him.

Without being able to get inside the house, there was nothing more for Julianne to do. She called Kira Mae. "The house is a burned-out shell," she told her. "The smoke has done as much damage as the fire. I can't stay here. I'll have to stay with you for a few days.

"I'll drive over to the villa after I've run some errands. Do you need me to get anything for you?"

"No, nothing we need. I'll see you later. The girls will be happy; they like having you around."

With no destination in mind, she got into her car and drove aimlessly.

Her life was one huge mess and it occurred to her that she had not one real friend to turn to in her hour of need. Her thoughts paused on Dominic. The brief affair had added excitement and romance but the two had not made arrangements to keep in touch. In fact, the very opposite. Julianne was pretty sure that Dominic was married and she had been no more than a fling. He never intended to see her again. She had been foolish to hope for more. When would she learn?

She turned on the radio—Spanish flamenco music. "No thank you," she said out loud.

Julianne literally didn't know which way to turn. She didn't want to return to the villa just yet, not with this latest disaster on her mind. Perhaps a drive along the mountain road might give her some breathing space and restore her sanity.

She decided to drive to the medieval fortress of Guadalest. That would require all of her concentration to navigate the narrow roads.

By the time Julianne arrived, the village was deserted. The dozens of coaches that blocked the mountain roads all day, and packed the small hillside parking lot, departed the village by 4 p.m., taking their tourist passengers home in time for dinner. A blanket of quietness had settled over the picturesque village with its couple of hundred residents preparing for another quiet evening at home. Cafés, restaurants and shops were empty, and many had already closed for the evening. A slight drizzle added to the left-behind feeling of the town. The village no longer locked and barred its city gates at night, but it felt to Julianne as if they had.

She climbed the steep stairway to the small church.

Inside there was just one other person, an old lady dressed in black who looked like she spent a great deal of time on her knees praying.

Julianne made her way to the front of the church to light candles and then slipped into a pew close to the open doors at the back. The irony of lighting candles to ask God to give her peace, when candles had already sent her house up in flames, did not escape her. But she did not know what else to do. She needed to try to make a direct connection with a higher force to take the heaviness from her heart.

"Please God, have mercy on my soul," she prayed. "Relieve my burdens. Let me know that You are close and, even though I feel bereft and hopeless, You will protect me."

Her tears fell and Julianne knew that even if relief did not come immediately, the fact that she retained her faith and entrusted herself to God was a good sign. She gazed at the statue of Our Lady, head wreathed in flowers from an earlier festival, and offered up a prayer.

"Holy Mary, please keep my daughters safe and give me the strength to be a mother to them," she whispered.

In the distance, Julianne heard a bell toll, signaling the time, five o'clock, and she left the church to make the journey up to the bell tower several steep staircases above. The climb up the mountainside challenged her. Her legs hurt and her chest was beginning to ache. *When did I become so unfit?* she wondered. On her journey upward she saw only a couple of older people, healthy ones in shorts with stout shoes and stout hearts. Her white flowered flip-flops were not really equal to the climb, but she kept going.

I can't give up, she told herself. I have to persevere. Life is hard and mine is a nightmare, but I have to believe that somehow, someday, I'll see a way through and the tough times will be behind me.

At the highest point of the village, the bell tower, she looked down at the wild countryside, admiring the cultivated terraces all the way up the mountainside and the abundant flowers.

From where she now stood, Julianne could not see another human being. Her long journey to the hilltop had culminated in this place of sanctuary from where, way before the day of mobile phones, the villagers would relay news to the surrounding villages and warn of possible invasions.

Relief poured into her heart. Her problems had not magically disappeared but here at the top of a rocky mountain, all alone, she felt a sense of protection. She stood there for so long she lost track of time. All is well, a voice deep inside her seemed to say.

On the road down the mountain, Julianne had promised herself a treat. First, she would take a trip to the overhanging parapet, below which a mirror-like blue reservoir stretched out. The sight was so beautiful and surreal, it always took her breath away. She imagined that deep down in the valley, the clear cool water flowed and her soul was indeed restored again.

But she also knew another way to do that.

In the village, high on a small outcrop and overlooking the small parade of shops, was a favorite place that she and Kira Mae often visited. The British café. The large sign on the rock face attracted those in need of a good cup of tea, made in a freshly heated teapot with boiling hot water, left to brew, with the milk put in the cup before the tea.

"A pot of tea for one and a buttered scone please," said Julianne as she sat down, shaking a few stray drops of rain from her umbrella onto the rough wooden floor.

Service was prompt. She was the only customer in the café although she suspected that the bar could get lively in the evening, judging by the number of times she heard the owner, a down-to-earth Londoner, tell callers on the phone, "Yeah, see you later for the match."

"A pot of tea and a buttered scone," repeated the affable owner, "coming right up."

Then he added a greeting he probably offered customers dozens of times a day. "You're a long way from home."

"So are you," she replied.

As an afterthought, he added, "Funny that, we had a couple of local guys in here earlier, asked me if I'd seen a beautiful British blonde. Rough types, if you don't mind my saying so." He leaned forward. "You look like you need that cup of tea. Is everything alright, love?"

Before she could reply, Julianne heard voices on the staircase outside the café. She perched on the rickety chair by the small wooden table and did not move a muscle. The door clattered open and a noisy group entered. Mother, father, kids, elderly relatives. Soon several tables filled up with the family along with their bags, coats, backpacks, raincoats, maps and water bottles.

Anxious to remove herself from the discord of chatter and high-pitched laughter, Julianne quickly gulped a half a cup of tea, covered the barely eaten scone with a napkin and rose from her seat. Busy now with a café full of customers, the owner gave her a brief wave as she left.

Julianne looked around trying to see if she could spot the strangers in town who were enquiring about British blondes, but there was no one to be seen. But maybe she was being completely neurotic. There must have been plenty of tourists in the town a little earlier, including some British blondes. Julianne felt her shoulders relax. She was imagining the worst-case scenario for no good reason, just as she had done on the beach with the girls.

Before she returned home to face the next installment of the drama her life was fast becoming, she could take a few minutes to visit Casitas de Muñecas, the museum of miniature dolls' houses that she and the girls always enjoyed visiting. It would be a welcome reminder of happier times. The museum was a fairyland of hundreds of architecturally accurate scale models of Spanish and European buildings with awe-inspiring scenes all individually created by artist Antonio Marco.

Julianne stepped through the door to the museum and immediately entered the fantasy world she remembered. She was lost in wonder as she peered into glass cabinets and imagined life in miniature, wondering at the beauty and artistry.

"Antonio, he never sleeps," said the museum curator with pride. With no other customers she was happy to have someone on whom to practice her few well-rehearsed phrases of English. "All night he works making his own special world in miniature. We have no room for more models but still he works. What a man."

Julianne smiled. She had heard the story of Antonio and his all-night working many times. No doubt it was true because the museum was filled to the rafters with tiny model houses and overcrowded furnished rooms.

A huge collection of tiny shoes and handbags in a palace bedroom caught Julianne's eye. She stared deeper and deeper into the imaginary world, delighting in the abundance of extravagant and glamorous styles, delicate fabrics and glorious feathers, jewels and pearls—all no bigger than her fingertips.

Way too close to her ear, a harsh voice and the unmistakable whiff of a smoker's unfiltered breath broke in on her reverie. He was not particularly tall but his bulk and gnarled features made him look menacing. Without preamble, he ordered, "Come with me."

Julianne jumped and looked round for the museum assistant. She had returned to her duties and now performed her Herculean task of keeping the many dozens of floor to ceiling glass cabinets polished and fingerprint free.

Unable to see around him, Julianne did not know if there were any other customers in the gallery. She was upstairs above the winding staircase. There was no other way out but down.

She looked at the man and, in an effort to buy time, said quizzically, "And why would I do that?"

He was not fazed. "Come with me," he said again with more emphasis this time.

Everything about him was at odds with the refined world of Antonio Marco's miniatures. His mere presence in the place threatened to endanger the fragile exhibits.

Julianne's heart pounded and she recognized the bitter taste of fear in her mouth. She considered her options. Fight or flight? She could identify no opportunity for either. And what if he had a weapon?

The man suddenly gave her a little push, galvanizing Julianne into action.

Shoving him out of her way, she ran downstairs to the smallest room in the house of small rooms. Along the way, Julianne checked for a window or door through which she could make her escape. There was none. She checked her mobile phone and wanted to scream. How often did she berate herself for not keeping her phone fully charged? Her power cable was in the car.

Changing her plans, she ran through the museum past the glass cases that reflected her image and outside to the narrow street, then back toward her vehicle in the parking lot by the small parade of shops at the bottom of the hillside. There were just two other vehicles parked. Wheelchair access signs on the rear identified the large silver camper as being the property of the family in the café. Other than a battered old car beside hers, the car park was deserted.

Julianne felt in her bag for her car keys—right at the bottom, she cursed—while looking wildly around her for any signs of life. Where did everybody go when the tourists had left for the day? At least there was no sign of her assailant.

She finally found her keys and as she fitted them in the lock, with a shiver of horror she felt him before she saw him. He must have strolled down after her. Now he was leaning against the wall behind her, watching.

"Vamos," he said, pointing her toward Rent-a-Wreck. "We take my car."

He opened the passenger door. "Get in," he said. "You'll be safe with me. As you will see I am the expert driver. I will make sure you get home safely to those little girls."

The implied threat ensured that she knew she had to do as he commanded.

Julianne looked back at her car longingly. If she'd arrived one minute later she wouldn't be in this mess. Another man seemed to appear from nowhere, and before she could even react, he snatched the car keys she held from her grasp. She tried to wrestle them from him, but he simply ignored her efforts and let himself into the front seat.

Julianne stared at the ungainly presence now taking up every inch of space in the front seat of her beloved car.

"He is the expert driver also," said the first joker as

he waited for Julianne to get into the filthy passenger seat of his car. Well past the car manufacturer's ambitions for it to look at its factory best, the beat-up old vehicle had seen better days.

"Get in and close the door," he told her, "We're late."

Without warning he leaned over, roughly grabbed her arm and tugged her inside the car. He started the engine and pulled away and Julianne was left frantically holding on to the half-open door in an attempt to ensure that it did not fly open.

The high-speed ride and unpredictability of the drive down the mountain road would have been great fun had it been an amusement park ride. Julianne prayed that she would not throw up.

"Please slow down," she pleaded. "You'll get us both killed."

The maniacal laughter and his cryptic reply, "No, *one* of us may get killed," convinced Julianne that she was being driven by not only a madman but more than likely a madman on drugs.

Above the noise of the clanging engine and the juddering of the body work, she shouted, "Where are we going? What is this all about?"

"Questions make my head hurt. You see when we get there."

Julianne checked the wing mirror again—the man driving her car was coming up close behind. She gave thanks that they had avoided running into the tourist coaches that often forced drivers to make heart-stopping passes on roads that overlooked deadly drops to the valley below.

Whenever she tried to ask a question that cried out for an answer, her captor insisted on taking his eyes off the road to look at her. Finally he told her, "You are very pretty. I see why Romero fell for you."

"Romero?" she asked. "What has he got to do with this?" He indicated the car and driver behind. "He sent Gio and me to get you. Romero wants to see you."

Julianne had already suspected that Gio was behind her ordeal. What she had not realized was that he was literally behind her. And driving her car. That news should have shocked and horrified her, filled her with fear. Instead she felt an odd surge of excitement.

Romero wanted to see her.

chapter twenty-eight

"Then love-devouring death do what he dare."

—Shakespeare's *Romeo & Juliet*

A silver helicopter landed on the vast stage and a team of James Bond lookalikes in black tuxedos pointed guns as they descended from a zip wire. The James Bond theme lived up to its promise of high energy, drama and excitement.

A saber light presentation flashed to dramatic effect across the cityscape. The cast of international female dancers dressed in glittering black cat masks, black tights and black leotards were in the process of stealing the crown jewels from the Tower of London.

Kira Mae sat in the almost empty auditorium watching rehearsals for the spectacular new show about to go into production at the Benidorm Palace, a space-age silver-domed venue alongside the Benidorm Circus.

Approached from the highway, Benidorm looked like a space-age city with skyscrapers and angled buildings piercing the sky. Fifty years before a traditional sleepy small fishing village, now a tourist mecca. The incongruous city between the sea and the mountains holds the distinction of having the most high-rise apartments per capita of the entire population in the world. Driving into Benidorm through the rural countryside and familiar orange and lemon groves, Kira Mae had been initially dismayed by the city. With little natural landscaping to speak of, the trees had been aggressively cut back and would not flower again till later in the summer. Stark steel pylons with triple lights illuminated new buildings. Apartments were heaped on top of each other.

The stretch of road from the top of the town where the Benidorm Palace was located down a hill to the seafront had little to commend it. Stores sold cheap clothing from China and cafés served British breakfast or fish and chips; sports bars showed English soccer. Apartments were in need of a new coat of paint, with balconies and awnings that were now faded and in need of repair. Few European visitors who preferred more traditional Spanish towns would admit to having a good word to say for Benidorm, but the hundreds of thousands who flocked there every year seemed to enjoy it well enough.

Kira Mae had not known what to expect when the unexpected call came asking her to go along and discuss the opportunity to design costumes for the Benidorm Palace extravaganza. So far Kira Mae was most impressed with what she had seen. The show was a combination of Las Vegas style showgirls, a Cirque du Soleil–style experience and a handful of local variety acts for good measure.

A traditional Latin crooner opened the entertainment, a mature romantic singer probably grown too old for the cruise ships, and the show ended with a group of acrobats whose bodies were coated in gold paint. Sketching as fast as she could, Kira Mae was grateful that the dancers regularly returned to the stage, giving her the opportunity to note the finer details of their costumes and how they were highlighted under the footlights.

She knew she was going to have to use all her creative imagination to come up with costumes to rival those she had seen. Male dancers in black suits, black fedora hats and black sunglasses flanked the ladies who appeared in sugar pink fur tutus.

The finale lived up to its name of Spectacular. Kira Mae paid extra special attention as it was this part of the show for which she hoped to be able to offer a unique costume presentation.

Dazzling in the spotlight, the lead dancers appeared in pink glitter gowns. But not for long. These were peeled off to reveal black bikinis with flowing pink cloaks, black gloves and pink and black Lurex accessories.

Kira Mae was delighted that she was invited to be a part of this exciting venture. Thousands of people attended the show every week and Kira Mae's costumes would be up there on stage for everyone to see.

She had hoped that her mother would be able to come with her to do a reconnaissance on the show, until her mother received the phone call from the police that her house was on fire. The last time Kira Mae talked to Julianne she had said that she would come to Kira Mae's villa after she'd finished her business. Strange that she had not rung to suggest a time when she might arrive.

Kira's head buzzed with ideas for the stage costumes; she wanted to share them with her mother. Although the two had their differences, their love of fashion, design and fine arts always brought them together.

Even though Rosita would feed the children and put them to bed, Kira Mae had begun to worry that she had neglected her business for way too long. Whatever else was going on, she had to get back the Galleria. She tried calling her mother yet again, but the phone was switched off.

chapter twenty-nine

"Some cupid kills with arrows, some with traps."

—Shakespeare's *Much Ado About Nothing*

Julianne clung on for dear life as her demented companion drove the car higher and higher on winding wooded mountain roads. Only a metal guardrail marked the demarcation between pavement and the deadly threat of a plunge straight off the clifftop into the valley below.

The wild ride tore her nerves to shreds and twisted her insides. She gripped her seat and prayed she would not end her life as a helpless victim in this car wreck waiting to happen. Whether to cover the sound of her gasps or to add to the excitement of his fairground ride, the driver tuned the radio to an exuberant Spanish dance channel. A cacophony of sound blared out, and Julianne allowed her anger to get the better of her as she shouted, "Turn the bloody music down."

Romero wanted to see her. In the craziness of her situation, she did not even know how to process the information. "Thank you," she said as the boy racer, who now held her life in his hands, did as she had asked and turned down the music.

Instinctively she smiled. In the middle of all the madness, that simple human gesture calmed him and he turned to her and smiled. "I'm a good driver, yes?" he said. "We're almost there."

Fear gripped Julianne. The devastating consequences of a meeting with Romero could not be underestimated. She had gathered all her courage and she decided it was now or never. She leaned close. "Please, I need a favor."

He turned and stared into her eyes.

In a soft, seductive tone, she told him, "My little girl, she is sick. She cries for me. I need to phone and at least say good night. Please, let me use your phone."

Her approach to him was outside his range of experience. Beautiful women did not come on to the drugged-up skinny kid, though given half a chance he often forced himself on them. This was different. Romero's woman was putting out to him. He intended to take full advantage.

He weighed the situation. Once he was sure that Gio in the car behind could not see what he was about to do, he slipped the phone from his trouser pocket and handed it to her. Then he demanded, "What's the number? Make it quick. And don't try to mess with me."

Julianne prayed that the call would not go to voice mail. Kira Mae answered. "Put me on to Angel," Julianne said immediately. "I need to say good night. I've been held up; don't know when I'll be home."

Having second thoughts about the wisdom of allowing her to make the phone call, he leaned over and snatched his phone back. Julianne used the last seconds before he pressed the disconnect button to say, "We need help, love you."

The expression on his face showed that he thought he had been taken for a ride, but before there was time to do anything, the phone rang. Julianne prayed that Kira Mae had understood she was in trouble. Her hope was that Kira Mae would call the police and get them to track the device, but the call had been barely a minute long. The driver took a call.

Gio called the driver. "We're here," she heard him say. "Take the next right."

They swerved into a small roadway overhung with branches. It was possible the car might not be able to make the potholed journey up to a small finca barely visible at the top of the rock-strewn lane. There were no other buildings in sight.

A barking dog that looked as if it had not been fed recently ran out to greet the car. The mangy hound prowled and growled as the two cars came to a halt. The dog did not waste much energy on his guard duties and sloped off to lie down on an old piece of carpet that marked out his home under a tree. Julianne noticed that a water bowl and feeding tray were empty, but their presence indicated that someone, sometimes, cared for the dog.

Perhaps someone here would care for her.

Julianne reached for her handbag, pulled a brush through her hair, reapplied lipstick without the benefit of a mirror and gave herself a quick spray of perfume.

Always the lady, even on the way to the scaffold. Or as best as she could achieve in these difficult circumstances.

She saw her car pull in. Gio got out and walked on ahead into the run-down farmhouse. Outside the place appeared almost derelict, with crumbling plaster and moss growing on the sides of the building. Garden furniture had been discarded and piles of rubbish and rubble littered the yard.

Julianne did not dare contemplate what her fate might be once she entered the ramshackle old building. She threw her shoulders back and followed the driver into the house.

It took a few minutes for her eyes to adjust to the gloom; shutters were closed and the only light came from a couple of strategically placed oil lamps. Far from being the abandoned building Julianne had expected, the interior of the main downstairs room was painted and reasonably furnished in the traditional Spanish dark wood style, and there were pretty curtains and carpets in place. She judged it might even have been a holiday home. Simple but comfortable. There was a small extension at the rear and Julianne noticed a kitchenette and a bathroom.

Gio was nowhere to be seen. The male who had driven her pointed toward the room at the back. He said nothing, but Julianne assumed she was being given permission to use the bathroom. She took the opportunity and then stuck her nose into the kitchen. The basics were in place. Crockery, cutlery and an open jar of coffee and creamer on the kitchen counter.

Julianne jumped as he pressed himself into her as she stood in the doorway. "I'm José. Coffee?" he said, though she wasn't sure if it was a question.

"Sure, thanks, shall I make it?" she said.

"You think we have maids here?" he said with what she took to be sarcasm. "You're not in your fancy villa now."

Fact was the little house was not that different from her own that had so tragically burned down. Julianne did not argue but asked: "My daughter's villa? You know it?"

"Yes, I delivered packages to the lawyer, Mr. Paolo."

"What was in the packages?" Julianne asked, not that she expected an answer.

He shrugged. "Why should he tell me? I didn't ask questions. You ask too many."

Anxious to do anything that would keep her far away from José for as long as possible, Julianne took her time to find a small metal pot in which to heat the water on the Calor gas hotplate. She filled it with more water than was necessary to allow extra time to boil and, while she waited, found a mug and spooned in coffee and creamer.

Somewhere in the house she heard a television or radio being turned on. Coffee in hand she made her way back into the living area and squeezed into one of two hardback wooden chairs that were part of a dining set in a tiny alcove just under the staircase. She presumed this led up to sleeping quarters. José was stretched out on a two-seater couch in front of a small television balanced on a wooden chest.

She watched while he channel-surfed through the three available channels with a remote control. A sports channel kept his attention for a while and then he switched to a noisy game show.

Beside the alcove she could see through a grubby side window to the yard outside.

Gio's absence gave her some relief but also increased her anxiety level. She hoped to avoid being alone with José for any length of time. Nor did she think that being alone with Gio was going to be a viable option. She hardly knew what constituted the worst-case scenario. To be raped by the young guy or killed by Gio. Damned if you do and damned if you don't. How strange, she observed, to sit there sipping coffee and contemplate her own death.

The contestants on the game show that blared out in the corner of the room had better options. To successfully answer just one question and win a car or get it wrong and lose everything. Right now she envied them.

Grateful that she was not tied up, Julianne moved from the living area to the bathroom to the kitchen, trying to work out what to do. José did not stir from the TV. The lock on the bathroom door did not work—that would have been too much to hope for—so she jammed a three-legged wooden stool under the door handle. Seconds later it rattled. She fumbled for her phone, which she had thrown to the bottom of her bag. Hoping against hope that it had regained a spark of power.

"What are you doing in there?" José shouted. "Open the door."

Julianne pulled the stool out of the way and threw the door wide-open. She stared straight at him. "What do you think I was doing?"

"Making yourself beautiful for me," he said with a leer that made her regret her challenge. Without warning he reached out and grabbed her arm. "You're coming with me," he said. "Upstairs."

This was exactly what Julianne dreaded. She had no response. His eyes were full of menace. His whole demeanor had changed from the person he was earlier. Julianne wondered again if he was on drugs, or maybe in withdrawal. His mood changes were so sudden and unpredictable.

He pushed her roughly toward the stairs, and she struggled to loosen his grip. The staircase was narrow and in his efforts to manhandle her, she lost her balance, stumbled and fell against him. They both crashed to the bottom of the stairs. Enraged by her refusal to give in to him, he drew back his fist and hit her square in the face. The force of the blow made her scream in pain, and, as she put her hand to her face, she felt the flow of blood.

Not to be defeated, José began to undo his trousers there and then. "You asked for this," he said as she backed away, looking for something to protect herself with.

The television, still at full volume, masked the sound

of the front door as it creaked open on its rusty hinges. Gio pushed his way into the room and stopped in his tracks.

"Get away from her," he said in a voice that brokered no argument.

José staggered to his feet and even offered a hand to help Julianne up. The blood poured from her wound, and he could see that her eye would be black the next morning.

"Clean her up," Gio demanded. "Romero has sent for her."

Julianne was unsteady on her feet and felt dizzy as she sat down on the first stair. José staggered toward the bathroom to get water and towel. She screamed as he attempted to clean the blood off her face. "I'm sorry," he repeated over and over again.

Gio had taken up a guard position in the main doorway and watched the proceedings. His face was expressionless, but his voice was loud as he competed with the volume of the television to tell José, "You will be when Romero finds out."

"Please don't tell him. Just say she fell down the stairs," he pleaded.

The look from Gio said it all. "Now, get her in the car. Her car. I'll drive. You follow."

As they crossed the yard, the dog sprang into life and started barking. Gio lifted his foot to kick it, then caught sight of the look of fury on Julianne's face and thought better of it.

Her injury had emboldened her. She knew from his anger with José that they were going to have to be careful about any reports that went back to Romero.

Julianne now had a request. "In the trunk of my car I have a change of clothes. Can I get something clean?" She was pretty sure Gio would consider it a good idea not to present her to Romero wearing bloody clothing. Julianne was a fashion plate and she intended to look as good as possible whatever the circumstances.

She persuaded Gio to let her rescue her makeup bag from the trunk, along with a fresh dress. He climbed into the driver's seat of her car. "Hurry up," he said losing patience as she sheltered behind the open trunk and pulled the bloody top over her head and stepped into a short denim dress.

As Gio drove, with the help of the sun visor mirror, Julianne used the opportunity to make herself look presentable. Gio shook his head in disbelief. Where the hell did she think she was going? To a dance?

Julianne questioned herself. *Why did she need to look good for that murderer, Romero?*

She despised herself, but she knew the answer. Because she still craved his touch. His poison was in her veins. The love she felt for him refused to die.

chapter thirty

"I'll follow thee and make a heaven of hell,
to die upon the hand I love so well."
—Shakespeare's *Midsummer Night's Dream*

In the dark, the journey down the mountain was even more hazardous, but Gio in the driver's seat felt like a safer pair of hands. He was not one for conversation and that suited Julianne just fine.

The only time he took his eyes off the road was when she twisted around in her seat to pick up a pair of glamorous red high heel shoes from the floor. He barked, "What are you doing now?"

"Sorry, I just needed to get my shoes. That's everything. I won't move a muscle from now on."

Hands folded in her lap and her eyes on the road ahead, Julianne had no choice but to wait and see where the journey would end. They zigzagged across the mountain from one high point to another and continued traveling on unpaved local roads.

"Can I ask you one thing?" said Julianne. He did not reply so she asked anyway. "Did you kidnap my granddaughter?"

"What do you think?" he answered. He shrugged.

"I'll take that as a 'yes'?" said Julianne. Not expecting confirmation, she ploughed on. "And what about the lawyer Paolo? Did he work for Romero?"

"You ask too many questions," he rebuked her.

"You sent me the bouquet, didn't you?" she challenged. "You don't need to deny it."

As an afterthought he added, "What does it matter when people are dead?"

Now they took a direct route down the mountain to the bottom. When they reached the main arterial road, they dipped even lower until they came to one of the picturesque harbors that dotted the coastline. Passing fancy new apartment blocks and resort hotels, they wound around the waterfront past restaurants and high-end designer shops.

Alongside a newly built harbor wall, Gio pulled up in front of electronic gates, inserted a code and drove into a small private parking lot. Julianne stayed in the car as she waited to be told what to do. Fearful and vulnerable, she hoped the cavalry would arrive to rescue her, but she wasn't sure that was what she wanted. What she wanted was to see Romero one last time.

She knew Gio was no gentleman, and it would never occur to him to open the car door for her. A curt nod was his signal that she should get out of the car and follow him. They walked to the end of the jetty where half a dozen yachts were moored. At the end of the jetty was the biggest and best of them all. A gleaming luxury yacht, all polished wood and sparkling chrome.

Gio stopped in front of the ocean-going yacht, unhooked a red silk rope and disappeared down the stairs of the high-speed cruiser. He reappeared almost immediately to signal that she needed to hurry up and follow him.

Julianne paused before following Gio onto the yacht. A thousand times over the years and especially over these last few days, she had rehearsed what she would say to Romero if she ever saw him again. She tried to make sense of her feelings—was she terrified or excited?

She stepped down the stairs and into an expansive downstairs saloon. A glittering chandelier lit up the room and reflected in the floor to ceiling mirrors. Plush red leather couches lined the stateroom and the soft furnishings, carpets and curtains were antique gold. The whole effect was luxurious and regal.

The man who tormented her dreams for so long sat behind a huge marble table.

Romero did not smile as he stared at her down the length of the table and, in a move she knew was designed to intimidate, took his time as he looked her up and down from head to toe.

He broke his silence with just one sound. "*Mmmm*. You are a class act, Julianne. I've been looking forward to seeing you again. Come here."

Julianne hesitated and held back until the request became a demand as he thrust out his right hand and gestured for her to come closer.

She could hardly believe her eyes, even now. He was as handsome and seductive as ever.

What had Romero been doing all this time? Where had he been? Was it too late to run?

Her heart was pounding and she could still taste the blood from the blow José inflicted.

But, as knockout punches go, that one was not within a mile of the one Romero had just delivered. She had to admit he looked gorgeous. Dressed in a black silk robe, he wore no shoes and looked as if he had just stepped out of the shower.

"Get out of here," he said to Gio, who still hovered by the bottom of the silver staircase. "And lock the door on your way out. I have a key. I'll call you."

Gio exited as fast as his legs would carry him. When Romero gave an order he knew better than to hang around.

Romero turned his full attention to Julianne. "You look like you've seen a ghost," he said, clearing the distance between them in his bare feet.

Like an animal about to attack, he suddenly reached out and grabbed her face. He tightened his grip, and Julianne attempted to pull away. Just as quickly, he removed his hand. The games he played had always been a mystery to her. She knew only not to antagonize him.

"I can assure you I am alive and well," he whispered as he reached out and this time increased the pressure on her cheek further. It wasn't an unpleasant sensation. She did not know how to react; she knew only that right now she was in his power.

She gazed into his eyes as with the tenderest of touches he stroked her face.

"You look beautiful," he told her, as he led her toward a banquette. "Come and sit here with me. We have a lot of catching up to do. *La Dama Escalata.* Gorgeous, as ever," Romero teased. "Come, let me look at you."

He inspected her by a window that framed the yacht's view of the sea. The opposite set of windows overlooked the harbor. After removing the guitar that he had been tuning when she arrived, he patted the seat beside him. On his wrist he wore a solid gold Italian designer watch, not so much a timepiece as a computer and phone. In his left ear he still wore the flashing ruby that she remembered from their earlier encounters. A warning sign she had refused to heed.

Everything about him screamed money, wealth and the confidence that came with them. From the top of his shiny, jet-black hair to his manicured toenails with just a hint of a gloss, he was polished, pampered and groomed. This man was certainly high maintenance.

Julianne's skin both repelled his touch and tingled at the closeness of him. Fresh from the shower there was no doubt that he scrubbed up better than any man she had ever known. Even better than Dominic. He smelled of the sea and sky and sun. A force of nature. His energy vibrated in the room, and she had to exercise restraint to stop from falling into his arms.

To remain aloof was becoming impossible, and she feared that the seething cauldron of emotions bubbling inside her would boil over and force her to do something dangerous or disgraceful.

She was on fire. Her body temperature was off the chart, and she felt like a teenager as a glow spread across her face. Her whole body pulsated when she was close to him. No wonder she had wanted to die when he left her.

Effortlessly, it seemed, he had pressed a primordial switch and evoked uncontrollable emotions within her of love and hate and revenge. How could this be? How could the man who had betrayed both her and her daughter trigger these feelings in her? The shame of it was nearly overwhelming.

In her dreams and nightmares she had been here a thousand times before.

Now Romero stroked her hand, her arms, her face, and looked deep into her eyes.

"Do you have anything to tell me?" he enquired, giving her no clue as to the answer he required. Julianne returned his steady gaze even as her heart pounded and she bit the inside of her cheek. He sat motionless but alert like a coiled spring.

She was reminded of a rattlesnake she had seen in the souk when she was with Dominic in Casablanca. Part of her dearly wished he was here now to step between her and Romero.

Stories of Romero's ruthlessness were legendary, she remembered. An international criminal who had clawed his way to the top of a murderous operation, he would certainly not maintain the respect and fear of a bunch of criminals by displaying any signs of weakness.

Romero followed through on his threats.

"You tricked me," he reminded her now, not that she had ever forgotten. "In the last letter I received from you in jail, you promised you were waiting for me. That I would be safe. Instead you tried to persuade Gio to kill me. You betrayed me. You know I can't allow you to get away with that. You made me look a fool."

"My heart was broken, Romero," she tried to explain. She clasped her hands as if in prayer. "I loved you, but so many other people had been hurt. My daughter, Kira Mae, had just been released from prison. She had given birth to her daughter, your daughter."

Romero softened. "How are the girls? Did the little one get home safe and sound?"

Julianne stared at him. So he had known about Angel's kidnap.

"Please Romero, I beg you. Do what you want to me but not them. You once told Kira Mae that you loved her and Angel is the result of the love you shared with her."

"Don't talk to me of those things," he said with anger in his voice. "It's not becoming for a mother. The child is not a matter for me to consider."

She dared to move closer and lower her voice seductively.

"Please. I'll do anything. Just tell me you won't hurt my family."

In one swift movement he grabbed his gun, a Glock revolver that had never been more than a few feet from his outstretched arm on the bench. With the gun in his right hand, he grabbed Julianne with the left. He pushed her roughly from the couch, and she fell on the floor in front of him. He held the gun to her throat.

"Beg for forgiveness," he growled. "Beg for me to spare your life."

Julianne was more scared than she had ever been in her life: she felt the sweat on her brow, her tongue seemed glued to the roof of her mouth and she licked her parched lips. Her insides were in spasms as she contemplated that he might indeed kill her there and then.

It was now or never. She gambled and took a risk, a gigantic risk. She looked deep into his eyes as she reached out and stroked his face.

"Please, Romero," she whispered. "You drove me crazy with desire for you. I didn't know what I was doing half the time. You bewitched me. I had never met a man like you and know I never will again. Please set me free. I am in hell. I fear so for my girls; please tell me we can now live without the threat of your revenge hanging over us. I know you are a good man. I know you can love. With all my heart and soul I ask you to set me, no, us, free."

Julianne had not expected to be forgiven, but she saw a glimmer of hope. The fact that Gio was still in Romero's employ might mean that some form of restitution was possible.

Romero spread his legs and held tightly to Julianne who was on her knees in front of him. He took her hair in his clenched fist and pulled her head back.

The gun was clenched in his right hand, his eyes bore into her.

"You and Gio owe me big time. Gio knows I will kill him for what he did," he told her.

An image of a cat tormenting a mouse sprang into her mind. "He just doesn't know where or when. Every minute of every day, he is in danger. He redeemed himself and prolonged his life because he came back to save me. He's a good Catholic boy, his family had hopes that he would be a priest, and his conscience did not allow him to leave me to bleed to death on the bare floor of an empty house. Even criminals abide by a code of honor. We are family. His mother is my sister. But one day he will pay for his crime. I will decide when the time is right."

Frozen shards of fear pierced her heart. Julianne did not dare move or speak. Romero's hand moved from her hair, to her face, to her breasts. He continued to stroke and caress her, his eyes accused her. She trembled with fear and longing.

"Stand up and take your dress off," he ordered.

She stood up and complied. Her whole body shook with stark terror, and she was aware of another emotion she wanted to deny. Anticipation. Expectation. Part of her craved for him to make love to her. She was weak with desire.

Passion and shame pulsated through her. She might be under his spell, but she was not completely powerless. She had to save the girls who were the real love of her life. She had to try to make a bargain. "I said I will do anything, and I will but will you do something for me? Will you grant me amnesty for my daughters?" she asked. "Will you let us live in peace?"

He was not the only one skilled in the art of manipulation. To hide her true feelings in order to subvert a situation was second nature to her. She had plenty of practice growing up with her father, trying to please him and avoid his overtures. He had taught her to hate but to pretend love.

Romero did not need to smell her fear, but she did intend to make him feel the passion.

With seduction in her eyes, she undid her dress, one button at a time. Slow and sensual. She unwrapped the denim belt from her waist and dropped it to the floor. Romero picked it up and ran it through his hands. Still wearing her heels she stepped out of the dress and kicked it away. She stood before him in her underwear. Black, frilly, flimsy.

Julianne knew her body was in great shape. She took pride in maintaining a slender figure, but from her Italian mother she had inherited full breasts and a shapely derriere. Romero was like a snake transfixed as she weaved her spell. With a subtle lift of her eyebrows, she tossed her head and shook out her long blonde hair. This was no time to be inhibited or shy.

"What will you do for me if I take off my bra and panties?" she teased.

She knew that Romero had only to snap his fingers to bring a bevy of lovelies running to his yacht, to his bed. Julianne was competing with an army of professional seductresses.

She could tell he was aroused. He pulled her toward him. Julianne felt an electric charge fly between them as he pressed his lips to hers. She returned the intensity of his kiss and gave herself over to his lips and his hands.

"What do you want me to do to you?" he murmured.

"I want you to spare my daughters," she whispered into his ear.

"I am not heartless," he claimed. "I know you have suffered enough. I promise not to harm any of them. I may not be much of a father or a husband, but I am a wonderful lover."

Now that she had his promise, she fell helplessly into his arms. Her passion matched and almost eclipsed his.

All the memories of his betrayal only fueled the flames of her eternal desire. She knew she had met her match. A man who could tame her. His darkness enflamed and enslaved her. Julianne knew she would have given up her life if it meant she could feel, breathe, scream, be submerged in the raw life-shaking experience of being with Romero.

Sweet, kind, gentle love was never going to break through the walls she had constructed.

From him she received depraved love. Lust and desire that threatened to overwhelm and consume everything in her life, but she was awakened. Her impossible love for Romero gave meaning to her very existence. If he meant to kill her, so be it. At least she would die happy.

Romero swept her off her feet and carried her to the master bedroom. He threw her on the unmade king-size bed.

He pulled a small pen knife from the top pocket of his black robe before he discarded the only covering that stood between him and his nakedness. The knife glinted in his hand as he expertly slashed at her underwear and hungrily ripped the flimsy lingerie from her body.

Romero told her, "Prepare to be ravaged."

He arranged her naked body in a star shape, arms outstretched, legs apart and, mirroring her predicament, climbed on top and covered her whole body with his until she was unable to move even one limb. Pressing his lips roughly to her, he forced her lips apart. Without warning he stuck his tongue into the deepest recesses of her mouth. She could hardly breathe. She felt his erection hard and firm, poised but not yet ready to enter her.

"You are mine," he whispered. "I control everything you see, everything you hear, everything you feel. I am your very breath."

Julianne succumbed willingly and swooned as he released his hold and, with unexpected tenderness, bent down and kissed every inch of her body from head to toe.

Truly she felt she had died and gone to heaven.

He spread her legs and inserted his tongue, gently teasing, licking and caressing. Julianne cried out with pleasure as he drove her to the very edge of ecstasy. And then withheld himself.

In her ear and against her mouth, breathing with her, Romero whispered words of love. "Your hunger drives me crazy," he told her. "I penetrate and capture your very soul."

To Julianne's ears it sounded like the words of a flamenco ballad. Erotic tales of longing, passion and, ultimately, treachery. His words matched the rhythm of the soulful guitar music that played softly on the yacht's elaborate sound system.

Julianne clung to him, she dug her fingernails into his flesh and craved the sensation of him pounding into her body. Orgasms rose and demanded relief but, at the last moment, Romero would withdraw and leave her burning with passion. His hands were surprisingly soft for a man who played the steel strings of the guitar, and he grasped her buttocks firmly as he penetrated her.

Like a master musician, he stroked, plucked and played her. "Give yourself totally to me," he demanded, "and I will fulfill your every fantasy."

"I'm yours," she conceded, "I want every part of you to fill my body and soul."

They clung to each other, first one on top, then the other, bathed in sweat, bruised and battered as they beat their bodies against each other and rode the furious wave of their passion.

When the great explosion came, orchestrated and choreographed by Romero, Julianne screamed his name and begged for her love and her life.

As the sea of emotion crested, rose and fell again, Romero sealed their union. "You are mine forever," he proclaimed. "No other woman gives herself to me so completely. You challenge me to go deeper, darker, further. You are the she devil."

At the climax, they came together in perfect synchrony and screamed and cried out with pain and pleasure. Two souls, bodies and hearts united.

In a state of altered consciousness brought about by fear, adrenalin and the roller-coaster ride of her exhilarating sexual encounter, Julianne imagined herself a black widow spider.

The creature kills her lover at the point of climax.

In a moment of pure madness, Julianne dared to focus her gaze and look around the opulent stateroom of Romero's yacht to see if she could find a weapon. The penknife he had employed to such erotic use earlier. *Was it in reach?*

She fantasized that she could transform the petit mort, the little death of orgasm, into the grande mort of death.

Now she really would drain the life blood out of Romero. He suspected nothing.

Romero was exhausted. Exposed. Naked, he lay on his back breathing deeply. One arm across his eyes the other stroking Julianne's thigh. It surely never occurred to him that he needed to protect himself from a woman he had just loved to within an inch of her life.

"Stay with me, Julianne," he pleaded. "I need you to make me whole. Come with me. We can run away together. Just disappear. I know many places where we can go. Where we can make love till our hearts are content. Maybe then I will get enough of you."

The words were music to her ears. Julianne experienced a kaleidoscope of emotions. She could not, would not, deny the depths of her feelings for him. They lay locked in each other's arms. Imprinted upon each other. Two of a kind.

Death itself could not be more earth-shattering than this experience, she reflected.

Julianne was at last at peace beside the man who had wrung every last ounce of emotion out of her. She loved him, hated him, feared him, and was obsessed and overwhelmed by him. Every emotion told her that she was indeed alive. She was a woman, and she had found her match in a man.

Conflicted and undecided. Deep in her heart she knew, much as she wanted to, she would not go with him.

"I can't abandon my children," she admitted. "They mean more to me than life itself. I have let them down so many times, now I intend to spend my life making it up to them. My love for you will never die. I know that now. I thank God I experienced it."

* * *

"Open up! Police," the angry shouts shocked them.

Thunderous pounding on the lower deck cabin door suggested that they were not going to wait for an invitation. Romero leapt off the bed and ran into the living area. He covered his nakedness with the black robe while Julianne retrieved her clothes from the floor.

Julianne watched in horror as Romero snatched up his revolver from the couch.

"The bathroom," he pointed out to her. "Stay in there."

She did not need to be told twice. As she made her

way across the stateroom she glanced out of the window and saw several police cars. Police officers were knocking on the cabin doors of all the yachts. If they found a door locked, they moved on.

Romero signaled to her to be silent. Julianne crept into the huge restroom where a circular Jacuzzi capable of seating about a dozen people took pride of place. She sat on the edge by the gold faucets and prepared to follow his instructions.

Gio hammered on the door and then shouted a warning, "Boss, it's all clear now. OK if I come in?"

"Bloody fool," Romero said to Julianne. "He almost gave me a heart attack hammering like that."

She came out from her hiding place, and Romero opened the door to let Gio in.

He locked it again straightaway.

"What the hell are you playing at?" Romero snapped.

"You must have missed my text saying we had police sniffing around," said Gio. "They've taken José off in the back of a police cruiser to question him. Perhaps they thought he had something to do with that girl being kidnapped. We've got to get out of here, Boss," he added. "Guardia civil are crawling all over the place. I don't know what José will tell them. He's not too bright."

"Neither are you," Romero told Gio. "José is always being arrested, his car's an occupational hazard."

The passionate atmosphere was well and truly shattered, and Julianne now questioned what would happen next. In the cold light of day, Romero was just a criminal with a score to settle. Why would he spare her or the girls?

"Where's her car?" Romero asked, as if Julianne was no longer present.

"Outside," said Gio. "I got the keys here."

Romero handed Julianne the keys and dispatched Gio to find her purse.

"She's leaving now," he told him. "In her own car."

"This is where we say good-bye, my fair lady," Romero said as he walked Julianne to the doorway. "Don't forget I gave you the choice to come with me. You are one wild lady in bed. It was a real pleasure to see you again," he added with a laugh. "I won't forget you."

"No regrets. The police will soon put the pieces together. Me, Gio and the dopey kid."

"You, Mr. Captain," he pointed to Gio, "*vamos*. Let's get out of here."

Romero kissed Julianne and almost before she had reached the top of the stairway and stepped out on to the jetty, Gio had winched in the heavy holding ropes, upped the anchor and, with engines fired and lights ablaze, the yacht cruised out in the direction of the open sea.

Julianne stood on the dock and, in case Romero was watching, she waved and blew him a kiss. Romero no longer would torture her. In fact he said he loved her. So why was her love life a succession of good-byes?

chapter thirty-one

"Is love a tender thing? It is too rough, too rude, too boisterous, and it pricks like a thorn."

—Shakespeare's *Romeo & Juliet*

Julianne rolled down the windows to let in the warm evening breeze and sang along to the radio as she drove south on the familiar coast road.

Village of Joy. The perfect place for her to be headed. She felt alive and vindicated. She had freed herself from Romero at last. No longer did the burden of her part in his death hang over her, or the threat of his revenge.

Without wishing to prolong Kira Mae's worry any longer than necessary, Julianne knew that she needed to gather her thoughts and come up with an explanation for the ordeal she had endured and the events that had led to her rescue.

It intrigued her to realize how much she had learned from Paolo about the process of constructing a defense to present a plausible scenario, without actually offering an admission of guilt.

"Most criminals indict themselves by talking too much," he had told her. "If only they learned to keep their mouths shut. But that's the point, they want to boast about what they've done and some of them even want to be punished."

Julianne would miss Paolo, her wise counsel. It was tragic that such a mature and noble man as he had fallen prey to the evils of drug addiction. Romero had a lot to answer for as a boss of one of the most powerful drug-smuggling organizations in the world.

Kira Mae and the girls rushed out to greet Julianne as they heard her car pull into the driveway. They hugged and kissed and laughed.

"Did the bad men get you?" asked Angel.

"Did a superhero save you?" asked Isabella.

"Let me catch my breath, and I'll tell you all about it," said Julianne, though she knew she wouldn't.

Kira Mae had realized something was wrong and alerted the police after Julianne's phone call from José's phone. But still Chief Xabia was fast losing patience with Julianne. As enamored as he had been of her previously, he was beginning to suspect that she wasn't all "butter wouldn't melt in her mouth."

He liked a quiet life. Crime in his area was low and that's how he planned to keep it. His recent media triumph when the Angel kidnapping had been successfully resolved was enough excitement for him for one decade. Now he was determined to close the case on this latest incident that involved the glamorous local celebrities.

Julianne was instructed to present herself at the police station the following morning. Chief Xabia called a conference, to include two of the police officers who had questioned her at her house.

Julianne had chosen a demure navy blue dress with a scarf at the neckline for the conference. Her blonde hair was held at the nape of her neck with an ornamental clip and her gold jewelry was understated. The defiance she felt was symbolized by her feet. She wore the red high heels she now saw as power brokers. While dressing that morning she had recalled the Marilyn Monroe quote, "Give a girl the right shoes, and she can conquer the world."

"Do I need a lawyer?" she asked when the chief arrived to personally escort her into the meeting.

He looked at her quizzically. "We are making no charges," he said. "This is an information-gathering exercise to ensure that everyone is on the same page."

Julianne felt some of the tension leave her body. In the middle of the night when she tossed and turned, first in shameful ecstasy at the memory of Romero's touch, then in a white-hot sweat as she imagined she would be thrown into jail, she had convicted herself of a long list of crimes. Murder, extortion, money laundering, drug running—and stealing a woman's heart.

Composed in her privileged seat next to the chief, Julianne listened as first the police officer, the young woman she had liked when she was on duty at the house, and then the detective offered a summary of the events leading up to today's meeting.

Chief Xabia beamed as the police officer recounted the successful conclusion of the child abduction case. He had become quite the local and national celebrity after all his television appearances.

"The child was reunited with her family and there were no casualties," the officer reiterated. "To the best of our knowledge, no ransom was paid but ultimately that decision was in the hands of the family. The lawyer, Mr. Paolo Grazia, dealt with everything. No arrests were made, but the case remains open in our files. We believe the suspects are not from this region." The chief was clearly happy with that observation. "Probably foreigners," he said, "or border hoppers. OK, now we move on," he told the policewoman as she scrambled through her notes to find the next report.

Nodding to the administrator across the room, behind the conference table, she appealed for help. "Can you give us the latest on the situation regarding the release of the body of Mr. Paolo?"

In a robotic tone, the note-taker answered. "Coroner inquest complete. Accidental death. The body is available for release to the family."

Julianne sucked in a lungful of air, which went down the wrong way, and the chief asked, "Do you want some water?"

"Yes, please," Julianne said, coughing.

She accepted the glass of water slid up the table to her by the administrator.

Chief Xabia took the opportunity to make a statement. "You are not the next of kin." He already knew the answer.

"No," said Julianne, "Paolo's family will come from

Italy to make arrangements. He was my friend and a consultant to my business, and we will take care of any legal matters through our company lawyers."

The chief was ready to move on again. "Next," he said and indicated the detective.

In an officious tone, he read from his notes.

"On the date in question, we questioned Señora Julianne about her relationship with Paolo Grazia. We wanted to discover what she might know about his death and the drug-trafficking activities that possibly led to his death in a swimming pool at her daughter's house.

"Paolo often stayed at another address, the house occupied by Señora Julianne. She was reluctant to let us search her premises when we told her the lawyer may have left evidence relevant to our enquiries."

The chief listened without interruption, but his eyes said, "Get on with it."

"We applied for and received a search warrant from the judge in chambers," the detective insisted on reading word for word, "and returned to the premises to carry out the search. The occupier was not at home nor could we make contact to gain access. We decided to return at a later time and if we were still not able to execute our warrant we would summon the owner of the house. Señora Julianne has a lease; she does not own the property to allow us access."

"What happened next?" said the chief in a bored tone.

"There was a fire," said the detective. "The house

was badly damaged so we were never able to carry out our search. The accident investigators think the blaze was caused by candles that had been left to burn in an upstairs bedroom and ignited a piece of fabric. We asked them to look for signs of an accelerator being used, but so far they haven't identified anything."

Julianne gave the detective a long hard look. "I told you it was the candles," she said.

The chief moved to sum up the situation. "Are police enquiries ongoing or is this now a matter for the insurance company accident investigators?"

"Yes," said the detective, his moment of glory over. "We are not pursuing enquiries."

Having sucked some of the air out of the room, the detective leaned back in his chair. Even he knew he had not covered himself with glory. Julianne was not under suspicion and he had no further basis on which to question her. Case closed.

Julianne flexed her shoulders against the back of the chair. Her muscles had been so tense for weeks. She promised herself that, at the first chance she had, she would head for the spa and a well-deserved massage.

Chief Xabia's voice broke into her thoughts. "That just leaves the incident we heard about from the next jurisdiction. Your daughter reported that you needed help. Our colleagues questioned a man who might have been up to no good when they tracked him to one of the harbors on their stretch of coast. What do you know about that?"

Julianne relayed the story she had prepared.

"There was a personal element involved," she admitted and allowed the element of mystery to shroud the facts. "It's embarrassing, I overreacted when I rang my daughter. The situation was not as intimidating as I had at first imagined. I had been drinking."

The chief had heard enough. "OK, drink had been taken. That usually explains a lot. Any damage to your person or your property? Do you intend to press charges?"

"No, nothing like that," Julianne assured him. "It's all over. Thank you."

"Anyone got anything to add?" asked the chief, as he pushed back his chair, clearly ready to dismiss the meeting and return to the quiet life of his office.

When no one answered, he turned to Julianne and said, "With great respect, Señora Julianne, I hope not to see you again too soon. You certainly seem to attract drama. It's almost like you are starring in your own reality show."

Julianne smiled, and he looked pleased with his little joke.

"Oh, I've got nothing on you," she joked back. "My life is nowhere near as exciting as pack-mule racing."

* * *

If Julianne had a hat, she would have thrown it in the air as she left the police station.

To skip down the street like the girls did was not an option in her red shoes, but her heart was so light she felt she could take off and drift high in the sky like a balloon. She was a free woman, no longer enslaved. She was guilty of no crime and no longer on the hit list of a master criminal. A celebration was in order.

She called Kira Mae.

"I'm at the Galleria. You'll have to come to me," said her daughter. "I'm up against the deadline for the Benidorm Palace costumes. A second opinion on what I've designed so far would be welcome."

"On my way," said Julianne. It was time to get their lives back on track and focus on business.

Julianne made a decision that from now on she would be there to free up Kira Mae from the pressures of running the Galleria. She had left her daughter to do all the heavy lifting and also to take responsibility for the upbringing of two young girls.

No wonder she and Paolo had fallen into each other's arms when Julianne was absent all the time. They must both have felt that they were not a priority in her life. It was easy for Julianne to justify that her globe-trotting was all for business, not pleasure.

It was time for Julianne to stop running away now and face the truth about her family. Even the fact that Julianne had maintained her own house instead of officially moving into the villa showed her determination to isolate herself.

Now fate had taken her house from her in a ball of flames. The cottage would be uninhabitable for some time and the decision whether to rebuild was up to the owner and the insurance company. Word was that Julianne would not be liable financially.

Julianne knew when she was beaten.

Forced to give up her independent lifestyle, she admitted that she never gave up anything without leaving claw marks. The fact was she had to let go or be dragged.

"Marry me," Paolo had begged her over the years. She would never know if he would have followed through if she had accepted. Whether he would have divorced his wife. Julianne now owed it to the family she still had left to make their lives as full and rich as possible.

She pulled up in front of her old house. The windows had been boarded up and a tarpaulin placed over a hole in the roof to prevent further damage if it rained before essential repairs were carried out. She walked to the back of the house through the side alleyway. A few steps down the garden path and she reached the shed.

Separated from the main house, there was no evidence of any fire damage. Despite the rusty lock, the door opened easily with the key on her keyring. Everything was as she had left it and inside she saw what she had come to see. There on the workbench lay a disintegrated wreath of what had once been red roses. Leaves withered, blooms long dead.

Palms outstretched she carried the blackened edifice, its thorns still prickly, to her car and laid it ceremoniously in the trunk. On the coast road, she headed to the nearest beach to perform a ritualistic burial at sea.

Scattering ashes in the ocean was a ceremony that Julianne had seen many times along this strip of coast.

Drifting across from the promenade she heard the plaintive flamenco guitar chords of an unsmiling Spanish musician who played at the restaurant tables for the tourists.

She lifted the wreath high and launched it into the sea. "Farewell," she called as the waterlogged bouquet floated out on the surface of the ocean.

The final ceremony complete, she turned and walked away. Still, like Lot's wife, she could not resist one last look. The surface of the water was calm. The wreath was gone. All the fears and doubts of the past had been cast to the bottom of the ocean. Her spirit threw off its shackles. Her soul was finally released.

Julianne sat in her car, stared out over the ocean and allowed herself the luxury of tears. Sobs wracked her body, but she felt a calm healing power settle over her mind and heart.

The past had been taken on the waves, and the future was full of promise.

In the sky there appeared a beautiful rainbow.

Julianne pulled her phone from her bag, congratulating herself that it was fully charged, and sent a photo to Kira Mae.

On the caption, she wrote, "Rainbows all the way. I love you."

Immediately came back the reply, "Love you more."

chapter thirty-two

"I will wear my heart on my sleeve."
—Shakespeare's *Othello*

Julianne arrived at the Galleria. The floor to ceiling windows were dressed to perfection. The beautiful garments she brought back from Bali on a recent trip formed the main theme. Sumptuous fabrics in rich sierra orange, kingfisher blue and ocean green were draped over make believe trees where exotic birds nested and Balinese fruits adorned the branches.

Accessories in antique gold and shiny silver offset the free flowing dresses. Paintings and framed photographs transported the onlookers to an idyllic island scene in a land of serenity.

The scenes reflected in the outer windows were in stark contrast to the activity inside the Galleria. Kira Mae was at the chaos end of the serene spectrum. There was even more fabric draped over her desk than decorated the windows.

"Too light, too dark, too matte, too shiny," she dismissed roll after roll of material that an assistant delivered to try to win the approval of her demanding employer.

"She's having a Goldilocks moment," the assistant told Julianne as the two attempted to pass in the doorway while the assistant manhandled sky-high piles of brightly colored silks and satins back to the stockroom.

"I know exactly the shade I need," said Kira by way of greeting to her mother. "You'll have to help me find it. Time is running out. I have to finish the first dozen costumes by this time tomorrow. Everything else that happened took up my time and attention and now I am really in the pressure cooker."

"You've never missed a deadline yet," said Julianne.

"No, and I never had my daughter kidnapped before," said Kira Mae.

"OK, let's get to work," Julianne told her. "What do you want me to do?"

"Look at the designs; they're on the table. Probably buried under stacks of material," Kira Mae instructed her mother.

"See if you can identify the shade of rose pink I asked Carmen to find. I know I used it for a client's dress only a few months ago. Check the stockroom. You can look through the manufacturers' catalogues. First check the British manufacturers we've bought from since the beginning of the year. Their names are in the ledger. Think Vivien Westwood—she used a tartan in the shade I want for her last collection.

"While you're at it, bring me all the pastel tartans you can lay your hands on. Color co-ordinate them with net for the bodices and bustles."

Julianne loved the sound of the design choices, but

most of all she loved being bossed around by her daughter. Kira Mae was in her element when she got her teeth into a design project and her energy and enthusiasm filled the workroom.

"Phone round and put half a dozen seamstresses on standby. I want people ready to sew for me as soon as I've finalized the design and materials."

Julianne lifted a pile of color swatches from the desk and found Kira's notebook.

"I better write all this down," said Julianne as she prioritized a schedule.

Music inspired Kira Mae and encouraged her creative juices to flow. The rock music that blared out in the small workroom had the opposite effect on Julianne, but she didn't comment. As long as her daughter was happy, that's all that mattered. And she would be happy when she had produced a set of showstopping costumes to make her mark as a new designer at the Benidorm Palace.

Mother and daughter worked side by side all day and late into the evening, and, even when the tension got to Kira Mae and she barked out instructions, Julianne did not react.

"Now," Kira Mae said. "Before you do anything else measure this hem. Carmen can't model and measure."

Julianne bent down on her knees to measure the hem on yet another garment and did not check the floor for pins.

The tip of a small tacking pin pricked her knee. Fortunately she was wearing linen trousers and the pin scratched the skin and drew a small amount of blood, visible through the fabric. As she hopped around on one leg, Julianne made a bigger fuss than was necessary, but she was determined to draw attention to the minor injury she had suffered. She jumped up and rubbed her knee. "That was painful," she said. "The pin stuck in my knee. It's bleeding."

Kira Mae exploded. "Don't get blood on the dress."

Even as she said it, she realized how mean she sounded.

"Sorry, Mama," she said.

The moment was awkward until all three women burst out laughing.

"Don't get blood on the dress," now became the rallying cry that accompanied them through the arduous and at times tense, creative process.

The perfect shade of pink satin was teamed with matching nets. The outfits had been measured and cut and tacked and pinned and each one was different but complimentary to the others.

There would be time, while the machinists sewed, to add finishing details in coordinating gloves and sky-high headdresses.

It was close to midnight when they agreed to call it a day.

Coffee and pizza and chocolate had fueled their energy all day. Now Julianne craved a proper cup of British tea. "You deserve it," said Kira as she drove home after they dropped off Carmen and thanked her yet again.

"That girl is a treasure," said Julianne. "She hasn't

complained once all day. She was as determined as us to get the job done. She really admires you and I watch her taking note of everything and asking questions when appropriate."

"I had the A team on today," Kira said with pride.

"This reminds me of when you first opened *Dama Escalata* and we worked together to build my reputation as a designer. It felt good to be working together again. Not just in the business but to build our dream and be there for each other. Thank you, Mama."

Mother and daughter looked in on their sleeping girls and dropped into bed exhausted.

chapter thirty-three

"We are such stuff as dreams are made on."
—Shakespeare's *The Tempest*

The Galleria was silent. Julianne had expected to be greeted by a hive of activity with Queen Bee, Kira Mae, buzzing around the place, instructing her subjects, directing operations, flitting from flower to flower. Instead Kira Mae was stretched out on the empty workbench, her eyes covered with a black velvet eye mask. No rock music today.

"Migraine," Carmen mouthed to Julianne across the soundless room.

"Where is everyone?" asked Julianne.

"We sent the machinists home. We have a power failure. No work today," answered Carmen as she took Julianne's arm and led her into the corridor.

"There's nothing we can do. The power went out less than an hour after we started work. Not one costume has been completed."

"You called the power company?" asked Julianne, searching her mind for a solution.

"Of course," Kira Mae heard the question and

answered. "They have no idea how long it will last. Could be all day."

She removed the eye mask and sat up. On the high workbench she sat swinging her legs.

"Everything is ruined," she said in a small defeated voice. "No costumes for the show tonight. I'm going to look like the biggest failure when I phone the owner to tell her. It's so unprofessional."

Kira Mae's frustration turned to bitter tears of self-pity.

"I've lost my chance. She won't ask me again."

Julianne walked to the bench and put a comforting arm around her daughter. "It's not the end of the world. I'm sure the costume department has spare sets of outfits. They could switch and change the finale. It is not all dependent on your designs."

"How can you say that?" Kira Mae had found a target for her anger. "It may not mean that much to you but it's important to me."

"Of course, it's important to me," Julianne soothed her, not quite making the "there, there" assurance sound she used on the children. "We'll figure something out."

"Go back to sleep," she told Kira Mae as she attempted to wrap her in a warm cover and settle her back down on the bench.

"I'm not asleep," Kira Mae pouted. "I'm resting my eyes."

"OK," Julianne spoke close to her ear and hushed her. "You rest your eyes. Trust me. I'll think of something."

The responsibility for worrying had now passed to

her mother, and Kira Mae soon lost her agitation. "I'll do the worrying. That's what mothers are for," Julianne had told her that all her life.

Mother and daughter had survived darker nights of the soul than this one.

Carmen was relieved. "What are you going to do?" she asked Julianne.

"No idea," Julianne admitted. "But I'll do everything in my power to make sure that Kira Mae's costumes appear on the stage of the Benidorm Palace tonight. Oh, yes, that's what we don't have. Power."

With no solution in mind, Julianne joked, "Now, where did I put my superhero cloak?"

Julianne poured herself a coffee and went and sat on the steps outside the Galleria to give the matter her full attention. She had learned over the years that to solve problems she needed to clear her mind and open up a channel to outside forces. Mysterious forces that she did not understand but she did believe in. Thinking was all very well, but the magic ingredient was a higher power.

"Higher power," she repeated as she sipped her coffee and entered a calm, meditative state. An idea formed and a small voice inside whispered.

"Higher power," she said over and over again.

"It's worth a try," she said to no one in particular, but a handsome young man who walked by with his large dog on a leash obviously thought the remark was addressed to him.

He smiled. "Always worth a try," he assured her, "what have you got to lose?"

Julianne appreciated the confirmation. A small angel moment. "Thank you," she said.

It took just minutes on Google to find the phone number for the local convent. She dialed the number and asked to speak to Sister Juanita, a long-time friend of hers.

Sister Juanita was active in the community, and she and Julianne had organized many charity events together. The convent where the nun lived and worked and prayed was less than an hour away from the Galleria.

Sister Juanita was pleased to hear from her. "First a question," said Julianne, "do you have electricity? I mean are you experiencing a power outage?"

"No," said the nun, who was well used to unreliable utilities, having come to Spain from a small village in Mexico. "Our area was out yesterday but not so far today. Why?"

"Second question," said Julianne, "your lovely nuns, the ones who are so talented and help the children make costumes for fiestas, would they be available to do an important rush job for me?"

Sister Juanita did not hesitate. "They are at lunch at the moment, but they'll soon be finished. For you to ask, I know it must be important. My nuns are always in the service of the Lord. How can we help?"

Julianne thanked her, explained her dilemma and outlined her plan.

"You have electricity and sewing machines and the expertise, so we will come to you."

"We'll be ready for you," said Sister Juanita, calm, unflappable and always game for an adventure.

Julianne was happy to find her daughter up and about when she returned to the workroom. Kira Mae looked uncertain but a further call to the power company produced no hope that electricity would soon be restored to the premises.

"It's worth a try," she conceded. "What have we got to lose?"

Julianne smiled. The plan was inspired.

Kira Mae's Range Rover was pressed into service as Carmen folded down the backseat and loaded the costumes into the back. Piled on top of each other, the costumes reached almost to the roof of the vehicle. There was no visibility out of the back window, but overloaded vehicles are a common sight on the one-track roads through local villages.

"I'll drive," said Julianne, as all three women squeezed into the front seat of the vehicle. "You two can hold on to the dresses to stop them from getting too tangled up in each other."

"What time are you due at the theater?" Julianne asked Kira Mae as they pulled into the gravel driveway of the convent and parked close to the statue of Our Lady.

"Don't ask," said Kira Mae before she answered, "five o'clock and it's at least an hour from here."

The deadline was just three hours away. "Say a prayer, best to be on the safe side," said Julianne as they passed the statue. "Everything will be fine. I have faith."

Sister Juanita, a senior nun whose job it was to represent the convent in the community, was her usual gracious self as she offered a warm welcome and opened the heavy double wooden door that led into the quiet confines of the convent.

"We are all very excited," she said, as if she and her nuns were the ones being done the favor.

"Follow me," she said and talked as she walked through the long stone corridors. Her gray habit swept the tiled floor, and a large beaded cross swayed on her chest.

"This is traditionally a quiet time of reflection and prayer, but the nuns also have personal time where they choose their own activities. You will be pleased to know that several of them chose to help sew your costumes."

"Thank you," said Kira Mae, "you are very kind."

Sister Juanita showed them into a room where half a dozen nuns sat around a large refectory table, sewing machines at the ready.

Kira Mae and Carmen assigned a costume to each person with instructions, including the intricate stitching on the bust area of the corsets and the need for doubled strength stitching to accommodate strenuous dance routines.

The nuns were delighted by billowing displays of silky satin material and colorful net that graced their table and looked like a giant confectionery. Good enough to eat. Work commenced and the whirr of sewing machines was the only sound in the room apart from the occasional whisper of mumbled prayers being said.

Carmen was dispatched back to Wear 4 Art Thou? to collect accessories that included an assortment of colored satin elbow gloves and plumed headdresses.

Kira Mae watched the nuns work and was delighted by their speed and accuracy. Their manner seemed unhurried yet the first set of costumes were turned out and ready to go in less than an hour. See-through gown covers had already been prepared with the name of each of the dancers on a small card in the front pocket. Kira Mae looked at her mother and smiled as she packed the first dresses hot off the press into their garment bags.

A quick phone call to the theater assured them that the costumes would be delivered on time. A dresser would stand by to assist Kira Mae and make any small adjustments required. It came as no surprise to learn that showgirls' weight yo-yoed depending on their diet, exercise regime, time of the month and commitment and whether or not they were in love.

One by one the dresses were finished and zipped up in their personalized bags.

Less than an hour to go but barring disasters, all the costumes would be ready.

Carmen returned with the accessories and loaded the packed bags into the back of the SUV.

The glittering silver and gold headdresses posed a problem. Because each was a four-foot-high elaborate tower of plumes and feathers, there was no room left for them in the back of the vehicle once the garment bags were in place.

Sister Juanita was not to be defeated.

"Load them in my car," she told Carmen, "I'll follow you and drive them to the theater. One of the sisters can accompany me."

Sister Juanita laughed with delight when she saw how the headdresses jostled for space in her compact two-door car. It threatened to burst at the seams. To avoid the need to bend them out of shape and prevent damage, all of the headdresses were laid lengthways from the backseat to the front, and feathers and plumes spilled over the tops of the driver and passenger seats. If they weren't careful, it would look like the nuns were wearing plumed headdresses. A possibility that did not faze Sister Juanita at all.

She drew herself up to her full height, a couple of inches over five feet, and confided to the nuns as they finished up their tasks and prepared to put covers on their sewing machines. "I've never worn a showgirl's plumed headdress. Now is my chance."

The afternoon flew by and the job was completed successfully amidst much good humor and fun.

Julianne, Kira Mae and Carmen needed no reminder to say a prayer of thanks as they passed the statue of Our Lady, drove out of the convent and headed toward the theater in Benidorm. On the way Julianne would be dropped off to collect the girls and bring them to the show later in the evening.

She might even persuade them to take a nap—it was

destined to be a long night. She certainly would be glad of a long, hot, bubble bath before she changed into her glad rags.

Sister Juanita promised to request permission from the Mother Superior to accompany them to the show. Julianne was pretty sure her dear friend would not ask.

Her usual refrain when anyone thanked her for her gracious service was always, "I don't need to be rewarded for doing God's work. But I will be with you in spirit."

chapter thirty-four

"The meaning of life is to find your gift."
—William Shakespeare

Angel and Isabella looked picture perfect. Julianne posed with them for a photograph and sent it to Kira Mae who was busy with last-minute preparations at the theater.

"Adorable," came the reply.

Their pink velvet dresses had come from Harrods and were part of a limited edition Princess Collection. Silver jeweled tiaras glittered in their waist-length black hair and sparkled in the reflection of their ebony eyes. Rosita had spent hours perfecting their ringlets and on their feet they wore high-heeled Cinderella glass slippers.

"Your daughters are destined to be heartbreakers," she told Julianne.

Julianne beamed. No matter that neither girl had inherited her coloring. It was obvious to see the dominant person in that gene pool. The strangest thing was that no one ever doubted they were all related. Some deeper essence declared them blood relatives.

For her own outfit Julianne chose all white, knowing

that whatever she wore she would be outshone by the girls.

Kira Mae had insisted that she did not want her mother to drive. Instead she sent one of the drivers from an airport limousine service to collect her three special girls. They were seated in the front row on a table so close it was almost on the stage. Dinner would be served as they watched the show.

The three-hour show was an action packed spectacular of music, dance, costumes, lights and lasers. Pure feel-good family entertainment. Angel and Isabella loved the circus acts, especially the high-wire trapeze artists, and they saw the humor in the comedy act where specially chosen audience members were encouraged to make themselves look silly while playing musical instruments.

Julianne could hardly wait to see Kira Mae's designs under the spotlight.

Two tired little girls were about to start asking, "Is it time to go home?" when the finale fanfare sounded and a dozen showgirls high-kicked their way on stage. Dressed in shimmering shades of tartan satin and extravagant net trains, the dancers looked divine. Tightly laced black satin corsets silhouetted their figures and elbow-length gloves flashed with giant sparkling costume jewelry.

Headdresses graced Las Vegas–style showgirls who looked twelve feet tall. The whole effect was truly show-stopping and the audience rose to their feet and gave the show, the dancers, the singers and the jaw-dropping costumes a standing ovation. Kira Mae had scored a personal triumph.

Julianne was on her feet clapping and cheering, and the girls stood on their chairs to get a better view. Across the room she saw a familiar figure.

There was no mistaking the tall, dark and handsome man who stood at the opposite side of the stage, clapping and showing his appreciation.

"Bravo," he called.

Julianne caught his eye, and Dominic laughed.

They both made their way through the enthusiastic crowds and when they finally made it to within touching distance, Dominic reached out, grabbed Julianne around the waist and swung her high into the air.

"Put me down," laughed Julianne. "Don't embarrass me in front of my children. What are you doing here?" she had to almost shout to make herself heard.

"One of those one-night engagements," he said, "took me to Valencia and I saw a poster for this show. You did tell me about your daughter and her fashion design business. So I re-routed and came along.

"I'm flying out again tomorrow morning. I have a car outside. Do you want to go somewhere and celebrate your daughter's triumph?"

Julianne hesitated and looked back to the tables where Angel and Isabelle sat now openly yawning. She shook her head sadly.

"I have a date with my three favorite girls," she told him. "We are all promised hot chocolate with marshmallows in bed to round off this special night. We are all very tired."

He smiled seductively, "I have a comfy bed back at my hotel."

"Tempting as it is, I'm afraid that invitation will have to be refused," said Julianne. She was genuinely sad to turn him down but determined not to be swayed. No longer would she allow romance, business or anything else to come before her children. There was a time when, after rationalizing her actions, she would have gone running off into the night with her handsome suitor on yet another not to be missed adventure.

Not anymore.

Knowing that she wasn't going home with him, she couldn't resist a jibe, "Is the redhead not joining you?"

He appeared confused.

"Your wife," Julianne challenged, "I saw her arriving at the hotel in Marrakesh."

Dominic took her hand and held it. "You jumped to a conclusion, lovely lady. The red head, her name is Petra, is my manager. I have no wife. A strolling troubadour does not have much chance to commit to a relationship. Have voice, will travel."

"I'm sorry. Thank you for putting me straight," said Julianne, sorry she had misjudged him. "Marrakesh was a very special, magical time, I did not forget it—or you."

"I felt the same," he admitted, "and now I have learned my lesson. The next time the opportunity arises, and I hope it does, and I wish to whisk you off into an Arabian Fantasy, I will give you notice."

Even before Kira Mae had reappeared from backstage, Dominic had disappeared into the tidal wave of audience leaving the theater.

But not before he and Julianne shared a lingering kiss so beautiful that it almost had her changing her mind about spending the night with him.

So maybe Romero was not the only one who could set her passion on fire.

Her gaze followed him as he left. What a big hunk of handsome man.

"Who was that?" asked Kira as she pushed her way from backstage carrying a huge bouquet.

"Just a friend," said Julianne, "he wanted to congratulate you—and me on having such a talented daughter." She turned to collect the little ones.

"Come on girls," she gestured for them to join her.

"What time does Cinderella have to leave the ball?"

"Midnight," they chorused.

"Well, we are going to have to get home at the speed of light or the clock will strike midnight and all our fine gowns will disappear. And our limousine will turn back into a pumpkin. Best make sure no one leaves behind a slipper."

chapter thirty-five

"For ever and a day."
—Shakespeare's *As You Like It*

Julianne threw fresh rose petals into the swimming pool to mark the place of Paolo's death. Time for the whole family to move on. Together Julianne, Kira Mae and the girls had chosen a new home. High up in the Altea Hills with magnificent views of the ocean, their new villa was state of the art. A tower-like construction, it had never been lived in. The height of luxury and technologically advanced, the exclusive design blended modern, contemporary and the feel of a family home.

The whole property was theirs to imprint with future memories, no ghosts of the past to hold them back. Mother and daughter treasured their restored relationship and valued the opportunities they had been given to heal and forgive after all the challenges they had endured.

One whole wing of the house was devoted to Kira Mae's design business. She and a team of seamstresses set up their workstations in a vast open plan space with views of the mountains and the ocean.

Carmen now held the official title of assistant to Miss Kira Mae, thus freeing Kira Mae to devote herself to all things creative, a large part of which promised to be the Benidorm Palace commission with new shows opening twice a year.

Julianne looked around the suite of rooms that she had chosen for her own. On the second floor of the building her bedroom was one uninterrupted wall of glass looking out to sea. There was ample room for her various collections of clothes in a giant, cedar-lined walk-in closet.

"Come and see this," she called to the girls the first time they all toured the house. Full of energy and enthusiasm, as always, the two of them bounded up the glass paneled staircase.

"My very own rooftop Jacuzzi," she pointed out and then revealed the winding outdoor staircase that led to the vast underground garage. "We can all live together but have our own privacy."

"I want privacy," Angel pouted. "Me too," said Isabella.

The girls laid claim to their own bedrooms on opposite sides of a T-cross with a shared en suite bathroom on the ground floor of the house. Whether they would actually ever sleep separately was debatable but at least they knew which room belonged to which girl. Kira Mae described her sleeping quarters as "above the shop," located as they were in the wing that housed the working engine of the house.

The beautiful whitewashed villa had two kitchens,

one indoors, one outdoors, and an outdoor barbecue area by the infinity pool.

Together Julianne and Kira Mae shared their passions and made all the decisions about furnishings and finishes in their dream home.

"Welcome to our forever home," Kira Mae declared minutes after she walked into the downstairs living area and saw the triple aspect lounge doors that led to a vast open air terrace.

The girls' beloved nanny, Rosita had agreed to live-in freeing Julianne and Kira Mae to pursue their business responsibilities while they shared childcare duties and the school run.

Angel and Isabella had been enrolled in a new school far away from the drama of the previous one and also in dance classes so that one day, "We will be ladies dancing on stage in Mama Kira Mae's dresses." That was the story they told anyone who would listen.

Joint decisions and inspired planning provided the perfect home and working environment for the whole family.

"I can do the school run on the way to the Galleria," Julianne volunteered. The manager at the Galleria who already did such a great job of managing and organizing the various aspects of Wear 4 Art Thou? was to share responsibilities with Julianne, who would work at the Villajoyosa headquarters.

"Villajoyosa does what it says on the tin," she reflected. "Brings me Joy."

Julianne and Kira Mae stood on their terrace and joined hands with Angel and Isabella.

"Thank the Universe for our good fortune," said Julianne. They bowed their heads.

"May the mountains protect us, the sky watch over us and the ocean surround us with waves of love."

The end

Acknowledgments

Thank you to the excellent creative and production team who applied their talents and expertise to this novel: Clare Christian at Red Door Publishing, Gary A. Rosenberg at The Book Couple, narrative editor Sadie Mayne, line-editor Lori Lewis, reader Pilar Uribe and editorial assistant Michelle Ruger.

I also offer thanks to Mina Gough, Spa Director at *The Standard,* Miami Beach, for her commitment to Enrichment Programs and especially the New Writers group at the Spa at the *Standard.* Also to Pastor 'Hunter' Thompson, staff and Board at the Miami Beach Community Church.

Blessings and gifts come my way every day: To my family, headed by brother William J. Beattie and his wife, Mary, who always "keep the light on for me;" special friends Jude Parry of the Gold Coast Theatre Company and Mily Soberon of EWM Realty in Miami Beach; plus my two champions, John Lee and Shaun Glennon. They brighten up my life. With the love and support of these wonderful individuals, I celebrate a joyful and fulfilled life.

About the Author

Ellen Frazer-Jameson is a professional communicator working in media, print, and theater. A former BBC broadcaster and Fleet Street journalist, Ellen is a published author, producer, theater director, and performer. She co-presented the largest late-night audience show in Europe on BBC Radio 2. Ellen lives in London and Miami Beach and to relax dances Argentine tango.

Ellen's other books include *Seven Steps to Fabulous* and *Love Mother Love Daughter* (Red Door Publishing), *Dark Hole in My Soul* (Fourth Dimension), and *Siobhan's Miracle* and *Making God Laugh* (John Blake Publishing).

You can contact Ellen through her website at
www.ellenfrazerjameson.com

Author photo courtesy of international photographer Dora Franco
www.dorafrancophoto.com

Printed in Great Britain
by Amazon